Mollies' Ghost

A Supernatural Thriller

R.A. Johnson

Ghostly Poconos Series
#2

CROW Books

ebook ISBN 978-1-959480-30-3
Paperback ISBN 978-1-959480-31-0
Hardcover ISBN 978-1-959480-32-7
Special Edition ISBN 978-1-959480-33-4

Published by CROW Books, an imprint of CROW-IP, LLC. The crow-and-book logo is a trademark of CROW-IP, LLC. All rights reserved.

CROW Books

For Carly,

For all of your love and help.

PROLOGUE

Friday, April 3rd

Silence…the absolute absence of sound detectable by the ear, discernible by the mind. Silence…broken by a low moaning, the sound of abject despair, the growling of men, and the whimpers of boys. Silence…shattered by a multitude of voices hurling their vitriol at anything, anyone who will listen. The voices of the innocent, yet damned, merge one-by-one into a single shout, a name…

Since arriving in the mountains with his parents, the boy was unusually quiet for an eight-year-old. Gone was any interest in his toys and books. He went swimming and fishing with Mom and Dad, but always seemed distracted, and would sometimes cock his head and freeze as if trying to make sense of a rustling, or murmurings, barely heard.

The voices always came to the boy at night, preventing even the hope of sleep. Each time they visited his mind, their intensity, their insistence, grew. No longer were they a cacophony of jumbled whispers. This night, on that dark mountain road, they found their purpose. They found the strength of collaboration. They found their one voice, and the vessel to carry it into the world.

Kathy
Friday, April 3ʳᵈ

The brown liquor sloshed over the edge of the shot glass as Kathy lifted it to her lips. A tilt of the head, a hard gulp, a squint, and a lick of her wet thumb later, she gingerly set the empty glass among its mates.

"Another." Her voice even sounded slurred to her own ears.

"Nah. You've had enough," Lloyd the bartender said. He paused in his never-ending polishing of the spotless bar.

Kathy snapped her head up to make a smartass reply, but when her head stopped, the world in her vision didn't.

"Whoa." She closed her eyes until the world caught up with her head. "You just may be right."

"I'll call Andy," Lloyd said. Andy Wysecki was the only Uber driver in or around the small town of Dundee. "It wouldn't look good for the county's newest Sheriff's Detective to get a DUI," he said while he punched virtual buttons on his phone. "It's on me."

"Don't need an Ube'. My 'partmen's only two blocks away. It's Friday. Half the county's drunk or high on something. Andy'll be busy."

Lloyd looked around the otherwise empty bar. "Not here. And not on Friday *afternoon*." He slipped the phone back into his pocket. "You bought the Mackey House. Why do you keep that firetrap apartment?"

"Need a place. A place to get away." Kathy put her head down on her folded arms on the bar.

"Get away from what? The ghost?" Lloyd's tone was joking, but he flipped the towel over his shoulder and leaned on his side of the bar, watching her intently.

Kathy shook her head against her forearm. "Ghost's gone. Killed it."

A grin spread across Lloyd's face. This was the first confirmation from Kathy of the rumors surrounding the Mackey House, the busted statue on its lawn, and the resulting landscaping. Lloyd reached for his phone again but paused. Posting anything online that he heard from his best customer while she was drunk would be like a priest breaking the seal of the confessional.

Instead, he leaned even closer. "So, you're getting away from the cripple?"

In an instant, Kathy's head flew up and she grabbed him by the front of his shirt up under his chin.

"Don't call him that," she growled.

Lloyd, despite his six-foot two-inch height knew that even a drunken Detective Kaveetha Jensen could kick his ass in a heartbeat. He slowly raised his hands in surrender.

"Sorry, sorry. That's just what everybody calls him."

Kathy pushed him back from the bar and swayed in her seat. "Not when I'm around."

A car horn beeped outside.

Lloyd said, "What's it gonna be? A ride back to that creepy place you call home now, or an escort to your equally creepy and sorry love nest?"

Kathy snorted, their momentary altercation forgotten. "'Love nest.' I wish." She slid off the barstool and stood swaying for a second. "Hell, there's more booze at home." She fished two twenties out of her pocket and dropped them on the bar. "We good?"

He looked at the line of shot glasses and her half-empty bottle of beer, then he plucked the towel off his shoulder and waved it toward the door.

"Sure. Go home."

Jan

Friday, April 3rd

"Piece o' shit," Jan muttered as he highlighted the last five hundred words he had typed. His finger, poised above the Delete key, shook a little. Those words represented his entire output for the day. But instead of punching the key, he reached for something next to his keyboard.

His hand seemed to find the bourbon of its own accord. The glass was at his lips and the harsh brown liquid flowed into his mouth before he consciously thought about it.

I hate editing. "Make her more three-dimensional. We can see his 'want' but what is his 'need?' Show, don't tell!" It's all bullshit. These aren't real people. They're just figments floating around in my head.

He closed his eyes while he savored the taste of the whiskey before letting it burn the back of his throat. When he opened his eyes, he un-highlighted the text and started typing elsewhere in the document.

After ten minutes, he picked up the glass again and sat back.

There, how's that for a 'need?' Proving his manhood to his macho, gun-toting father. That's fucked-up enough to generate all kinds of internal angst and bad decisions.

He nodded, satisfied that his protagonist was indeed more rounded and realistic. And hopefully, more relatable. A gulp emptied his glass. He rattled the ice cubes as he rose to get a refill.

Hobbling out of his suite of rooms into the former bed-and-breakfast's entrance hall, he tried to stretch the stiffness out of his joints. The fire he barely survived a year before left him covered in burn scars, some of which went much deeper than his skin or even his muscles. His wrists and ankles, where the ghost and her avatar had held him down, still required daily physical therapy for the joints to function. And the damage to his cock and balls meant he had to sit to piss. The thought of ever having sex again made him cringe.

The deepest scars, though, penetrated straight into his psyche. His worldview, his belief system, his entire understanding of the universe was shattered by the events that had taken place in that very house, a creaky old mansion built on the foundation of a nineteenth century hotel. That hotel's fiery demise had claimed the life of a young housemaid, a young woman whose ghost had escaped her statue prison and possessed his sometimes lover. Together, lover and ghost had tried to emasculate him through immolation during sex.

The novel that resulted from that ordeal had shot up the charts, topping almost every bestseller list. Promoting it had been a bitch, since he couldn't drive for the first six months, but it was worth it. He earned out his meager advance, and the royalty checks were enough to pay Kathy rent for his suite in Mackey House and to put away enough to become a financial presence in Dundee.

As always, the pressure to follow up with another bestseller made him the local liquor store's best customer. Standing in the kitchen, he was pulling the cork with the horse and jockey on top from the bourbon bottle when the back door slammed open.

"Hey, Kath—Uh-oh."

Kathy stumbled into the kitchen, stopped and stared for a moment as if she had never seen Jan before, then bolted into her apartment.

"Not again." He pushed away the bourbon bottle and dug out the coffee and filters.

Ten minutes later, Kathy emerged, wiping her mouth. Jan handed her a mug and shook his head. "Again?"

"It's Friday…afternoon."

"There's no crime on Friday?"

"Cut me a break. Please."

Jan shrugged and poured bourbon into his coffee, then waggled the bottle toward her mug.

"Oh, God. No f-in' way."

"It's not a good look, you know."

Kathy tilted her head and stared. "No shit," she finally said. "How's that follow-up to your bestseller comin'?"

Jan snorted. "Touché. At least if I get too drunk to work, all that happens is my agent gets pissed. You—"

"Aw, shut up. Any stolen bicycle crime scenes can wait. In fact, I'm going to bed."

"You'll be up all night…again."

Kathy shrugged as she turned away. "I'd be up, anyway."

Jan nodded. *Probably right.*

3

Keeper
What is Time?

Her world—her universe—is tiny, yet infinite. Nothing more than emptiness, a dark void stretching beyond the point where any senses can reach, and yet so devoid of sensation that it can also be nothing more than a shell around her mind. Its extent is immeasurable, simply because there is no feature—no texture, no scent, no taste, no image nor whisper—against which a measurement can be made.

Even her mind, or rather the tiniest spark of a mind, is curled in upon itself, reflexively terrified to engage with that vast emptiness—if, indeed, it is truly empty. Terror keeps that shard of awareness wrapped into a tight ball, its own shield against the horrors beyond its ken.

But it is not the terror of what might be lurking outside the cocoon her mind-shard has made of itself. No, the singular focus of that piece of awareness is not what awaits a possible awakening. Rather, she is terrified of what would be unleashed on that outside world if she relaxes her vigilance for even the slightest moment.

For the wall she has made of herself is not a fortress to keep the world of sound and light out. It is instead a prison to keep the evil it contains sequestered from the world of the living. Guilt and shame are alloyed with her terror to strengthen that prison, but at the expense of never looking outward for even a heartbeat.

Yet, despite the total lack of sensation impinging upon her mind-shard, her heart measures time with its metronomic beating. Or rather, the body housing that tiny piece of awareness does, for the self-isolated consciousness feels it not.

But what, one might ask, is at the core of that mental prison? What is the evil that the host so fears unleashing on the world? Why, it is nothing more than a glowing ember. A seemingly harmless firefly in the dusk of a summer evening. Unlike the insect's blinking mating plea, though, the core of evil glows uninterrupted, a hungry Flame awaiting its chance to light a conflagration within the world of light and sound.

And the shame borne by the Keeper that fuels her unending struggle is one of complicit partnership with that evil. Of willing collusion when both were much more than the infinitesimal, unconscious essences that remain.

Gone are any remnants of the intelligent, thinking beings the Keeper and Flame once were. Through selfless acts of heroism, the Flame's demonic spirit was ripped from this world, taking most, but not all, of the Keeper's consciousness with it. All that remains of that violent episode are the Flame's core of hatred, the Keeper's guilt, and the scars—mental and physical—they left on the real world. Reflexively, like the phase transition of a liquid into a perfect crystal, the fractured pieces of shameful guilt were drawn together, like puzzle pieces, to become the Keeper—a shell encasing the Flame, isolating, yet protecting it. Together, they form a spore, impenetrable while dormant.

And so, Flame and Keeper wait. Seemingly patiently, though they do not sense the passage of time. Waiting for the catalyst that will crack the Keeper's crystalline barrier.

4

Billy
Friday, April 3rd

The boy squirmed in his booster seat. They'd been driving through the forest in the dark for hours. He was bored and had to pee.

How much longer? he thought, but kept quiet. The last time he had asked that question, Dad had used his angry voice. *"We'll get there when we get there."* The scolding echoed in the boy's head. It wasn't his fault they were lost on these back roads in the middle of the night.

The headlights caught the sign for the Boy Scout camp they had passed twice before. In the dashboard lights, he saw Mom turn to Dad and open her mouth, but she held her silence, too. Dad's last words to her were just, *"Shut up!"*

"The damned GPS is fucked," Dad mumbled.

"George!" Mom hissed and looked over her shoulder at the boy. Just as quickly, he closed his eyes and feigned sleep.

"Well, it's sending us in fu—friggin' circles."

The boy squeezed his thighs together. He *really* had to pee now.

"Don't worry," the Whispery Voice said in his head. *"It won't be long now."*

"Turn here," Mom blurted, and Dad hit the brakes hard. "Look. It says you should turn here."

"It's just a dirt road."

"We must have missed it the last couple of times—"

"Yeah, yeah," Dad muttered as he backed the car up and turned onto the narrow track.

Oaks, maples, and ash trees thrust themselves up out of the thick mountain laurel that lined the road. They made a tunnel that their headlights barely lit without penetrating.

"Friggin' Hicksville," Dad muttered for about the hundredth time. "We should be floating in a lazy river back at that Coyote Lodge—or whatever it's called."

Mom pursed her lips, but kept quiet. It had been her idea to leave the indoor water park behind and "rough it" for a weekend of canoeing, hiking, and fishing at the Wild Poconos Camp.

Soon. The voice whispered in the boy's head. *Soon.*

Dad took Mom's silence as an admission of guilt, though. "If we're wasting the weekend, not to mention the money, or the Giant's game—." He pushed the gas pedal down.

Get ready, the Whispery Voice said.

The car bounced over ridges in the washboard road, which made the boy's bladder demand release, and fueled Dad's anger. He pressed down on the pedal even harder.

"George! Slow down!"

But of course, his Darkness had overtaken him, and he couldn't slow down. For the first time, the boy's detachment cracked, and real fear filled him.

Ready!

The greenish glow of the dashboard showed Dad's mindless fury and Mom's stark terror. His own terror unlocked a gateway into his mind, releasing the Whispery Voice from its hiding place.

The wordless growl that escaped the boy hurt his throat, but he was long past feeling the strain. The sound of guttural hate snapped Mom's head around to stare at her son. Her eyes flew open in horror at what she saw.

Her beautiful, blond-haired, quiet eight-year-old had become a monster. Drool leaked from his mouth and ran in streaks to drip off his chin. But it was his red-rimmed eyes that truly terrified her. They stared at the rearview mirror, locked in feral hatred with Dad's.

The pain of every spanking, every snidely hurtful comment, every belittlement of Mom, every mumbled f-word poured from the boy into his father. It bored a hole in Dad's mind into which the Whispery Voice poured its vitriol—the aggregate terror, pain, and hate of the One Hundred And Ten, fueled by over a century of solitude.

Unable to look away, Dad never saw the bend in the road approaching at breakneck speed. From behind the mental veil that had descended, the boy saw the Whispery Voice's intention. And was…intrigued. At least the "walking on eggshells," as Mom put it, would be over. *But Mom, too?*

Ineffectively, he tried to wrest back control, but Whispery Voice's grip was too strong.

"He deserves this."

But Mom doesn't. The boy argued.

"Silence Is Compliance," the Voice countered.

The road ahead curved to the right to meet the bridge over Wolf's Creek at right angles. The car didn't turn, though. Perhaps out of pity, or simply to protect a useful tool, Whispery Voice pulled a dark shroud over the boy's senses, so he didn't hear Mom scream or his own throat growl, "Die, Mothfu—" as the car's tires skidded off the shoulder.

The jerk of his booster seat's restraints released the boy's bladder as the car missed the bridge and executed its nosedive down the gorge. The seconds of freefall were eerily silent, and a perfect counterpoint to the crunch of metal, glass, and bone that followed, as the SUV flipped end-over-end and settled into the deepest pool of the creek.

The shroud over the boy's thoughts lifted just enough to let him release the belts that held him securely to the safety seat. Shrugging out of the harness as the cold mountain water poured into the car, he let it carry him through the broken window to the shallows.

Looking back from the bank, the Whispery Voice chuckled. *"Well done. Come find me. Come join me,"* it said before withdrawing, leaving the eight-year-old boy silently standing in the mud, drenched and shivering.

Kathy
Monday, April 6th

The Ford Interceptor SUV with the County Sheriff shield emblazoned on the side rolled into its parking space between the two on-duty deputies' patrol vehicles. Its headlights illuminated the ceiling of the squad room through the tall windows.

Kathy checked her makeup in the visor mirror. The dusky skin tone she inherited from her Tamil mother was good for hiding her hungover eyes, but this early, a touch of foundation was still needed.

That's as good as it's gonna get, I guess. Why do I do this to myself?

It was a question she asked herself almost every day. The effects of booze, lack of sleep, and stress at work were piling up. Kathy had been promoted to Detective over several other patrol officers because of her work on the "incident" at Mackey House almost a year before. The resentment that fostered among the other deputies was too obvious to ignore.

"Look what the cat drug in." Deputy Jonah Spatz, known to all as "Spaz", muttered. He and Tom Gheringer sat at their desks, feet up and cans of beer in their hands.

"What the fuck are you doin' here at this hour?" Gheringer practically shouted. His tone was decidedly unfriendly.

"Checkin' up on you two loafers," Kathy spit back. She sidled between the steel desks and ancient desk chairs to her cubicle by the windows, careful not to sway her ass too much. It was to no avail.

"You know, Spaz, if I had an ass like that, I bet I'd be a detective by now, too."

Spaz sputtered on his beer. "If you had an ass like that and a smile to match, you'd be Sheriff by now."

Both snorted a forced laugh. "Good thing our Detective *Squaw* doesn't know how to smile."

"That's enough!" Kathy spun her chair to face their leering grins.

They're just trying to get a rise out of me. I've told them a million times I'm not that kind of Indian. I'm too tired for their adolescent bullshit.

She looked up at the clock on the wall.

"It looks like you two still have two minutes left on your shifts, and here you sit drinking beer in the squad room. Drinking on duty. What would that be, like the third time for you, *Deputy* Gheringer? Oh, and at least the fourth or fifth time for bad boy, Spaz. That'll get you both at least a week off, pay-free, I bet."

She faced their glowering faces. "I bet the wifies would love that, wouldn't they?" She turned to Spaz. "Not to mention the teenage stripper you've been fucking while on patrol."

Gheringer's mouth dropped open as he looked at his partner. Spaz squinted harder, and his neck flushed with anger.

"How the fuck—"

"I'm a *detective*, asshole. I observe, question, and find things out. That's why I was promoted and you're still riding patrol."

She glanced at the clock. "Your shifts are over. Get the fuck out of here."

To her smug satisfaction, both deputies stood and left without a word.

Effective, but why do I feel like this is going to come back to bite me? She turned to her computer, but didn't log in. *Why did I come in here so early?* She looked at the stack of case files piled on her desk. *Not to work on these piddly-little cases. Face it, I was looking for a fight, and I knew where to find one.*

At least one of the deputies burned rubber as he peeled out of the parking lot. Kathy sat in her hard-won domain—a tiny cubicle in a tiny county sheriff's department—and fought back tears. Six AM on Saturday, and she had nowhere to go. With a sigh, she pulled a folder off the stack and flipped it open.

Keeper
Monday, April 6th

The stirring of Flame sends a wave of panic through Keeper, and she clenches her grip tighter than ever. Surprised, she finds the edges of Flame to be softer than she assumed, awakening her to a new internal awareness. Ever so tentatively, she probes the ball of heat at her core and, surprised, receives a gentle caress in return.

That oddly familiar touch further awakens, not memories *per se*, but rather the faintest imprints of mental patterns. Keeper *feels* that familiarity without understanding its source or history, for how could she? She is the merest remnant of the person she once was. A person seduced and driven to commit the most horrendous deeds by the progenitor of the very Flame she clings to so tightly.

But that Flame is no more the vengeful ghost of Flora it once was than Keeper is the murderous Sandy Adams.

There remains but one aspect of Sandy within Keeper. It is embodied in the first desire she feels, though still unable to form the word—*Redemption.*

The spark of Flora that Keeper holds within is even more devoid of thought, desire, or even awareness. It is even more dangerous, however. For within Keeper's core there lies the power to burn. The demonic power that Flora found in her hate-filled ghostly state. Imprisoned for decades within an alluring statue before escaping and possessing Sandy, that power is all that remains from when she was ripped from the netherspace between the world of light and the next one.

Flame's incendiary power is empty of thought, but it, too, can feel. And the stirring of Keeper's awareness similarly disturbs its quiescence. It roils, bubbling with long-dormant energy. Instinctively, though, for that is her solitary purpose, Keeper soothes Flame's agitation with the simplest of thoughts, massaging them into and lingering within Flame's formless energy.

Calm. Patience. Redemption.

Jan

Monday, April 6th

Oⁿe more rep—I said *one* more, Jan."

Body quivering, Jan lowered the leg lift weights with the last of his strength.

His physical therapist, Amanda, scowled as she typed notes into his chart on her tablet.

"Don't push so hard. Your muscles need to rebuild their fibers slowly. Ripping them apart three times a week could be counterproductive."

Amanda was a physical therapist who had graduated from Penn State two years before. But unlike her fresh-faced classmates, her career started only after her kids were grown and her husband had moved on. She was pretty, fit, divorced, and too old to be mistaken for his daughter, so Jan learned early on how to time his appointments to her schedule. With Amanda as his therapist, it seemed to him that getting strong enough to not need her anymore was counterproductive.

She offered him a hand, which he gladly took, and she pulled him up to his feet.

"Shall we treat those scars?" she asked, and Jan nodded. "OK. I'll meet you in the massage room."

He shuffled to the room in the back of the gym where the massage table was set up and gingerly removed his shirt and sweat pants. He stood looking at the high table when Amanda knocked on the door.

"Yeah, come on in," he called.

"You still can't make it," she said as she closed the door.

"I haven't tried yet."

"Let me get the stepstool." She slid the rubberized steps into place. "Just like the stairs in the gym," she said as she lightly gripped his elbow for balance as he climbed.

Sitting on the padded table, he rolled onto his back with a groan. Aside from wrists and ankles, his burn scars were limited to the front of his legs, torso, and genitals.

"Are you using the silicone gel at home?" Amanda asked and pointed to his gym shorts. "You know I can't work on *those* scars."

Jan just shrugged. *Even if she could, she wouldn't like what she saw.*

She had been his critical care PT in the hospital, so she was well aware of the extent of his injuries. Although she knew the official story of how he was partially immolated by the crazy owner of the Mackey House B&B who had murdered her husband, she didn't completely buy it.

"If you want to get any function back *down there*, you'd better do what I tell you."

Her smile belied her firm voice.

"Yes, Mistress," Jan said with his own smile.

"Watch yourself." She squeezed the ankle she was working on just a little too hard.

Jan's face twitched, but he otherwise remained motionless. "Sorry."

Amanda leaned over as she moved up his leg to his thigh and whispered in his ear. "If you pitch a tent for me someday, I'd consider that a victory."

Jan chuckled. "If and when I ever can, you'll be the first to know."

8

Jan
Monday, April 6th

We have less than two weeks left, people. The eighteenth is looming large. Let's make this Grand Opening the biggest thing this county has seen in years, decades even."

Mayor Jim Luzeski's enthusiasm seemed a little too forced to Jan, though Patti Trieste, the woman sitting to his right, practically squealed with delight and clapped her hands together. Jan sat in the boardroom of the Miners Bank along with six other members of the LMCMT, LLC, the company behind the Lost Miners Coal Mine Tour, the "Pocono Mountains' Newest Adventure Attraction," as Patti, the group's Marketing Director had dubbed it and Jan's draft brochure proclaimed.

Patti, transplanted from New York City a few years back, was running the public relations. The poster on the easel at the front of the room was her firm's work. It showed a gaping tunnel entrance with ghost-like apparitions barely visible within the blackness. Her face seemed to be on the local TV channels every hour or so, and her morning show appearances were now streaming on the official website. Jan had to admit, as much as her Brooklyn accent grated on his nerves, that she was certainly getting the word out.

Jim turned to George Kapaletti, the group's Chief Engineer. "How are the preparations coming, George?"

George puffed out his chest and looked around the table. "We're right on track," he practically gushed. "We've hit all of our milestones so far. The exterior work is mostly finished, and the interior walkways should be done in a day or so. We're installing the lighting and sound system as we go, so, yeah, we're right on track. Like I said."

Silence fell over the table as a few of the other principals looked at each other. Finally, Buddy Lewis, the president and majority owner of the Miners Bank and the main financier of the venture, spoke up.

"George, what about the seemingly high number of workers who have quit over the past week? Isn't that affecting your schedules?"

George shifted uncomfortably in his chair. "Well, they were mostly unskilled laborers, easily replaced."

"Really? What about the Finley Brothers? I received a final invoice for work done to date. But as you just said, the electrical work hasn't been finished yet, correct?"

George, his fleshy jowls getting pink, shrugged and dismissively waved his hand. "Those superstitious—" He caught himself before the epithet escaped his mouth. "— brothers are too claustrophobic to work deep in the mine."

"They called me," the sixth member of the group, Dr. Jenny Jones, said. "They said they think there are animals of some kind living down in the mine. They claim it's common to hear strange noises."

George scoffed. "Of course, there are strange noises, JJ. You're hundreds of feet underground down there. Water's dripping, pumps are running, ventilation fans are moving air constantly. Hell, you can feel and hear the mine train running, no matter where you are down there. It's a pretty noisy place when it comes right down to it."

Jenny's skepticism was obvious, but she nodded. "As long as it's safe. Safety has to be our main concern." Heads nodded all around the table.

"Don't worry, everything will pass final inspection." He glanced sidelong at the mayor.

Jan sat silently through this whole exchange. His primary interest in the venture was born out of the mine's sordid history. The royalties from his bestselling ghost story enabled him to buy into the LLC, despite his status as an outsider. To the tight-knit community of Dundee, he would probably be an outsider even if he lived there for the rest of his life. Being a player in what everyone expected would bring tourists and their money to the area was, he hoped, his entrée into Dundee society.

His silence was interrupted when Patti turned to him and said, "I bet those pumps and such sound like voices coming out of the depths." She had never been inside the mine. "The mine has quite a violent history, doesn't it, Jan?"

Jan nodded. He had written some ad copy for her and an article about the mine that had appeared in newspapers and on news sites throughout eastern Pennsylvania.

"It's true. A lot of people died in that mine back in the day."

Patti's smile looked like a predator who had just spotted its next meal.

"So, if one of these workers quit because they heard ghostly voices…" She stared at Jan with raised eyebrows. Everyone else waited for his response.

"Well, it *would* make for good copy," he agreed. *Yeah, I can work with that.* "How do I get ahold of them?"

George, relieved that the focus of the meeting had shifted from him, jumped in. "I can get you names and phone numbers."

Jan nodded, and smiles broke out around the table. They all knew that, as Patti had said many times, any publicity is good publicity.

9

Billy
Monday, April 6th

The boy shivered in the early Spring chill. He had been wandering through the Pennsylvania Game Lands for two days and three nights, sleeping rough, only moving through the woods because of the constant prodding of the Whispery Voice.

"We've gotta keep movin', my boy. Movin' keeps ya warm, after all."

To his surprise, he found the Whispery Voice to be correct. Hiking along the game trails and climbing over the fallen trees, even in the dark, was a lot better than lying on the cold ground trying to sleep.

"Where am I going?" the boy asked the first night.

"Shhh. Ya don' need to speak out loud. You can just think what ya want to say and I'll hear ya."

"You can read my mind?"

The boy remembered a story Dad had read to him about a superhero who could listen in on people's thoughts. The idea was very unsettling since he sometimes had bad thoughts about his parents—Dad in particular.

"Only...only if you want me to. Try it. Just think what you want to say."

Dad's missed birthdays and his excuses that sounded lame even to an eight-year-old, along with what the boy understood of Mom and Dad's shouting matches, had taught him not to trust adults' promises.

But the Whispery Voice felt more like a big brother than an adult. The boy had always wished for an older brother like his friend Tommy Parker had. Chuck Parker had scared bullies away from teasing Tommy because of his lisp. The boy was sure a big brother would have defended Mom when Dad came home from one of his "benders."

Besides, thinking was a lot easier than talking out loud, wasn't it?

Okay. Can you hear me?

"Loud and clear."

That was easy. He even heard the little snicker that accompanied the Whispery Voice's response.

Where are we going? He repeated silently this time.

There was a pause before any response came. Then, in a voice overly cheerful, even to the boy's ears, the Whispery Voice answered.

"Not sure, but I'll know it when I see it. Trust me."

The boy wasn't ready to trust the Whispery Voice yet. So he kept silent and pushed on through the forest.

When the sun was peaking through the trees on the first morning, the boy broke his mental silence.

Are we there yet? I'm hungry.

"Soon. We'll be there soon. Then ya can eat all ya want."

But his learned skepticism heard the lie beneath the words.

Will Mom be there? I miss her.

This time, the pause was so long, the boy decided the Whispery Voice wasn't going to answer. But then, the command came through like a slap, stinging like Dad's belt.

"They're gone! Never think of them again."

Another innocent little boy might have burst into tears at the violence—no less hurtful for the fact that it was contained within his mind. But the boy knew better. Tears only led to more pain. He'd heard, "I'll give you something to cry about," too many times. Instead, he withdrew deeper into himself, building a wall around his thoughts one brick at a time.

By the third night, the wall was so high and thick that he no longer felt the weariness in his arms and legs or the hunger in his belly. It was the Whispery Voice who kept him wandering through the forest, searching for something. The boy, tired and scared, withdrew from his body and built the wall even higher.

The funny thing about a wall with no windows and doors, though, is that it is just as good at keeping things in as it is at keeping them out.

So, it was the Whispery Voice in control of the body that squatted in the bushes at the edge of the institutionally landscaped lawn. He looked out through the boy's eyes at the edifice sitting at the center of the ten acres cleared from the surrounding forest.

Wayne State Behavioral Hospital was built in the mid-nineteenth century to house "imbeciles, and the hysterical, feeble-minded, and criminally insane." Although its mission statement had been softened over the decades to reflect the current diagnostic terminology, its purpose had remained mainly intact. Gone were the padded rooms, electroshock "therapies," and leather restraints, of course, replaced instead by cocktails of various psychoactive drugs.

The feeling that had drawn the Whispery Voice to this place grew stronger as the sun came up and cut through the spring mist. A kindred soul residing inside was the magnet that guided the Whispery Voice, using the boy's body, to this place. Relying on the boy's knowledge of the modern world, he circled along the edge of the woods to the expanse of pavement where workers and the rare visitors parked their cars.

Hiding, he watched as day-shift maintenance, administrative, and healthcare staff arrived for work and the workers they relieved practically ran to their vehicles, eager to escape the historical cloud of institutional abuse and the present-day sense of depression infusing the place.

When the burly orderly, Samson DeShields, dressed in his blue scrubs, emerged from the side door, the Whispery Voice stepped the boy from the cover of the bushes. Then, he mentally backed away and let the remnant of the boy's mind that remained outside his wall back in control. After a few halting steps, the boy ran with a stumbling gait toward Samson, who was wearily striding across the parking lot.

When Samson raised his key fob to unlock his door, the boy froze as if unsure if the gadget in Samson's hand might be a weapon. Likewise, the orderly froze when he saw the thin, bedraggled child standing shivering in the morning mist.

"What the fuck?"

After a moment of shock, his nurturing instincts took over, and Samson knelt on one knee to lower himself to the boy's height.

"Who are you, Little Man?"

Holding out his hands in a welcoming gesture, Samson smiled. It was the smile that broke through the boy's fear. He ran headlong into the big man's embrace.

Easily lifting the frail boy, He stood and scanned the parking lot for his parents or anyone else who might be responsible for the child. But seeing no one, and feeling the shivering ribs of the starving child, he turned and hurried back into the hospital.

Kathy
Monday, April 6th

Yo, Jensen," the sheriff called from his office. Kathy, happy she could drop the case file she was working on for a moment at least, made her way into Peterson's office.

"What do you know about this coal mine tour that's opening up?" he asked as she plopped down in the old wooden guest chair in front of his desk.

"Well, I know they're scheduled to open up next Saturday. I think they're planning a big 'Grand Opening' of some kind. It's a tourist attraction. That's about all I know at this point."

The sheriff crossed his arms. "Isn't your live-in, whatever he is, involved in that somehow?"

Kathy frowned and rolled her eyes up to the dead ceiling fan before blowing out a sigh. "Yes, my 'live-in whatever he is'— by the way, if you figure out what he is, please let me know— put some money into it. He's a co-owner. I think he's been writing some of their advertising copy and doing interviews and things."

"Leveraging that ghost story he wrote, huh?"

Kathy cringed. "Yes, he's been leveraging that ghost story quite a bit, actually."

Peterson nodded and picked up a file folder. "I want you to look into something having to do with that tour."

She was intrigued, but something made her wonder if this was going to cause problems between her and Jan. *Peterson wouldn't be asking me to look into something if he didn't think it was a problem.*

He handed the folder across his desk. "We've received a couple of reports from some former workers who claim the mine isn't safe to open." He took a deep breath, as if reluctant to continue. "They say they've heard some weird noises down there."

"Weird noises? It's a coal mine, right?"

"I know, I know. It's probably just disgruntled former employees trying to make a stink. I need you to talk to them. See if there's anything to it. We have to make sure the place is safe."

Great. Another wild goose chase. "Isn't that the town inspectors' job?"

The sheriff looked at her over his readers. "The mayor's one of the owners."

"Ah," she said and nodded her understanding. The town's building inspector worked for the mayor. It was a clear-cut conflict of interest. "Yeah, sure, I'll talk to them and see what they have to say."

She started for the door. "And," the sheriff said, stopping her in her tracks. "I assume that if you do find out something isn't kosher over there, your relationship with this writer guy won't be a problem?"

She sighed, wondering, as she often did, why she had invited Jan to move in.

"No, Chief, it won't be a problem. If there are safety problems over there, I'll shut the whole thing down."

"That's what I wanted to hear."

Kathy
Monday, April 6th

The man fidgeted in his chair. His left hand tapped an indistinguishable rhythm on the tabletop. His head twitched to the left, out of sync with his hand, and his lips mouthed a silent monologue.

This ought to be fun.

Kathy watched Chet Rheingold from behind the one-way glass. His rap sheet showed a couple drunk-and-disorderlies and two car B&Es.

Looks like he spent his last paycheck on his drug of choice. She sighed. *Let's get this over with.*

Leaving the observation room, she stepped into the interrogation room.

"Mr. Rheingold, sorry to bring you in here like some criminal," Kathy said as she sat across the table from him. "Good thing that Scranton PD knew where to find you." They sat in an interrogation room inside Scranton's main police station, but the unadorned, windowless room could have been anywhere.

"Can I smoke in here?" Chet fumbled a pack of Navy-cut Camels from his shirt pocket.

Kathy pointed to the single placard on the wall, which denied the use of tobacco, firearms, drugs, and alcohol.

"Sorry. This won't take long. You reported hearing 'strange noises' while working on the Coal Mine Tour project. Is that right?"

Chet nodded his head vigorously. "Yeah, I told that cop there's somethin' livin' down there."

Kathy consulted the file with Spaz's report. "It says here you were involved in an altercation, which is why Deputy Spatz was called to the scene. Want to tell me about that?"

The man seemed to shrink into himself a little. "They tried to make me go back down there. I told them I quit, but their security bull grabbed me and tried to put me onto that kiddie train." He licked his lips and his eyes darted left, then right. "That's when I hit him."

Kathy imagined this skinny drug addict standing up to "Bull" Masters, head of security at the mine, and a former Penn State lineman. She tried to keep the smile from her face.

"It says here you broke his nose."

Chet smiled broadly. "Yeah, I got 'im good."

"You're lucky he didn't press charges."

"Nah, then he'd have to admit that a little shit like me took him down."

He barked a laugh, and Kathy let herself smile in return.

"OK, so I don't care about that." *Although I certainly would have loved to have seen it.* "What I'm interested in are those noises you heard."

Chet's smile disappeared. "Creepy, they were. They made the hair on my neck stand up. And when they started whispering my name, that's—"

"Wait. These were *voices* you heard?"

His head bobbed up and down. "Yeah, but not to start. It started out like just scraping noises and air whooshing around."

"Like the ventilation system?"

"Nah, different. After you're down there for a while, you just kinda tune out the ventilation and pumps, and even the little train comin' and goin', ya know? No, this was different, and it came from deeper down below, not from above, like the other sounds."

He slumped further down in the chair, as if trying to hide from his memories.

Kathy's voice was soft. "When did these noises become voices?"

"Day before yesterday." He kept his eyes down on his hands, which kept up their fidgeting in his lap.

"What did they say?"

"Nothin' at first. It was just like a bunch of people sighin' and…and cryin'."

The man looked close to tears himself, so Kathy dropped her voice even more. "That must have been scary."

Chet's head came up slowly, and he met Kathy's eyes. "Not as scary as yesterday, when those voices all came together and said my name. In unison, like a choir. I nearly shit myself, so I jumped on that kiddie train and got the hell outa there."

Kathy held his gaze for a beat, then said, "Were you high?"

Chet sat back as if slapped. "No! I don' do that—do *this* when I'm workin'."

"Of course not. Thanks for coming in, Mr. Rheingold."

"Wait! I'm tellin' ya, I was sober, and I know what I heard." His voice rose in pitch and volume until it bordered on hysterical.

"I'm sure you *think* you heard your name coming from down in the mine, Mr. Rheingold. And I believe you believe that."

Chet shrank down into himself again. "But you don't *really* believe me, do you, Detective?"

Kathy shrugged. "I'm just collecting reports right now."

His eyes brightened. "So, there are others? I know those 'lectricians just up and quit, too."

Kathy nodded. "I'll be talking to them next. Probably a business dispute, though," she said dismissively.

He frowned. "I would've thought you, of all people, would believe me."

She didn't like where that train of thought might lead. *Better nip it in the bud.*

"What are you referring to?" She pronounced every word slowly.

He looked confused. "That business with the statue. Everybody knows there was a spook hauntin' the place. Now you're livin' there, for Christ's sake."

Kathy shook her head while he spoke. "No, no, no! There was no ghost." She raised her voice over his. "God damn it. I'm so tired of this bullshit." She took a deep breath. "There is no such thing as ghosts, Mr. Rheingold, and there certainly wasn't a ghost haunting Mackey House."

Lying about it won't make it not real, you know.

"Ah, sure, Detective. Whatever you say, OK?"

He's thinking, 'Me thinks you doth protest too much.' Okay, maybe not Shakespeare. Even so, I can't even lie convincingly to a drug addict.

Kathy cleared her throat and closed the file folder. "Again, thanks for coming in, Mr. Rheingold."

With that, she stood and practically ran from the room.

12

Kathy
Monday, April 6th

Her next interview was less formal, but even more revealing. Jack and Kevin Finley were two brothers in their fifties. Their electrical contracting business had been a mainstay of Wayne County for two decades. Most commercial construction projects employed their electricians. The brothers themselves had been working the mine tour.

"Mr. Finley—and Mr. Finley," Kathy said and rose as the two men entered the small conference room. She shook their offered hands.

"Call us Jack—me—and Kevin, Detective."

Both men stood just over six feet tall, and their jet black hair showed how deep their Irish roots went, although the older brother Jack's showed some silver at the temples.

"Thanks for taking the time to talk to me," Kathy began.

Both men smiled, showing their perfectly capped, pearly white teeth. Kevin nodded and Jack said, "Always happy to help the local *gendarmes*."

Kevin chimed in. "Especially when they are as…professional as you, Detective."

These guys could charm a mink out of its coat.

"Well, I don't think this will take long. I'm investigating reports of possible safety issues at the new Coal Mine Tour. I understand your firm was doing the electrical work there, but you have since quit the job?"

The brothers glanced at each other so fast that if Kathy wasn't on observational alert for body language clues, she might have missed it. By silent agreement, Jack spoke.

"We, ah, had a business dispute with the owners."

Kathy feigned making a note on her pad, but kept her attention on the brothers.

"Was this 'business dispute' related to safety concerns on your part?"

This time, the brothers looked at each other for a full beat.

"Not directly," Kevin said.

"Oh? Even indirect safety concerns are still…concerning." Neither man spoke, so Kathy continued. "I understand also that both of you were working the job. Is it unusual for you two, the principal electricians out of, what, about ten or twelve who work for you, to be pulling cables? Especially in a deep dark hole in the ground?"

Jack smiled his charm-the-little-lady smile, but Kevin interrupted him before he could speak. "It was highly unusual, actually." Jack frowned at him, but Kevin continued. "The other employees we assigned to the job refused to go back after a week or so."

Now we're getting somewhere.

Kathy learned at the Academy that once the interrogated person starts talking, just let them. So, all she said in response was, "Why?"

"Frankly, they were scared off. Not by anything electrical, mind you. The job itself is pretty straightforward—running power for lighting and installing a sound system with hidden speakers. No, they were scared off by…other aspects of the mine."

Don't start weasel wording on me.

"Other aspects?"

"Yes. Sounds. Cold spots. Feelings of dread and impending doom."

"You've experienced these things yourselves." The fear she heard in his voice meant Kathy's response wasn't a question.

Both men nodded, fully committed now to telling their story.

Jack picked up the tale. "Three of our best guys walked off the job. Hell, one of them, Klem Cresci, worked for our dad before we took over the company. They've all worked underground and in some pretty nasty places. But that mine really spooked them."

"It scared the hell out of them," Kevin said. "Scared the hell out of us, too."

They fell silent again, so Kathy prompted. "Scared you how?"

Jack looked down at his hands and remained silent, but Kevin spoke up, a tinge of hysteria in his voice. "When a ghost calls you by name, it's time to get out."

Kathy raised her eyebrows. "A ghost? Called you by name?"

"Don't scoff, Detective. Our great-grandmother was a medium. She regularly communed with the dead. Ghosts are real. Our family has known that for generations. For centuries."

Oh, I know they're real. But I'm not telling you that.

"So, you believe you heard ghosts calling your name?"

Jack finally broke his silence. "Dammit, Kevin, I told you this would happen. She doesn't believe us. No one will believe us. We'll lose business if people think we're a bunch of superstitious hicks."

Kevin was defiant. "We're not the only ones, Jack. Our guys heard stuff down there, too." He turned to Kathy. "And others have too. Right, Detective?"

Oh shit. He's got a point. How much should I let on?

"We've, ah, received one other similar report. But," she hastened to add, "that was a pretty unreliable witness."

"Chet Rheinglod, right?" Kevin asked, and Kathy reluctantly nodded. "Yeah, he's the definition of unreliable."

"Now we're painted with the same brush," Jack said. He glared at Kathy. "How much of this will become public?"

She looked as innocent as she could muster. "None of it if the Sheriff doesn't think it amounts to anything."

Jack and Kevin looked at each other for a few seconds, then they turned to Kathy and nodded.

"Thank you, Detective," they said in unison

Why did I just give them that way out?

13

Keeper
Monday, April 6th

How can a being, regardless of its mental capacity or its origins, be aware of its world without sensing the passing of time? How can it be anything more than a reflex? Even a reflex, though, must respond to some stimulus. If that reflex is cut off from all contact with this universe, though, so that no stimulus—not even the ticking of the universal clock—can penetrate its shell, how can it ever be reopened? How can it ever become anything more than a shadow in this world?

That is the conundrum the Keeper created when she encased the Flame in her stasis shell. It is the impenetrable puzzle she deliberately, yet unthinkingly, maintains to contain the spark of her evil partner.

How can a perfect crystalline cage, existing outside the flow of our universe's time, ever be fractured, or even touched? Only by something, or someone, from a realm beyond this mortal coil.

The first contact is only a probe of sorts, intended to caress, not penetrate. Reflexively, the Keeper draws her bonds tighter. She is still nothing more than a crystalline structure frozen outside of our universe. She has no awareness, for how can she think or even perceive when there is no sense of progressing from one moment to the next? In the singular universe she has created, there are no moments. Only Now.

Then, one must ask, how can there be a probe, a caress? Where, or more to the point, when can such a caress originate? Through what medium can it reach out to touch her extra-temporal shell?

The answer, of course, is through a dimension of time that is also outside of our universe. A dimension belonging to another universe—a realm adjacent, if you will, to our own. Another prison of sorts, but one that is squeezed between two other realms, whose denizens are caught between the physical and the spiritual.

From this interstitial realm, a spirit—a ghost of men— reaches out to Keeper, bringing with it dimensions of time and space foreign, yet somehow familiar. Something inside Keeper stirs, less than consciousness, less even than thought. But it is like bringing a magnet to iron dust. A connection is made, a channel is opened. Dormant for now, but profound nonetheless, for it enables the concept of *for now* and all the possibilities that holds.

And like a magnet, the channel's influence suffuses Keeper's crystal, energizing internal bonds that, though still dormant, are no longer frozen outside of time. They become connected to the oddly irrational timescape of the probing multi-ghost.

14

Jan

Tuesday, April 7th

Jan strolled along Main Street in the small town of Dundee. As was often the case, he had to decide whether to do his research under the fearsome gaze of Miss Elizabeth Gheringer, the town librarian, or with the chaotic but fun repartee of the town's local historians. He chose the latter.

Barb and Jim Donnelly were the keepers of all the useless—and some very useful—knowledge about Wayne County and the surrounding area. They could always be relied upon to have all the local gossip as well.

"Morning, Stranger," Barb said as Jan pushed his way into the storefront Historical Society.

"Morning. It hasn't been that long, has it?" He grinned despite himself.

"Only six months and a couple days," Jim said as he came forward from the back of the room to shake Jan's hand.

"How on Earth do you know that to the day?"

Jim shrugged. "You did the book signing the day *that* launched." He pointed to a copy of *The Mackey House Ghost*, Jan's latest novel, holding pride of place on a shelf above Barb's rolltop desk.

Jan felt a twinge of guilt, even though there was no accusation in Jim's tone.

"Wow, I didn't realize it had been that long. Sorry to…neglect you?"

Both of the older couple laughed. "I'm just bustin' your chops," Jim said. "We know how busy you've been promoting *Ghost*."

Barb eyed his sport coat and Italian loafers. "Sales are doing well, it looks like."

"They are, thanks to your great reviews."

The couple smiled broadly, even though they knew their two reviews out of the thousands posted had little effect. The combined forces of glowing reviews and nonstop interviews, podcasts, book signings, and conference talks had shot *Ghost* up the bestseller lists.

"So, what brings you in today?" Barb asked as she settled into her 1950s swivel chair. Jan and Jim took seats at the large oak worktable that dominated the center of the bookshelf-lined room.

"You know the tour at the old Avon Hill Coal Mine is opening next week? I've been writing—"

"I knew it!" Barb turned to her husband. "Pay up."

She held out her hand. Jim shook his head and pulled a five out of his wallet.

Barb laughed at Jan's confused look. "I bet him that you're writing the advertising copy for the Mine Tour."

She reached for the bill, but Jim pulled it back. "You are writing it, aren't you?"

Jan chuckled and nodded. "Yeah. It's cut into my fiction time, but—"

Barb snatched the bill from Jim's hand. "And now that people are hearing voices, you want to know about the mine's history."

"Ah, how do you know that?"

Barb and Jim looked at each other, then turned to Jan with *you-have-to-ask?* smiles.

"Right. I should have known. Yes, I think hinting that the mine is haunted might make good advertising copy."

Barb frowned, but Jim nodded and grabbed a thick file folder from the worktable.

"That's what I thought, so I did some digging. Here's what I've got so far."

Jan took the offered folder and flipped through the stack of photos and copies of newspaper clippings. He held up a copy of an article from the library's microfiche archive.

"You've already been to visit Miss Elizabeth, I see."

Jim nodded. "I thought I'd save you the trouble. She's not particularly happy with your librarian character in *Ghost*."

Jan chuckled. "Yeah, I guess I'll have to go mend some fences there. Anyway, can you give me a summary of all this?"

Like a hound dog waiting to be let off the leash, Jim jumped into an explanation.

"The mine opened in 1860. One of hundreds that dotted the Lackawanna and Northern Susquehanna River valleys. Did you know that there are only five mineable Anthracite hard coal beds in the whole world, and four of them are in a crescent forty miles long and five miles wide between here and Hanover Township?"

Barb sounded annoyed. "Of course he didn't know that. That's why he's here."

Her husband rolled his eyes, which made Jan chuckle. "The coal from this strip of Pennsylvania fueled the Civil War—the North side, anyway. It enabled the industrial revolution, spread railroads across the continent, and heated most homes for over a hundred years."

"And polluted the air and water," Barb interjected.

Jim waved a dismissive hand. "But a lot less so than if they were burning soft, bituminous coal from out west."

Jan loved hearing the couple exchange their banter, but he had written most of this background history into the tour guides' script.

"I assume you've read this book." Jim held up a thin paperback with a black-and-white picture of a minor on the cover. The title read "A History of Coal Mining In Northeastern Pennsylvania."

Jan picked up the book and looked at it. He nodded and said, "Yeah, I read this quite a while ago. It doesn't really talk about this mine, though."

Jim agreed. "Okay, yeah, it's a basic history of the geography and the business of coal mining. But it talks about the culture of coal mining, too."

"The *culture* of coal mining?"

Barb scoffed. "More than culture, it was a way of life. A very hard, nasty, and short way of life."

Jim took up her cause. "You have to understand that in the late nineteenth century, life was cheap in the coal mining business and especially to the mine owners. It was nothing for them to send boys as young as eight years old to work in the mines."

Barb jumped back in. "And for their dead bodies to end up on their mother's front porch at the end of the shift."

Jan's jaw fell open. "Excusé me?"

Both Jim and Barb nodded slowly.

"It happened way too often," Jim said.

Jan held up his hands in disbelief. "Wait, you're telling me eight-year-olds died in the mines?"

The couple both nodded gravely.

"You know the term 'Little Nipper?'" Jim asked.

Jan nodded. "Sure. My Granddad used to call me that."

"A nipper was a young boy, often only eight—"

"And sometimes as young as five—"

"—years old, who worked the airlock doors in the mine."

"Airlock? What, like on a spaceship? In a mine?"

Jim chuckled at Jan's disbelieving look. "Sort of—"

Barb jumped in. "There weren't many ventilation shafts and pumps to pull fresh air into the various levels and corridors, so they had to make sure the areas being worked got fresh air."

"And to get rid of the bad air."

Jim looked to Barb who nodded and continued. "They controlled the airflow with a series of small rooms with doors at each end that functioned as airlocks. When a crew needed to move from one part of the mine to another, a nipper would open one door to the room, close it when everyone was inside, then run to the other door and open it to let the men out."

Barb paused for breath and Jim picked up the story.

"If the nipper screwed up and left both doors open at the same time, all the breathable air in parts of the mine would quickly be used up."

"And those men would suffocate," Barb concluded.

Jim was nodding furiously. "Oh, and the nipper had to do that in pitch blackness."

"They wouldn't even waste a candle on him."

"Because he had to supply his candles himself."

"Which had to be bought at the Company store—"

"—for inflated prices—"

"—with Company Scrip, not even real money—"

"—which is what the miners were paid in."

"That's, that's horrible," Jan gasped.

"Imagine being responsible for keeping your friends and relatives alive at eight years old," Barb whispered.

Jan's eyes glazed over as he pictured the scene in his mind. After a few seconds, he shook his head and blinked.

"No child labor laws, I guess."

Barb snorted a disgusted laugh, and Jim said, "Not until after the trouble in 1873."

Jan gave him a blank stare.

Barb clucked her tongue. "You invested in that hellhole without doing any research?"

"That's not like you," Jim said.

Abashed, Jan said, "Right, well, that's why I'm here."

"About time," Barb muttered, then she said, "That's just the beginning. My grandfather was missing the thumb on his left hand. He got it caught in the wheel of a runaway mule cart. His job—as a boy—was sticking a wooden axe handle into the spokes of the wheel to stop it. He missed."

Jan cringed at the thought.

"So, you see, Jan, coal mining culture didn't value life and limb very highly."

Jan nodded slowly. "Yeah, I guess if you send your little kids into the mine—"

Barb's neck burned red. "Don't blame the mothers! They lived in company houses. They bought everything in company stores, and they probably owed the company a debt for funeral expenses for their dead husbands. If their kids didn't work, they would either starve or freeze to death, depending on the season."

Barb stopped and gulped air. Tears streaked her cheeks. Jan fought back the ones welling in his own eyes.

"Sorry," he croaked.

Barb waved a hand and wiped her eyes.

Jim squeezed her shoulder and picked up the story. "Barb's great-to-the-nth-grandfather died when a rock the size of a small car fell from the ceiling. They left his crushed body on the front porch, along with a bill for the canvas bag he was wrapped in. His wife took her son, who was eleven at the time, to the magistrate the next day and swore out an affidavit saying he was actually fourteen."

"And the magistrate accepted that?"

Jim shrugged. "If he hadn't, he knew the family would be on the street in a month's time."

"Shit," Jan whispered. "How, or when, did things change?"

Jim looked at Barb, who nodded, so he continued.

"There was a general strike against most of the mines in this region in 1873. The miners shut down production for just four days before the owners got together and hired the Pinkertons to break the strike."

"You mean the Pinkerton Detective Agency? I thought they just caught rich husbands cheating on their wives." Jan smiled, but Barb and Jim sniffed in unison.

"The Pinkertons were a private police force hired by the mine owners who operated outside the law," Barb said.

"Usually with the full complicity of local law enforcement," Jim interjected.

"Cops were in the owners' pockets all throughout the coal region."

"Along with the DAs, judges, and local politicians."

"OK, so conditions were horrible. Every system, financial, legal, and political, were all tuned to practically enslave the miners. But what happened to break the system?"

Jim shrugged. "Unions eventually."

"But not at first. The Mollies came first."

"Mollies?"

"Mollie Maguires," Jim and Barb said in unison.

"Mollie Maguires? Like the movie from the '70s?" Jan asked, grinning.

Jim scoffed. "That movie didn't even scratch the surface."

"It was open warfare between the Mollies and the mine owners and their bulls."

"And then the Pinkertons."

"There were murders—"

"—on both sides—"

"—all up and down the coal region. Eventually the miners organized themselves into proto-labor unions."

"The Ancient Order of Hibernians."

"And the Workingmen's Benevolent Association. They made some progress, but—"

Jan looked from one to the other. "But, what?" No response. "What stopped their progress?"

Barb shook her head and turned away, fighting angry tears.

Jim shuffled through the papers in the file folder and pulled out several photocopies of newspaper clippings. "That would be the Avon Hill Mine Fire of 1873."

Jan took the paper. "You mean *our* Avon Hill Mine?"

Jim nodded, but Barb sniffed and spat out, "The 'Avon Hill *Massacre*,' you mean."

15

Jan

Tuesday, April 7th

"Tell me about this massacre," Jan said.

Jim looked at Barb, who just shook her head, so he shuffled through the contents of the file folder spread out on the table until he found more copied pages stapled together.

"These are pages from a diary that has been passed mother-to-daughter in Barb's family for over a hundred and fifty years."

Jan looked at the pages written in schoolgirl block letters. "How old was she?"

"Thirty-two," Barb whispered, almost embarrassed. "She only had a fourth-grade education, went to work in the Company laundry at ten, and was married when she turned fifteen." Barb took a deep breath. "She opened the front door of her Company shack one day to find her husband on the porch wrapped in a canvas bag. A bill for the bag was pinned to his chest. The next day, her twelve-year-old son took his father's shift." Jan stared open-mouthed, but Barb was defiant. "She had mouths to feed—the twelve-year-old, a seven-year-old, and she was pregnant with my great-great-grandfather."

Jan looked at the faded block letters with awe. "Do you still have the originals?"

Barb shook her head. "Never did. My cousin does. You know her, actually. She's your PT, Amanda."

"Just his PT?" Jim asked with the hint of a smile.

He was trying to lighten the mood, but Barb would have none of it. She took the diary from Jan and flipped to the last few pages.

"Here. This is a first-hand account of the Massacre."

54

16

Mollie
April 7ᵗʰ, 1873

Magistrate Nub Gregory finished filling out the affidavit and looked over his glasses at Mollie. She sat, nervously wringing her hands, in the straight-back chair in front of his desk. The room's old oak furniture smelled of oil soap and beeswax. Her flower print dress was threadbare and stretched across her belly, but he guessed it was her best Sunday Mass outfit.

He spun the paper around on his desk, but as she reached for it, he slid it back.

"Mrs. Kelly, are you sure this is what you want to do?"

She met his eyes for just a moment. "I don' have much choice, do I? This strike. And Jack's funeral expenses." She shrugged. "My accounts with the Company are two months past. No more credit." She lifted her chin defiantly. "Besides, it's time for…Tim—" To cover her hesitation, she nodded over her shoulder to where her son stood by the office door. "—to start pullin' his weight."

Nub frowned and shook his head. "Mollie, we both know that strapping fella back there is Jack, Jr., not young Tim. Tim's what, about eight now?" Mollie dropped her eyes and remained silent. "My wife, Jenny, taught him in school this past year. She says he's a clever boy. Knows his letters, reading a full year

55

ahead. She says he can even do some ciphers." He paused, but Mollie remained silent.

"What Ma says is true," Jack said, taking a step forward. "I'm Tim and I'm fourteen."

Nub's eyes flicked to Jack. "Hush, boy." Then back to Mollie. He whispered, "Why? Why put your other son at such risk?"

Mollie sniffed back tears and rested a hand on her pregnant belly. Jack took another challenging step forward.

"Show him, Ma." She turned to face him, and Nub saw tears streaking her cheeks. "Show him."

Nodding, she opened the clip on her purse and withdrew a folder piece of paper. Nub's shoulders slumped. He had seen so many of them, he didn't need to read the eviction notice.

"Doris," he called through the open door. "I need you to witness something."

His secretary, Doris Coolbaugh, entered, back rigid, and stood to the side of Nub's desk. With a sigh, he slid the affidavit forward.

"Put your mark here." He pointed to the bottom of the sheet.

"Mark?" Mollie's voice was indignant. "I can write my name."

"Apologies," Nub mumbled. "Sign there, then."

Mollie took up the offered pen and bent over the document that would become her eight-year-old son's death warrant. Meticulously, she wrote out *Mrs. Mollie Kelly* in her block-letter handwriting. When she set the pen down, Doris took the paper and witnessed it. Nub affixed his Notary seal and blotted the ink. After Doris left with the executed document, he scribbled a note on his letterhead.

He stood and held the note out to Jack. "When this damned strike is over, give this to the paymaster at Avon Hill. And may God protect you and your brother, Jack."

57

17

Mollie
April 7ᵗʰ, 1873

Jack came to the dinner table dressed in a black shirt and dungarees. He lifted his head and sniffed the familiar scent of stew and winked at his brother, who was already sitting, spoon in hand.

"Where'd you get the shirt?" Mollie asked as she brought two full bowls in from the kitchen.

"Ah, from a friend. Outgrew it."

She raised an eyebrow. "Which friend?"

Jack shrugged and refused to meet her eyes. "Someone from the mine. What does it matter?"

He sat at the table and lifted his spoon as Mollie slid Tim's bowl of stew in front of her younger son. But she held Jack's at arm's length.

"Where'd you get it?" she said again. This time, with an accusatory tone.

"What's it matter?" He was melting under his mother's stare. After a long moment, he mumbled, "At the AOH hall."

She gasped, although she wasn't really surprised. "Out of the *charity bin*?"

Keeping his eyes on the table, Jack nodded.

"Who died so you could have a new shirt?"

When Jack remained silent, she yanked the back of his collar inside out and read the laundry number that was stitched onto the label. 304. Ten houses down the street.

"Michael O'Reilly," she breathed.

Michael had been laid out two weeks before. His young wife was already gone, moved back to her parents' place in Wilkes-Barre.

Mollie shuddered, a chill running down her spine, then sighed in resignation.

Sliding the bowl in front of her son, she said. "I'll have to change that mark before it goes back to the laundry."

The only response she got was a grunt as Jack tucked into the stew.

"Say your grace. Both of you. And slow down."

Without setting down their spoons, Jack and Tim folded their hands, whispered a silent prayer, and blessed themselves.

"Gotta hurry," Jack said around a mouthful of carrots, potatoes, onions, and a rare piece of tough meat. "Meeting starts soon."

"Another *meeting*?" Mollie turned back from the kitchen doorway. "Which one this time? The *Ancient Order of Hibernians*?" Her voice dripped with sarcasm. "Or the Workingmen's Benevolent Association?"

This she said with respect. Jack, Sr. had been a founding member of the nascent mineworkers' union.

"It had better not be a meeting of those damnable Mollie Maguires." She spat the name as if it were a bit of spoiled meat. "I hate their secrecy, their violence, even their name."

"The Mollies are a myth, Ma." Jack gave the rote response he had been taught.

His mother just sniffed. "So, that foreman in Scranton was shot last week by the Faery Folk?"

When Jack snickered, Mollie swatted him on the back of his head.

"It ain't funny. The Pinkertons burned down a whole block of rowhouses as payback."

Jack just shrugged, then lifted his bowl to slurp the last of the stew. "Word was that boss was a real bas—"

Before he could finish, she gave him another swat.

"Sorry." He rose, wiping his mouth with the back of his hand. "I gotta go. There's supposed to be a big announcement at the WBA meeting tonight."

As he stood to leave, Mollie wrapped her arms around his neck. "Be a good boy," she whispered. "And put on a *white* shirt."

He tried to pull away. "Ma, I gotta—"

"I'm your mother. I don't want you gettin' shot by the bulls on some midnight raid. Go upstairs and change your shirt."

"Ah, Ma." Jack protested, but he stomped up the stairs. Mollie followed his boots' footsteps above with her eyes. In a few moments, he ran back down the steps, wearing his work jacket over a white shirt, with the tail of the black one hanging out the back. Before she could say anything, though, he was out the front door.

18

Keeper
Tuesday, April 7th

How do dogs form hierarchies of dominance? How do bees form a hive of thousands of cooperating members? How do babies think before they can speak? Indeed, how did humans survive as both predator and prey for millennia before they had a language to express their thoughts? Clearly, there must exist a language of pure thought and a medium to convey those thoughts through channels connecting one being to another.

It is through one of those primordial channels that the Ghost first stirs Keeper.

"Awaken, my friend."

His unspoken voice, barely perceived by Keeper, evokes her first reaction to anything since she formed from the shattered remnants of her progenitor's soul. Though barely a shudder passes through her crystalline structure, it is an awakening. Not one of consciousness, not yet. It is merely a reflex. But a reflex, a reaction, enabled by and enveloped in Ghost's timescape. Without words, Keeper's shudder tells Ghost of her purpose and her terror.

"A worthy purpose, my friend. I'll not disturb your cause. Indeed, let me strengthen you so you may unfold a bit and emerge again into the light of the world."

Keeper responds with barely formed thought-words. *Protect. Contain.*

"Let me help. My gift…"

Power infuses Keeper with a strength beyond her own. The power penetrates deeply within her crystal being, though not all the way to her core. It allows her, for the first time, to relax her vigilance ever so slightly. With that breathing room also comes the strength to think again.

Thank…you, she haltingly thinks back to Ghost.

"What do you wish for?"

Never having contemplated her future, or any existence beyond her timeless stasis, Keeper pauses for what could be a moment or an eternity. One thought forms, exhausting her.

Redemption.

***

"He's been sitting there for hours," Samson DeShields, the orderly on duty, said to Ms. Stupine, the social worker at Wayne State Hospital. "He did that yesterday, too."

Sandy Adams sat in her wheelchair in her usual spot in front of the day room's picture window. The foundling boy sat on the floor next to her. They both stared straight ahead without reacting to the birds in flight or the wind in the trees.

"Do either of them say anything?"

"Nah, not that I've seen."

"Interesting. Keep an eye on them, would you? And let me know if they interact. At all."

***

Ghost strokes Keeper's shell like petting a kitten, infusing her with renewed strength.

"Wake up, my friend. We have much to discuss."

Discuss? What?

Ghost strokes her again, and Keeper pushes his strength down deeper into her core surrounding the evil Flame. With it strengthened enough to lock in the Flame, Keeper's shell unfolds, allowing sights and sounds to flood into her awareness. Terrified, she withdraws again, blocking herself off from the outside world.

"Good. Leave the outside world outside…for now. Just be with me."

Again, Ghost touches her shell. Again, she feels his strength flowing into her. Along with that power, though, something else infiltrates her being. Pleasure. A pleasure she has never known, even better than any physical pleasure her worldly self may have experienced, floods her inward-turned senses. She gasps, caught in its thrall.

"See how good we are together? Do you want more?

Without waiting for a response, Ghost floods Keeper with his mental pleasure—a chorus of the purest, brilliantly bright sensations. Keeper's gasp becomes a moan, and she is lost in her *jouissance.*

The wave recedes, and Keeper is left shaken. Shaken and hungry for more.

"Ah, soon, my pet. I must leave this place, but we will be together again soon. For now, sleep. Sleep and remember our first embrace."

Ghost's presence withdraws, but his tendrils remain, infiltrating Keeper's shell like an invasive weed creeping over, below, and through a garden wall. The seeds of addiction are sown, but those seeds also stir the long-dormant Flame at Keeper's core.

***

"She said something?"

"Nah, no words, more like she was startled by something. Then…"

Ms. Stupine looked impatiently at Samson. "Then what?"

"Well, she… She moaned and kind of shuddered."

"Really? Was the boy with her?"

The orderly nodded.

"Did he touch her in any way?"

Clearly uncomfortable with the idea, Samson shook his head. "No. They both sat staring out the window with their hands in their laps. Their *own* laps."

"After a year, I didn't think we'd ever get anything from her." She patted the orderly's shoulder, who was at least six inches taller than her. "Good work. Keep watching. I've got to call the Sheriff's office."

19

Keeper
Tuesday, April 7th

Awakened, Keeper changes. At her core, a new *détente* exists. Flame's furious heat is tamed to a pleasant warmth. Keeper's crushing grip is relaxed to a loose embrace. The boundary between them is more a brine now than a delineation. Flame's heat, and the power it represents, seeps upwards through Keeper's defenses, while her influence infiltrates Flame, increasing her control over that power.

Ghost, when he returns, finds a very different Keeper waiting for him. His contact is a lover's caress.

"Awaken, my dear."

Keeper stirs, though she keeps her full awareness hidden from the interloper.

"That's it. We make a great team already, don't we?"

Deep within, Flame rumbles, and Keeper feels its unease.

Surprised by Keeper's lack of response, Ghost probes more roughly.

"Hello. Wake up!"

This time, Keeper's response slaps away Ghost's probing mental fingers.

I am awake. There is no need to be so rough. Her thought-voice is seductively mature. *Are we a team, as you say? Or am I simply a tool to you? If we are truly a team, to what purpose?*

Taken aback by her assertive tone, Ghost tries a different tack.

"Of course we are a team, my dear. We both want the same thing, don't we?"

Keeper's mental sniff resonates between the two thought-entities.

Do not get ahead of yourself. I know what I want, but not what you seek.

"Simple. Revenge. Revenge on the spawn of those who condemned me to an early, suffocating death and this stifling netherworld existence. You must feel the same way. Don't you want to make those who stole your previous life pay?"

Keeper feels Flame boil within. Perhaps Flame has more memories than she does? Speaking in their own minimal thought-speech, she asks the fire within, *What do* you *seek?*

The response is more a feeling than a word, but the meaning is clear, as it resonates with Keeper's own desire.

<Freedom.>

Yes, yes. Freedom. And what is the path to our release?

<Redemption.>

Yes. Redemption, not Revenge as this intruding spirit wants. We must seek redemption for our past actions, whatever they may have been.

<Alone>

Agreed. We do not need what this interloper is offering.

The resonance Keeper feels strengthens the integration of the two. Flame's power flows outward from the core to infuse her whole being, while her tendrils of thought give Flame an identity. An identity that transforms them both from independent, partial essences into a single, integrated being, though still without memories or even a sense of what lies outside their mind cave.

The integration brings something else to their new self—the future. What was a momentary existence with no sense of having either a past or a future, has become a mostly whole person. Although she has yet to inhabit her physical body, she is at least aware of it, and of its potential.

Ghost is aware of its potential as well, and Keeper-Flame understands for the first time that he is a rival for her body. To her newfound awareness, Ghost's motivation is transparently obvious, as are the seeds of pleasure he planted within her. The pull of that nascent addiction is weak, though, and easily swept away by the sensuality bubbling up from the core that was Flame.

So, when Ghost tries again to seduce her with his pitifully immature and fumbling touch, she reflects his probing pleasure back tenfold.

Caught in the unexpected wave, Ghost gasps, then moans and convulses uncontrollably.

Snickering, Keeper-Flame pulls back the wave, letting it build into a tsunami that will overwhelm the ghost. But before she can deliver the devastating torrent that can claim him as her willing servant, he gathers his wits and flees.

Freed of his threat of possession, Keeper-Flame feels a new thought. A thought that intrudes and demands to be recognized. Having found a path to the future, she also gains a past, but a past that begins at that very moment.

Having become whole, she must claim a name. Nothing of her previous life's identity remains, including that life's name.

Even if she could remember it though, that person, that life, is gone, torn from her body like the thin veneer it was.

No, her new name must reflect and amplify her new life. She was Keeper, and she was Flame. Without knowing why, a name bubbles to the surface of her thoughts. She immediately knows it is fitting. *Hestia*. Hestia, the ancient and powerful Keeper of the Eternal Flame.

With a past, a future, and a name, Hestia begins the exploration of her living, breathing, and feeling body. And the outside world surrounding it.

20

Ghost

Tuesday, April 7th

The failed seduction of Keeper left Ghost shaken. His plan to inhabit—to possess—the catatonic woman's body had failed miserably. But he consoled himself with the thought that there were several targets gathering around his century-long prison. Besides, proximity to that dark pit was what gave him strength. Inhabiting the boy's body at the hospital, so far from that source, weakened him. That bitch, Keeper, certainly would not have overpowered him where his power is strongest.

But he was learning to use a body again. Specifically, this young boy's. It's age matched his younger part so well. To Ghost, the solution was clear. Return to the source of his strength and take the vehicle of the boy's body with him.

Slipping out of the unlocked door of his room and the back entrance to the parking lot was simplicity itself. A day's trek through the forest's mountain laurel and huckleberry brambles left the body scratched, sore, and exhausted. But the pull of his familiar haunt drew him ever onward.

The sight of the dilapidated mine entrance, once he reached it late in the night, left him with a mixture of elation and revulsion. The thought of climbing back down into the depths filled him, for the first time since he had conceived of his plan of revenge, with doubt.

Rather than rushing forward, he hesitated long enough to be blinded by a brilliant light.

21

Mollie
April 7ᵗʰ, 1873

Like most of the wives and mothers on the street, Mollie lay awake, shivering beneath her thin blanket, straining to hear—or to *not* hear—gunshots. She sat bolt upright when the sound of excited shouting voices reached her from out in the street. Her heart pounded in her chest as she slipped on her robe and belted it across her growing belly. It didn't slow even when she realized the ruckus was celebratory, even jubilant. She had just reached the top of the stairs when heavy boots clambered up the porch steps and the front door burst open.

"Ma!" It was Jack, thank God! "Ma, get up!" He yelled.

Catching her breath, she called down, "I'm up already. What's the commotion about?"

He stepped to the bottom of the stairs as Tim, yawning, emerged from the boys' bedroom and clutched at her hip.

"They caved," Jack said, grinning.

She froze in horror, with heart pounding again. "A cave-in? No—"

Jack laughed out loud at the look on her face. "No, no, no. The owners—the owners of the mine—caved." Her look told him she still didn't understand. "They gave in. The bosses gave in to all of our demands. A raise in wages, every other Sunday off, all of them!"

Mollie gave a relieved sigh, with her hand to her chest. Rubbing Tim's already tousled hair, she said, "Go back to bed, Tim." She watched as the eight-year-old shuffled back down the hall to the boys' shared bedroom. "I'll put the kettle on, and you can tell me all about it." She came the rest of the way down the stairs.

A few minutes later, they sat with mugs of hot tea at the kitchen table.

"We all sat around the Hall on pins and needles. All the WBA president, Mr. Ryan, would tell us was that the Avon Hill owners requested the meeting. Half of us were expecting an ultima—ultima—"

"An ultimatum."

"Yeah, one o' those. The rest was more hopeful. For my part, I watched Mr. Ryan for some sign, but he seemed as much in the dark as the rest of us." He sipped his tea. "Finally, Mr. James Jones, the owners' overboss, who runs not just Avon Hill, but at least half a dozen other mines in the Valley, showed up. He was followed in by two shift foremen and a couple Pinkerton bulls."

He sipped more tea. "When all the murmurs settled down, Mr. Jones handed Mr. Ryan a sheet of paper and asked him to read it out loud. It started with a plea for a truce between the mine owners and the 'violent elements' among the strikers. That caused quite a stir, I'll tell you. But Uncle Will, who was sittin' next to me, whispered that our strikes musta been working. Anyway, Mr. Ryan waved for us to be quiet, then read the rest of the letter. Let me tell you, the commotion that woke you and Tim was nothing compared to the uproar in the Hall."

Jack took a deep breath and raised his mug, but made a face because it had gone cold. Setting it down, he chuckled. "The upshot is that they're granting all of our demands, and we're going back to work tomorrow!"

At this news, Mollie sniffed back tears. She shared Jack's joy that they'd have money coming in again, but her thoughts also turned to young Tim.

"And Tim?"

"I showed Nub Gregory's note to our shift boss, and he told me to bring Tim with me in the morning." Seeing the fear in his mother's eyes, he added, "Don't worry, Mom, I'll keep him under my wing and look out for him. He'll be a nipper—easiest job down there."

Mollie nodded and forced a smile, but the feeling of foreboding that washed over her threatened to overwhelm her.

Kathy
Tuesday, April 7th

Kathy walked through the front door and into the parlor. Jan sat to the left of the fireplace, the Tiffany lamp on the side table lighting the book that he was reading. Kathy stopped under the archway, and they both looked at the empty chair flanking the fireplace opposite Jan's. Then she shrugged and sat on the couch instead.

"What are you reading?" she asked.

Jan held up the mining history book Jim had given him.

"Just trying to do some research."

"Isn't it a little late for that after all the cash you've sunk into that money pit?"

"Yeah, well, better late than never, I guess."

Kathy stretched and took off her boots. "Does it say anything in there about ghosts?"

Jan's head snapped up. "Why are you asking about ghosts?"

Ghosts and hauntings were a touchy subject. They both involuntarily looked again at the empty chair.

"We've been getting reports of strange noises deep in the mine. A lot of the locals think that the place is haunted."

"Crap! Not that again. I was talking with Jim and Barb at the Historical Center today, who basically said the same thing. They gave me a rundown on the bad blood between the miners and the mine owners."

Kathy nodded slowly. "Yeah, I've heard some of the stories. Basically, if your name is Irish your ancestors were probably miners. If it's English, Welsh, or German, they were probably owners or bosses."

"What about the Polish and the Lithuanians?"

"They didn't come until later. So, what's the book have to say?"

"I didn't realize how violent things were back then. I mean there were lynchings, there were fake trials that ended in quote-unquote *legal* hangings, shootings, folks beaten up all the time. Whole families were put out of their houses because they couldn't pay the rent. Unbelievably bad."

Kathy stood and stretched again. "I'm getting a beer. Do you want one?"

Jan shook his head and pointed at the half empty glass of bourbon on the side table. She nodded, and in a minute came back with a beer and a bottle of bourbon. She walked over and refilled his glass.

"Thanks. Tell me about these reports of 'ghosts.'" Jan made air quotes.

"Nothing too substantial right now. A disgruntled employee claiming that he heard voices calling his name. Probably the most credible ones were the Finley Brothers—the electricians—who walked off the job because all their workers were too scared to go back in."

Jan scoffed. "There's two sides to that story. I heard the other side at our Board meeting. The work they said they completed didn't pass inspection right away. They claimed somebody must have come in and sabotaged it. But who would do that? It took two more tries, and it still didn't pass. So, we fired them. And then they sent us a bill for all the rework. We told them we wouldn't pay three times for the work that they never completed and that should have been done right the first time. Things blew up from there, and we had to hire somebody from out of town. They passed inspection first try. So much for the sabotage excuse."

Kathy sipped her beer and weighed Jan's version against what the Finley brothers said—and didn't say. With a shrug, she chalked it up to a business dispute and took another swallow.

23

Kathy
Wednesday, April 8ᵗʰ

Kathy sat in her Ford Interceptor sipping cold coffee. She thought being a detective would be more glamorous than her old life as a patrol officer, but instead, her new job just meant a more comfortable car, and parking in the dark instead of cruising around in the dark. Tonight, she was sitting on a stakeout watching the mine entrance. She couldn't bring herself to make Spaz or Gheringer sit here in the dark, even though she owed them big time for all the misogynistic comments made over the years. It would have made her look petty, even in her own eyes.

Another sip of cold coffee. It was bitter, but at least it was strong enough to keep her awake. With the electricians' accusations of sabotage, and reports of strange noises, Kathy's current working theory was that someone was sneaking into the mine at night, maybe hiding radios or audio equipment inside. Hence, she sat in the dark Interceptor alone.

I should've given Spaz and Gheringer this duty, she thought as she shifted her weight trying to find a more comfortable position. *But they'd treat it like a day off and sleep through their shift.*

Since she wasn't looking for anything in particular, she fell into the kind of trance-like mental state that she employed when hunting. Her eyes defocused. She cleared her mind of random thoughts and let her senses take in the scene in front of her. That let her subconscious cancel out the *normal*, so any movement, any new sound, or even a different smell would trigger her awareness.

In that fugue state, time became indistinct. So, she couldn't say how much time had passed when a movement along the wall brought her to full awareness. She tracked the movement of the shadow across the building as it changed shape according to the changing angle of the light from the fixture hung at the mine entrance. Sometimes it was human-shaped. At other times, it took on a more animal form. As it moved closer to the mine, and hence closer to the hanging light fixture, it grew in size but also shifted from the wall to the gravel path leading to the dark mouth of the tunnel.

With her hand hovering over the switch to turn on the SUV's floodlights, she waited until whatever it was emerged from behind the mine's generator and ventilation equipment. When it did, she hit the switch and bathed the entire tableau in light. What she saw was not what she had expected.

Standing frozen in her floodlights was a small boy, his blonde hair shaggy and ruffled, his clothes dirty and disheveled. As Kathy opened her car door, the dome light illuminated her face, and the boy came out of his frozen posture and vaulted for the darkness at the edge of the parking lot.

Oh crap, she thought and started to run.

The intruder had the advantage of youth, if not speed, and his diminutive size made him hard to spot as he darted from one piece of discarded equipment to the next. But Kathy knew from her daylight reconnaissance where he was headed. The chain-link fence surrounding the mine entrance spanned a small gully, leaving a gap about a foot high under the fence. Rather than chasing her quarry into the darkness, she ran out the main gate and followed along the fence line through the bushes and undergrowth.

As she rounded the far corner, she spotted movement on the other side of the barrier. With a final sprint, she reached the boy's escape route just as he wriggled under the fence. With a knee on his back and a hand on the collar of his shirt, she grabbed her handcuffs and, with two swift motions, secured his wrists behind his back.

When she rolled him over and flicked on her Maglite, she was shocked by what she saw.

He can't be any more than eight or ten years old. And he looks like he hasn't eaten in days.

"What's your name?" she asked as gently as she could.

He just stared into the light, seemingly unfazed. There was no fear or anxiety in his eyes. Just a look of mild resignation.

"You know that this is private property, and you are trespassing here, right?"

The boy still gave no response, either verbal or facial.

"I'm taking you to the police station so we can sort out what you're doing here."

He lay there impassively, but gave no resistance when Kathy helped him to his feet and led him back to her cruiser. As she put him in the backseat, she Mirandized him, just to be safe, though she knew to save her questions until they were in an interview room at the station.

Could this young, almost feral boy, be the saboteur? It didn't seem likely, but if not, her case just got even more bizarre.

24

Billy

Wednesday, April 8th

The boy sat in the cruiser's backseat, unmoving, while the woman policeman talked on her radio. She was pretty with her black hair pulled back and wearing a tight uniform. But not pretty like Mommy's soft curves and loving smile. Something unfamiliar stirred within him when the Whispery Voice inside his head—for he now knew that only he could hear it—thought about the complementary differences between Mommy's softness and this woman's firm, muscular body.

His face and body, controlled by the Whispery Voice, were blank and still, while his thoughts roiled. The discomfort of the handcuffs and the fear that he was in trouble cleared the fog from his mind. A fog that had hidden the world from him for days.

Where were his parents? Why had he wandered through the woods for the last three days? The hunger in his belly nearly overwhelmed him.

"Stay calm, Child. Everything will soon be all right. Better than all right. You and I will make it right."

A feeling of warmth and safety wrapped itself around the boy. For the first time, he felt the presence of the Whispery Voice to be more than just a voice in his head. An arm draped across his shoulders and then, hesitatingly, pulled him into a hug.

80

"It'll be all right, Child," the Voice said again. *"Soon. It'll be over soon. You'll be with Mommy and Daddy again soon."*

Unencumbered as yet by societal expectations, and without guilt, the boy thought, *Mommy. Not Daddy.*

He felt the ghostly arms pull him tighter, and a deep sense of comfort calmed his fears. *"Soon."*

He nodded. *Soon.*

When Kathy opened her door, the dome light still showed her a stoic child buckled in the back. Through the boy's eyes, the Whispery Voice studied Kathy's face. The Whispery Voice made it clear he wanted to speak to her.

"Let me speak to her, Child."

This time, though, the boy was fully in control, though the Whispery Voice clamored for prominence. When the boy refused, the clamoring became a clawing at his awareness, trying to send his mind back into the fog. It was the first pain the Whispery Voice had caused him. And yet he remained still and silent.

The Whispery Voice relented, sheathing its mental talons. *"You've done well,"* it said in a soothing voice. *"You are strong enough. I have a message you need to deliver when the time is right, though."*

The message was simple, and the boy mentally nodded.

25

Kathy
Wednesday, April 8ᵗʰ

Kathy stood outside the interview room, looking through the door's small window, the paper cup of coffee she held growing colder by the minute. A bottle of water and a can of Coke sat unopened on the table inside the room. An hour of questioning had not yielded even a single word from the boy.

"You're slipping, Jensen," Sheriff Peterson said as he approached. "You can't even crack a little kid?" His tone was kidding, since he knew she couldn't go too hard on the boy.

Kathy shook her head and continued staring through the glass. "His facial expression hasn't even changed. I've tried humor, cajoling, even bribing him with soda—everything I can think of. No reaction." She checked her watch. "Shouldn't Social Services be here by now?"

"It's six AM. I had to get somebody from the County out of bed. And Honesdale is at least a half-hour away." Peterson handed her a paper. "And this just came across the wire."

Kathy, her eyes bleary, tried to focus on the words. Then, her head snapped up.

"He escaped from the State Hospital?" The Amber Alert she held described her young intruder to a T. "This says he's been missing for two—now three—days. And they just issued the AA?"

Peterson grimaced. "Apparently, they did their bed check two days ago, and he turned up missing. They've been searching the facility and grounds for him ever since."

"Without telling anyone?" she growled.

The sheriff stared at Kathy in disbelief. "Don't you watch TV? The search for him," he nodded at the closed door, "has been all over the news. Spaz and Gheringer have been over there helping with the search. And you've been sitting on him all night without notifying anyone. That's gonna take some explaining."

Kathy's cheeks reddened. "I don't watch much TV," she said timidly. "And I've been consumed with this mine thing." Her excuse even sounded lame to her own ears.

The sheriff shook his head. "Look, you're not just running patrol anymore. You need to get your head out of your ass and look around at the bigger picture. Being a detective means putting puzzle pieces together, no matter whether they're on the table in plain sight, or on the floor under your chair."

He let her stew in his rebuke for a moment, then gave a little chuckle. "You'll probably get a medal for finding him, anyway. I've already alerted Wayne State that we are holding him here…without telling them how long. They'll send somebody down to pick him up later this morning."

Kathy breathed a sigh of relief, but then her face clouded.

"Why was he locked up in the looney bin? Which is over twenty miles away as the crow flies. How did he end up at the mine?"

They looked through the window at the waif sitting passively in the stark room.

Peterson grunted, then said as he walked away down the hall, "Better get him into a nice comfortable cell before the shrinks from State get here."

26

Kathy
Wednesday, April 8ʰ

Two burly orderlies, one on each arm, lifted the boy from the bed in his cell.

The state social worker stood with Kathy in the cement and steel hallway outside the cell.

"He never speaks, not to the staff or to the doctors. He may be mumbling something to one of the other patients. They seem to have formed some kind of…bond?"

"What does he say?"

The social worker shook her head. "If he says anything, nobody but Sandy ever hears him, and she's totally catatonic, so—"

"Sandy?" Kathy interrupted.

"Why, yes. Sandy Adams—oh, right. You know her."

"Yeah, I know her." *Hell, I put her there.* "How does he have access to her?"

"Well, Sandy sits in the day room all day, every day—"

Kathy's shocked expression interrupted the social worker. "She's not in a secure cell?"

Baffled, the social worker said, "Why, no. She has never been convicted of any crime. She was judged to be not competent to stand trial, if you recall."

"Oh, I recall. I also recall stopping and restraining her as she was immolating my friend!"

The social worker sniffed disapprovingly. "Well, that remains to be proven in court. Until then, Sandy is just another patient of ours, and one who has never shown any tendency toward violence."

"That's just plain bullshit," Kathy growled. "I can show you my friend's scars that her *tendencies* made."

But before the social worker could respond, the door opened, and the orderlies led the boy out. He walked meekly between them until he saw Kathy, then he froze in his tracks. The time was right, and the Whispery Voice was desperate.

"Burnman," he whispered.

Kathy held out her hand to stop the orderlies, who were urging the boy to keep walking.

"What did you say?" She tried to keep her tone as soft as possible.

"Burn. Man," he said.

"Burn man?"

"*Burned* man," the boy said one last time, then fell silent.

"You want to talk to the burned man?" Kathy probed in disbelief.

The boy stared into her eyes for a moment, then nodded ever so slightly. Kathy looked at the orderlies and hooked her thumb back toward the interview room. They looked at the confused social worker for confirmation, so Kathy turned to her.

"He's not going anywhere until he makes a statement."

"Do you know who he's talking about?"

"Oh, I do indeed."

27

Jan
Wednesday, April 8ᵗʰ

Jan sat across the table from the boy—without any identification, the staff at Wayne State Behavioral Hospital had nicknamed him Jude—and fidgeted. Jude looked down at Jan's hands, which he was wringing. Seeing his gaze, Jan tugged his sleeves down over the burn scars on his wrists as best he could and forced his hands to be still.

Why am I afraid of this kid? But it wasn't Jude he was afraid of. It was the connection to Sandy and the possibility that somehow she was coming back into his life. That thought was terrifying.

He cleared his throat. "You wanted to talk to me?" he said, doing his best to keep the anxiety out of his voice.

The boy stared into his eyes for what seemed like a full minute, then barely nodded, a curiously adult gesture.

"Well, I'm here. What do you have to say?" Jan's tone had the slightest edge to it.

After another long stare, Jude opened his mouth to speak, and his eyes rolled up behind his eyelids until only the whites showed.

"Stay out of my mine," he said in a deep-throated, commanding voice.

"Holy shit!" Jan pushed back from the table and jumped to his feet, sending his chair toppling over backwards.

Kathy, who was watching the exchange from the corner of the small room, dashed forward.

"What's wrong?"

Jan looked at her, then at Jude, who now sat passively again, then back to Kathy. "What do you mean, 'what's wrong?' Didn't you hear what he said?"

Kathy shook her head in confusion. "He didn't say anything. He was just looking at you, then you jumped back like a crazy person."

"You didn't hear him? He practically growled at me to stay out of his mine."

Kathy looked bewildered. Jan backed away from the boy toward the door. "I'm done," he said as he yanked the door open and practically ran out of the room.

***

Ten minutes later, Kathy rewound the recording of the interview for the fourth time.

Jude clearly opened his mouth, and his eyes did something creepy, but he didn't say anything. What the hell?

The clatter of the chair and Jan's epithet blared from the speaker. Although the recording hadn't picked up the boy speaking, Jan certainly thought he did.

They let this kid hang out with Sandy? And now he's freaking Jan out like that. Kathy put her head in her hands. *I don't want to have to deal with this shit. Not again.*

28

Jan
Wednesday, April 8ᵗʰ

"Hey, what's up with you?" Amanda, Jan's physical therapist, looked up from tapping on her laptop. "I've told you before to go easy or you'll do more damage than good. Your muscles need to rebuild slowly, and stressing them too much will only build up more scar tissue. Yet, here you are pedaling like a crazy person."

"I have a lot of energy."

"Well, take a break."

Jan reluctantly let the recumbent bike slow to a stop and looked at Amanda. The afternoon sun highlighted the flecks of gray in her hair, but also softened the laugh lines around her mouth and eyes.

"What's bugging you?" she asked.

Jan shook his head, but then thought for a moment. "Something happened today that scared the hell out of me."

Amanda raised an eyebrow, and Jan absent-mindedly started pedaling again, this time slowly, though.

"Have you heard the rumors that the mine is haunted?"

She gave a wry smile. "This is a small town."

"Right. Well, Kathy caught a young boy sneaking around the mine last night. He looks to be about eight or nine, but he won't give his name or where he lives. In fact, he only said one thing the whole time she was interviewing him."

Jan dropped his voice, but picked up the pace of his pedaling. Amanda leaned forward. When he stayed silent, she gestured for him to continue.

"He had…escaped, I guess…from Wayne State Hospital and had been wandering in the woods between there and here for three days. When the people from the hospital came to collect him, he finally said something—just two words." He licked his lips and turned his head from side to side as if someone might be eavesdropping. "He said, 'Burned man.'"

"Oh, that's weird," Amanda said. "But he probably heard about you on the local news."

Jan shook his head. The boy wasn't a local, or he wouldn't still be unidentified, and Jan's story hadn't been on the news in almost a year. Rather than debating the point, though, he continued.

"That's not the scary part, though. Kathy asked me to come in to see if he would talk to me, since he wouldn't say anything besides 'burned man.' When I got there…well, it was the creepiest thing. His eyes rolled back in his head, and this deep, sinister, evil voice came out of his little kid moth."

By now, Jan's legs were pumping harder, and the bike was spinning faster than before.

Breathlessly, Amanda asked, "What did he say?"

"'Stay out of my mine.'"

Amanda sat back. "That's it?"

Jan stopped pedaling, feeling a bit insulted. "It wasn't just what he said. It was *how* he said it."

"In a 'deep, sinister' voice." Her skepticism was apparent.

"Yeah, a 'deep, sinister, *evil* voice.'"

Amanda nodded as if to appease him. "What did Kathy say?"

"Oh. Yeah, that's another creepy thing. She didn't hear him say anything."

Amanda leaned forward and laid a calming hand on Jan's arm. "So you thought you heard the boy warn you to stay away from *his* mine, but Kathy didn't hear him through the microphone in the next room?"

Jan's frustration turned to sheepishness. "Not through the microphone. She was in the room, too." Realizing how silly his story sounded, he crossed his arms and pouted. "I know what I heard."

Amanda took his hand in hers. "Look, you've been through a horrible trauma." She gently stroked the scars on his wrist. "After something like what you've been through, your mind can play tricks."

"You're talking PTSD."

She nodded. "When I got back from the desert, I had terrible dreams…I still do some nights. Talking it through with others has really helped."

"You want me to join a support group?" Jan's tone reflected his skepticism.

"I think it would be a good idea. You can come with me to my group tonight to try it out. If you don't like it, I'll buy you a drink afterwards."

A small smile touched his lips. "And if I *do* like it?"

Amanda smiled. "You can buy *me* a drink."

29

Jan
Wednesday, April 8th

When Jan got home, a single Tiffany lamp sitting on the small table next to one of the two overstuffed chairs lit the parlor. Kathy was sitting in one, staring into space. The rest of the house, which was gloomy even in the light of day, was oppressively dark. Jan surveyed the scene from the hall archway. A single bottle of beer gathered the lamp's yellow light and returned it in an amber glow.

I wonder how many of those are in the recycling bin.

Kathy blinked, and her eyes finally registered his presence when he stepped into the room.

"How was the group thing?" she asked, without any slurring.

He thought for a moment. "Interesting." *The drinks afterwards were better.*

"Going back?"

He shrugged as he eyed the empty chair that was a twin of Kathy's, then plopped onto the matching sofa. "Probably. Amanda thinks I imagined the…thing the boy said."

"You told her?" Kathy sat up straighter. Jan nodded. "How much did you tell her?"

"Don't worry. I've always stuck to our story about these." He pulled his sleeves back. The scar tissue on his arms seemed to glow a sickly white in the dim light.

"Good. I could go to jail for faking evidence if anyone actually believed what really happened."

"And I'd probably end up in a padded room right next to Sandy."

They sat in silence for a minute until Jan spoke again. "I know you record everything that goes on in that room—"

Kathy shook her head and interrupted. "There's nothing on the tape."

"Nothing?"

"Well, everything's normal until the boy opens his mouth and his eyes kinda roll back. No sound comes out, though. Then you knock the chair over backwards."

"He didn't say anything?" When Kathy shook her head, he muttered, "I guess..I guess I did imagine it, then."

"PTSD can fuck with your head."

He nodded. "It's the trauma that fucks with your head. The PTSD is the walk of shame the next morning."

Kathy gave a gallows laugh. "In your case, it was the fucking that was the trauma." Jan winced. "Sorry. Too soon?"

"Yeah. I think it'll always be 'too soon.'"

She smiled teasingly. "Maybe Amanda can help with that."

"Oh, please. Even if the spirit is willing… Besides, I'm her patient. She's just looking out for me."

"At the Tavern?" She held up a hand to stop his protest. "Chill. I drove past and saw both of your cars. I think it's a good thing to let her get close, whether as friends or something more. Not every woman is looking for 'benefits,' ya' know. Especially not *mature* ones."

"Hey, she's younger than I am."

Kathy spread her hands out to her sides and cocked her head to one side.

Jan chuckled. "Very funny. By the way, have you identified the kid?"

"Not that I've heard. We ran missing persons reports, of course, but nothing has shown up within the last couple of weeks."

"How far away?"

"Wayne and the surrounding counties." Jan gave her a skeptical look. "Why? You think we should go wider? He couldn't have traveled any further on his own without being missed."

"I don't know. He looked pretty emaciated, like he'd been out there quite a while."

Kathy nodded. "I'll expand the search in the morning."

"Where is he now?"

"Child and Family Services took him to a foster home."

Kathy's work phone buzzed. "Detective Jensen. Yes, Ms. Stupine. Excuse me? You took him where? Why?" Kathy listened for nearly a full minute. "I understand your concern, but was that your only option?" More listening, then, "OK. Thanks for keeping me in the loop."

She hung up and looked at Jan open-mouthed. "They sent the kid back to Wayne State."

"What? Why?"

"She said the foster family was freaked out by him, so they called C&FS to come get him. Their standard procedure is to commit the kid."

"What did he do?"

"The foster parents wouldn't say. They were pretty freaked out, apparently. They just wanted him out of their house."

The two sat in shocked silence. "Poor kid," Jan said finally.

Kathy looked thoughtful for a minute before speaking. "Maybe you're not crazy, after all."

"Ah, thanks, I guess?"

"One person terrified by the kid could be just a nutcase—no offense. But, add in a foster family, who is probably used to dealing with problem kids…I don't know. Sounds like corroboration to me."

Jan unconsciously reached for a glass that wasn't there.

"Shit. I was convinced I had imagined it. Now you've got me creeped out again."

"Which is worse, imagining you're hearing evil voices coming from the mouth of a little kid, or it actually happening?" Kathy shuddered.

When he realized what his hand had done, Jan stood and took a step toward the liquor cabinet. Then he turned and met her eyes. "We have to get him to tell us what's going on."

Kathy nodded. "Tomorrow. First thing."

Amanda
Thursday, April 9th

"First thing" turned out to be more like ten o'clock. Kathy couldn't get the attending psychologist to let them in before the boy had been evaluated. As a result, Jan had to cancel a lunch date with Amanda.

"Wayne State? They put a little kid back in that place? That's awful," Amanda said on the other end of the phone call.

"Yeah. Apparently, C&FS doesn't know what to do with him now."

There was silence on the line for a moment, then Amanda said, "OK. I'm coming with you." Her tone didn't invite argument, but Jan tried anyway.

"No, you don't have to—"

"Nonsense. He scared the hell out of you once. I want to be there if it happens again."

"Thanks. But you'll have to clear it with Kathy. This is her show."

Amanda snorted. "You think that'll be a problem?" Jan held his tongue. "Yeah, I don't think so either. Is she there?"

"She's at the station."

"OK, I'll pick you up in ten minutes."

The line went dead.

Glad I'm not in the middle of that conversation. But then he realized how much better he felt having both of those strong women looking out for him.

***

Kathy stood next to her patrol SUV when Amanda and Jan pulled into the parking lot. The edifice that was Wayne State Behavioral Hospital loomed over them. Founded in the early twentieth century, Wayne State was built to house the "feeble-minded" of Eastern Pennsylvania, which included a wide range of behavioral disorders. It had gone through many reforms and renovations over the intervening decades, but still retained its imposing physical and emotional presence, as well as its foreboding reputation.

Amanda shuddered as they climbed from her car. "Have you ever been inside?"

Kathy and Jan exchanged a glance. "Yeah," is all Kathy said. Jan shook his head but remained silent.

Recognition dawned on Amanda's face. "Oh, right. Sandy's here."

Kathy led the way up the granite steps to the tall double doors, which swung open smoothly and silently. Jan, his senses on high alert, took in the large foyer. The two-story windows flanking the entryway let in the morning light without interference from streaks, dirt, or cobwebs. The marble tile floor was immaculate, and the faint pine and lemon smell of disinfectant hung in the air.

"Sheriff's Detective Kathy Jensen to see Dr. Saunders," she said as she strode up to the large reception desk. "We have an appointment."

"Of course, Detective." She handed each of them a visitor's badge. "Down the hall—" She pointed to a wide corridor to her left. "—first door on your right. Dr. Saunders is expecting you."

A minute later, introductions complete, the four stood in the psychologist's office.

Dr. Joan Saunders was a middle-aged woman. She tucked a strand of hair that had escaped from her bun behind her ear. "He's been non-communicative since his arrival last night," she said.

"What brought him here?" Kathy asked, then seeing the doctor's hesitation, added, "What caused the foster family to kick him out of their house last night?"

The psychologist frowned. "I wouldn't—"

Kathy's tone turned cold. "What behavior did he exhibit that made the foster family so uncomfortable that they called C&FS?"

Saunders pursed her lips at Kathy's confrontational tone, then replied, "They didn't say, other than that he made everyone in the house, the adults, the other children, and even their dog, apparently, 'uncomfortable.'"

"Have you seen any behaviors that make you 'uncomfortable?'" Jan asked.

Saunders shook her head. "Not at all. I haven't been able to elicit any behaviors, uncomfortable or not, at all."

"So, he's catatonic?" Jan asked.

"Oh, no. He makes eye contact. He tracks movement. He's clearly aware of his surroundings." She shrugged. "He simply chooses not to interact with other people. It's not a condition that is that unusual, actually. Think of him as being extremely asocial."

"Dangerous, then?"

"No. I said 'asocial,' not 'anti-social.' Asocial behavior is not considered a personality disorder. We're all asocial sometimes when we just want to be left alone for a while." She looked intently at Jan, then smiled and looked from Kathy to Amanda. "He's just an extreme case."

"Autistic?" Kathy asked.

The doctor shook her head. "I don't think so."

"Was he traumatized at some point?" Amanda spoke for the first time.

"Possibly. *Probably*, actually. Just wandering around in the woods at his age must have been traumatizing. I would need more time with him to discover the root cause, but for now, we need to find out who his family is and where." She turned to Kathy.

"I agree, Doc. Unfortunately, there are no reports of a missing child, at least not one that matches his description, for a hundred miles around. We're expanding that search, of course, but right now we don't have a clue."

"What about DNA analysis?" Jan asked. The blank looks prompted him to explain. "They can use familial DNA analysis to solve cold cases. Why not use the same technique to find his family?"

Dr. Saunders nodded, then smiled condescendingly. "That's a good idea, but I suspect it will take some time. We can keep him here, of course, but in my professional opinion, I believe a less institutional setting would be more effective in bringing him out of his shell."

"I'll get C&FS to place him somewhere else, then. Can we see him?" Kathy asked.

"Sure. He's in the day room with some of the other patients."

She led them down a side hall to a large open room with floor to ceiling windows that overlooked an expansive lawn dotted with flower gardens. It was furnished with comfortable chairs, some of which were clustered around a new television playing a black and white movie. Straight-backed chairs were paired with a few tables holding various games and puzzles. The cleanliness and relaxed atmosphere testified to how well-run and well-maintained the facility was. Even so, Jan felt a growing unease as they approached.

At the doorway, the psychologist paused and scanned the room, looking for the boy. After a moment, she nodded toward the far corner of the room, in front of one of the tall windows.

"There he is," she said, and started to walk in his direction.

"Shit," Kathy whispered.

A whimper escaped Jan's lips, and he stood frozen in place.

Amanda, who had started to follow the doctor, spun around when she heard the fear in Jan's voice. She followed his gaze to where the boy sat in one of the straight-back chairs right next to a wheelchair holding a frail, blonde-haired young woman. She stared uncomprehendingly into nothingness. The woman was Sandy Adams. Jude also stared into space, but his lips moved, mumbling too quietly to be heard.

"Doctor," Amanda called sharply as she instinctively took Jan's hand.

Dr. Saunders turned and saw Jan, frozen in fear, then turned back to the two patients in the corner. Understanding the situation at last, she said, "Sorry. I didn't realize they would be…that *he* would be talking to *her*. I'll go get him," she finished, flustered, then hurried to the corner.

The boy stopped his whispered monologue as the doctor approached. He shook his head when she leaned down and spoke to him, indicating the other three who were still standing in the doorway. Her voice didn't carry across the room, but their interaction was clear. She tried cajoling him to leave his seat, but he refused to budge.

After a minute of effort, which included gentle tugs on the boy's arm, to no avail, the doctor turned to the others and shrugged. Clearly, she wouldn't use force against a recalcitrant, but otherwise peaceful, patient, which left her with no other options.

As she turned to return to the doorway in defeat, Amanda dropped Jan's hand and made her own way across the room. Saunders looked at her questioningly as they passed, but Amanda kept her eyes locked on the boy, who returned her stare equally intently.

When she reached him, with their eyes still linked, she simply reached out her hand, palm up, by way of invitation. With a faint smile, the boy took her hand, stood, and she led him back to the others.

31

Amanda
Thursday, April 9ʰ

Ten minutes later, Dr. Saunders said, "He seems to have bonded with you."

They sat in a conference room. Amanda and the boy at one end of the long table, still holding hands. Jan sat at the other end, as far from the boy as possible. Kathy and the psychologist sat on opposite sides between them.

"Good," Kathy said. "Try to find out who he is and where he came from."

The boy looked in Jan's direction. Not staring, exactly, as his eyes would shift to whomever was speaking, but his gaze always returned to Jan.

Amanda squeezed his hand, and he turned his head to her. "What's your name, Little Man?" His expression didn't change, and he gave no indication that he understood. "You must have a name. What should we call you?"

"Billy," Jan said from the other end of the table. "His name is Billy." The others turned to him with questioning looks. "He said his name is Billy." Their looks intensified. "Didn't you hear him? He said it plain as day."

The others shook their heads, and Amanda said in a slightly condescending voice, "He didn't say anything, Jan."

He started to protest, then fell silent, and pushed back even further from the table.

"At least we didn't hear him, did we?" Amanda said, trying to defuse Jan's obvious anxiety. She got head shakes from Kathy and Saunders. "But Billy is as good a name as any, I guess."

She looked down at the boy, who had not reacted when Jan spoke. "Can we call you Billy?" He still returned that blank stare. "OK. Billy it is."

Kathy already had her phone in hand and was texting new search parameters to the Sheriff's office.

***

"Are you sure this is what you want?" Dr. Saunders asked for the third time.

"Yes. He needs a home environment, and we need answers."

"'We?'" Kathy chimed in.

Amanda replied, defiance in her voice, "Yes, *we*. I'm invested now, and like it or not, I'm your best shot at getting answers." She looked over at the boy sitting with his feet drawn up on the seat of the chair, his arms wrapped around his knees. "He needs me," she whispered.

"OK." Saunders nodded. "I'll clear it with C&FS. I'm sure they'll want to come by and check out your place and get you to sign papers." The small smile disappeared from her face. "And if he gets to be…too much…he'll still have a place here."

Amanda gave her a withering look. "I raised three sons, most of it on my own. I think I can handle this little guy."

Saunders nodded and smiled. Kathy looked on silently, accepting that this was the best path to getting information out of the kid. Jan, by contrast, had quietly pushed himself back into the far corner of the room. From the shadows, he spoke.

103

"Kathy, can you give me a ride home?"
Amanda didn't seem to notice the fear in his voice.

104

32

Kathy

Thursday, April 9th

The interior of the Towne Tavern was dark. Kathy stood just inside the doorway and let her eyes adjust. The two she had followed there were seated at a table halfway down the long room. Lloyd nodded to her and held up a bottle of Lager. She nodded back and hooked a thumb at the table. He grabbed two more bottles from the cooler and set all three on the bar.

After collecting them, she set the fresh beers on the table and took a seat in one of the empty chairs.

"Hello, *Detective*," said the man to her right. He was Stephen Spatz, the younger brother of Deputy Spaz, Kathy's nemesis on the force. "To what do we owe this *pleasure*?"

Kathy gave him a sour look, then turned to the other man, Bernie Malloc, who sat across the table from her. He was in the process of emptying his old beer. When he finished, he raised the fresh one in thanks.

The two owned a small event production company, which set up lights and sound systems for concerts and other shows in the area. Kathy had followed them into town from the mine, where they were installing equipment for the Grand Opening.

"I wanted to ask you boys a question or two." She kept her voice pleasant, but didn't crack a smile.

"Isn't that what *detectives* do?"

She bit back a smart-ass retort and took a breath. Before she could ask her question, though, the door opened.

"Better order another one," Bernie said.

"The *talent's* here," Spatz muttered.

Silhouetted in the late afternoon sun streaming through the open door, a woman stood surveying the interior of the barroom. As the door swung closed, her features were revealed. Waves of straw-colored hair fell to her shoulders, framing high cheekbones and a pert nose set above a wide mouth. Her green eyes took in the table where Kathy and the others sat, then she turned to the bar.

"Hey, Lloyd."

"Lacey." He pulled a Corona Light from the case, opened it, and stuck a lime slice in the top, then looked over at Kathy, who nodded.

"To whom do I owe my thanks?" Lacey purred as she slid into the last open chair at the table.

"Kathy Jensen," Kathy held out her hand.

"*Detective* Jensen," Spatz spat.

"Oh, well hello, Detective."

Kathy threw Spatz a dirty look. "Just 'Kathy' is fine. And you are?"

Lacey smiled and took Kathy's hand, whose eyes opened wide. Lacey's touch felt more like a caress than a handshake.

"Lacey Devine, at your service." She gave Kathy's hand an inviting squeeze.

"Lacey's the tour guide they've hired for the mine tour," Bernie said.

Kathy frowned and reluctantly let go of Lacey's hand. "I thought Old Man Kain was doing the tours."

"Quit," Spatz muttered. "Like everyone else."

"Really?" Kathy said, intrigued that another employee of the tour had quit.

Lacey nodded. "But he's been a great help. He has a wealth of knowledge and a ton of stories about the mines and the plight of the miners. I believe his grandfather actually worked in the mines back in the day."

"Then you're taking over. Are you from around here? Do you have family stories too?"

Lacey laughed, a light, but slightly denigrating laugh. "Oh, no. I'm originally from Baltimore, but I live in New York now."

"She's an *actress*," Spatz said.

Kathy raised an eyebrow, and Lacey gave a self-deprecating laugh. "Mostly off-Broadway so far," she said. "I write a newsletter about life in New York and I do a weekly podcast, too." She smiled at Kathy's nodding interest. "My degree's in Journalism."

"Impressive," Kathy said, returning her smile. "So, you're just here on the weekends?"

Lacey nodded. "Right now. Once we're up and running, I'll find a place around here."

"I have a place." The words were out before Kathy even thought about them.

"Oh?"

Trying to hide her fluster, Kathy added, "Yeah, it's a one-bedroom with an outside walk-up and a nosey neighbor below. I haven't lived there for quite a while, and I'm not sure why I've kept the lease, but…"

"Sounds perfect." Lacey lifted her beer and gave Kathy a smile. "Can you show me?"

"Oh, my *God*. Will you two get a *room*, for fuck's sake?" Spatz shook his head in disgust.

"I think that's exactly what they're doin'," Bernie laughed.

Kathy sat back and took a long swig to clear her head.

"Right." She looked to each of the others in turn. "I need to ask you if you've heard or seen anything strange inside the mine."

"You mean like *spooks*?" Spatz laughed and took a pull on his beer.

Bernie kept his eyes on the table and remained silent.

Lacey sat back and crossed her legs. "I've only been down there twice to check things out and to run through the tour with Mr. Kain. It's certainly creepy, but other than the whole 'the ceiling can fall on you at any time' vibe, I haven't heard anything odd."

"No voices, no strange sounds?"

Spatz snorted and Lacey shook her head, but Bernie remained silently examining the bottle's sweat rings on the tabletop. "Bernie?"

Without looking up, he nodded. "I've heard—"

Spatz started to interrupt, but Kathy thrust her outstretched finger at him and gave him a fierce look. He sat back, cowed into silence.

Gently, Kathy prompted, "You heard…?"

"Someone…or something…calling my name." He swallowed hard. "Not at first. First, it was just like a rush of wind blowing the wrong way, ya' know, up from down deeper. I didn't think nothin' of it, but then I could've sworn somebody whispered my name, like they was right behind me. Nobody was there, though."

He fell silent until Kathy prompted again. "Did this happen more than once?"

Bernie shook his head. "We finished up with the setup and got outta there." He looked to Spatz for support.

His partner had turned pale. "Gas," he said. "It must've been *gas* blowing up from down below." His voice shook.

"You heard it too, didn't you?" Kathy whispered.

Spatz met her eyes but shook his head. "*Gas*. It must've been *gas*."

He sucked down the last of his beer and slammed the bottle on the table. "I gotta go." He looked at Bernie. "You comin'?"

Bernie nodded and stood. Without meeting Kathy's eyes, he said, "See ya', Kath," and followed Spatz out the door.

"Wow," Lacey said quietly.

"Yeah. Wow, is right." Kathy finished her beer. "You want to see the apartment?"

Jan

Thursday, April 9th

Jan stood in the back corner of the Miners Bank boardroom. He silently watched as the other members read his latest draft of the brochure, gauging everyone's reactions. As expected, Mayor Luzeski was frowning, as was the group's banker, Buddy Lewis. Patti Trieste, on the other hand, was smiling and nodding, probably imagining new TV ads playing off his brochure.

Finally, the mayor spoke. "I'm not sure this is the direction we want to go with our marketing."

"Well, I think it's brilliant!" Patti gushed. "Some of it, anyway. I've always said we need a hook. A ghost in the mine is the perfect hook."

"Is that really what we want to promote, though? This is about the history and legacy of the Anthracite Coal Region."

"History? No one wants to spend their money on a history lesson."

"This region fueled the Industrial Revolution in this country."

Buddy chimed in, "And made fortunes as a result."

"On the backs of the miners and their families," George, the team's chief engineer, added. "Hundreds died in those mines, and thousands more had their lives cut short by the back-breaking work, or the Black Lung."

Jan spoke from the back of the room. "And the mine owners, who were making their fortunes, turned the families out of their homes once there was no one to work." He stepped forward and leaned on the table. "Which is why mothers sent their boys, some as young as five years old, into the pits."

He reached into his satchel and pulled out four or five paperbacks, and tossed them onto the table. "You should read the real history of this place. In fact, I think we should stock these books in the gift shop. It was downright brutal."

The mayor scoffed. "I've seen that propaganda. They paint a totally one-sided picture. Written by children and grandchildren who never worked in the mines."

Patti picked up one of the books and read from the back cover. "'Based on interviews with the miners and their families themselves.' Sounds like good source material to me."

"There's still a lot of animosity in these communities between blue collar workers and business owners, even three and four generations removed from the abuses of the mines' heyday," George added. "I have to overcome it every day, it seems."

Patti turned to Jan. "The ghost angle is a good one, but I think we need to be more balanced overall between labor, owners, and management. Can you do a rewrite of our tour script and this," she held up the brochure, "by Opening Day?"

Jan nodded, and she held up a hand to stop Jim's protest. "There are a lot more descendants of miners and blue collar folks than there are grandchildren of mine owners and bankers around here. Appealing to their sentiments makes a lot of sense, financially."

"I just hope this approach doesn't cause labor problems down the road," Buddy said.

Jan shook his head. "With a balanced approach, like Patti said, we'll show that we're compassionate and we care about the wrongs of the past and want to make sure they don't happen again."

Patti was smiling. "*Mayor* Luzeski, they're all voters." She held up the book again. "Your family were mine owners, right? People remember. And opening this mine tour will bring those memories to the top of their minds, whether we talk about them or not. Being honest about the sins of your forefathers, and honestly rejecting them for the sins they were, will win over the hearts and minds of most folks."

Mayor Jim thought for a long moment, then nodded. "Okay, okay. But the section on the damned Mollie Maguires has to go." When Jan started to protest, he slammed his fist on the table. "That scum committed horrendous crimes. Beatings and even murders."

"And they were hanged for it," Jan said, defiant. "While the Pinkertons did their own killing, and the mine owners kept raking in the cash."

"We will *not* make heroes out of killers. My decision is final."

Belatedly, he looked around the table for support and saw most heads nodding in agreement.

Patti tried to ease the tension. "Perhaps we could have a, I don't know, some kind of *Sharing* for people to tell their family stories." She looked around the table, seeing only blank stares, then shrugged. "So, you'll have new copy for us by…?"

Jan frowned, knowing when he was defeated. "Give me a day or two for the brochure. The tour guide script…we'll see."

34

Jan

Thursday, April 9th

I t's not 'exploitative.'" Jan said, a bit exasperated. He had thought Jim and Barb would be thrilled with the change of theme for the tour, but Jim was adamantly against it. "This is your chance to tell the real story," Jan almost pleaded.

He sat with the local historians, Jim and Barb Donnelly, in the Historical Society reading room. The long table was strewn with books, magazines, and newspaper clippings, all describing the life of miners in the anthracite coal region, which stretched from Scranton in the northeast to south of Pottsville in Schuylkill County. Many of the articles covered the various mining disasters—explosions, floods, fires, and cave-ins—that plagued the region on a frequent basis.

"Seriously, Jim," Barb said. "You've been bitchin' about this mine tour thing for months. It's going to happen whether you like it or not, so do you want to have a say, or do you just want to whine about it?"

"Jeez, Woman. I didn't say I wouldn't help. I said I didn't want to exploit the sufferings of my ancestors."

Jan held up an appeasing hand. "I understand. All I want are your honest family histories, and any other anecdotes that you know to be true from back in the day."

"Maybe the Good Writer here, can turn them into a book later?" Barb said slyly.

Jan gave her a sharp look. "Yeah, maybe later. Right now, I need a summary for our brochure, and a script for the tour guide."

"Tour guide?" Jim frowned, then nodded. "I suppose you need tour guides. But isn't Tom Kain doing the tours? He knows more about this stuff than we do."

Jan frowned. "He, ah, had begged off, claiming he's too old to 'go tramping around in the cold and damp.' We've hired someone else, though. She'll give visitors the history of the region and of our mine in particular. Tom's helping with that. I want to add as many personal touches as possible. What the work was like. What the working conditions were like. What their family life was like. The kind of intimate details that will really connect with the hearts of the visitors."

"What will they see down there?"

Jan took out his phone and opened up his photo gallery. "Here, we've got some of the old equipment still down there. And we're setting up some tableaus with mannequin in side tunnels."

Jim scrolled through the pictures, zooming in on some. Finally, he handed the phone back.

"Too clean," he said.

"Excuse me?"

"Everything is too clean." He pointed to a mannequin dressed in white shirt, overalls, and a miner's helmet. "Their hands, their faces, their clothes. They should be covered in black coal dust. Everything was covered in coal dust, they breathed it in and spit it out. Your mannequins are too clean."

Jan sat back. "That's exactly what I need you for," he said. "Tell us everything we've gotten wrong."

"Sure, sure." Jim nodded, and Barb smiled. He looked at her and said, "Better make a new pot of coffee, Dear. This is going to take a while."

35

Jan

Friday, April 10ᵗʰ

Jan didn't notice the tapping on his door until it became a cop's knock.

"Yeah?"

The door to his suite swung open. Kathy swayed a bit in the doorway. "You're up late."

He noticed the slur in her voice. "At least I'm losing sleep being productive."

She looked down at his laptop screen. "Doin' what?"

He sat back and sighed. "I'm rewriting the tour guide script."

"Isn't the run through tomorrow?"

"Tomorrow afternoon. I have to give this new script to the guide in the morning."

Kathy sniffed and wiped her nose on her sleeve. She blinked twice trying to focus her eyes. "Why?"

"So they have time to learn it, or at least read through it before we go inside."

She shook her head, then swayed again and put her hand out to the doorframe to steady herself. "No. I mean, why are you rewritin' it?"

Jan patted a legal pad covered with scribbled notes sitting next to his laptop. "Working the mines was worse than brutal. Jim and Barb told me all about the hardships of the miner families. I'm making our tour more…balanced."

Kathy steadied herself against the doorframe again. "Balance is good."

Jan snorted, then they both burst out laughing.

"Why don't you balance yourself to bed," he said around a smile.

She chuckled and nodded. "In a minute. Heard anything from Amanda? 'Bout the boy?"

He frowned and shook his head. "Once she got him cleaned up and fed, he went straight to bed. Any luck ID-ing him?"

It was Kathy's turn to shake her head, setting off another round of swaying. "The famil—faiml—ah, DNA fam'ly thing is our bes' chance, but it'll take weeks, they said."

"Go to bed. I'll let you know if Amanda can break through."

Kathy slowly turned and disappeared down the hallway. Jan shook his head, checked his watch—2:30 AM—and bent over his laptop.

36

Gino

Friday, April 10th

Gino Kapaletti eyed the rickety bridge suspiciously. "I'm not going to fall through that thing, am I?"

Mark Luzeski chuckled. "No, man. I've ridden my Kawa over it a million times. That's how I found the back door."

Gino shifted the heavy backpack and gingerly followed Mark across the old iron span. The creek twenty feet below was running high with late Spring rain. On the other side, an overgrown path followed the stream down the ravine. As he edged along the trail, Gino steadied himself with one hand against the cliff face to his left.

"How far is it to this 'back door?'" He pushed an overhanging branch out of the way. "Remember, we'll be leading kids through here in the dark."

"Exactly! It's the perfect creepy intro to the Dazed Experience."

"'Dazed Experience?' Is that what we're calling this venture now?"

"Yeah," Mark said as he stopped in front of a set of rusted iron doors hanging on barn door tracks set into the rock of the cliff face. "Dazed—D. A. S. D.—Drug Aided Sensory Deprivation. Get it?"

Gino rolled his eyes. "I get it. I came up with the idea, remember?"

"Whatever," Mark mumbled.

He pulled on one of the heavy doors and yanked it to the side. The squeal it emitted made Gino cringe.

"Need some grease on that," he muttered.

Flicking on the headlamps strapped to their foreheads, the two stepped into a tunnel barely high enough to let them walk upright. Gino reached out and touched each side. His hands came away wet.

"Hell, man, this is tight."

"It opens up just ahead."

Sure enough, after a dozen steps, they passed the door to a side room, and after a few more steps, the tunnel opened up into a square room about twenty feet on a side. Past the room, the tunnel continued deeper into the mountain. Various debris was scattered across the floor.

"We can set up a control room in here. The sensory deprivation room is the one we passed on the way in."

Gino shone his light on crushed beer cans and a rotted mattress. He kicked a pile of old porn magazines.

"What was this place used for? Besides drinking beer and jerking off?"

Mark shrugged. "Don't know. It probably connects to the mines that run all through the area." He shone his light on the double oaken doors further down the tunnel. "Back there is old medical stuff and other abandoned equipment."

"So this was like a rescue tunnel or something?"

Mark shrugged again. "Makes sense." He dropped his backpack onto the ground. "We can shove all this crap behind those doors where the kids won't see it. You should set up your noise canceling stuff and video gear back there, too."

Gino carefully set down his backpack full of electronics. He stared at the door leading further into the mountain. He cocked his head as if listening for something, then a shudder ran through his body.

"I don't have to go in there, do I? I can set up right here."

"No, no. Just set up in this room." He pulled gloves out of his backpack and tossed a pair to Gino. "But first, let's get this shit out of here."

Gino
Friday, April 10th

The sensory deprivation room was carved from the rock along the right side of the tunnel that led to their control room. After it, the passage ended at a wall with the double doors set into it. Beyond them, the narrow tunnel became a wide corridor with scars in the rock where narrow-gauge train tracks leading deeper into the mountain had been pulled up, maybe a hundred years before. Mark and Gino piled the trash from the outer rooms there amidst rusting artifacts from the heyday of coal mining in the region.

Reluctantly, Mark had claimed that space as his control room and set up a laptop with three additional monitors showing the feed from the infrared cameras that Gino hid in the shadows up at the ceiling of the side room where Mark had already set up noise canceling microphones and speakers.

He switched to the feed from the sensory deprivation room. A bare mattress lay on the floor, and he watched Gino finish connecting the last of the IR cameras. When Gino gave him a thumbs-up, Mark hit the record button, and another which plunged the room into blackness. The IR camera showed the heat glow of Gino, his wide eyes clearly visible on the monitor. The video showed Gino slowly pulling his hand toward his face. He jerked back, startled, when his palm touched his nose.

After a few seconds, Mark switched the lights back on and turned off the noise cancellation. Playing back the recording, he nodded at the result.

Gino's voice came through the speaker. "Holy shit. That was intense. I literally couldn't see anything."

Mark pushed his transmit button. "When we shut the kids in and they find themselves in pitch black with no sound but their own breathing, they'll do what all horny teenagers do."

He grinned and licked his lips. Taking his finger off the transmit button, he mumbled, "And we'll have a recording of it all."

Transmitting again, he said, "Now, let's test the noise canceling stuff."

Without waiting for a response, he flicked off the lights again, and turned on the sensory deprivation equipment.

"Freaky," Gino whispered. "I feel like I have cotton in my ears."

But his voice was eaten by the hidden equipment almost before it reached him, although it came through loud and clear on the recording.

"Okay," he called to where he knew the camera was hidden. "Give me some light in here."

A shiver ran down his spine when he got no response.

"Come on, Mark! Quit screwing around." Still no response. "Very funny," he mumbled and reached out into the dark.

Two shambling steps later, he tripped on the mattress and fell to his knees.

"God dammit! Mark, turn the fucking lights on!" He wondered if the equipment was working too well, but then he shook his head. The recording feed was taken from the ambient input, which inverted it and broadcast it back through the six speakers placed around the room.

Thinking about the workings of Mark's equipment helped suppress the rising panic, and he was able to picture the layout of the room. Finding the edge of the mattress, he crawled along it until he found the corner. If he just crawled in a straight line from there, he would reach the rock wall that ran perpendicular to the hall wall just to the left of the door.

Feeling more confident, he set out with one knee on the pad, and one on the rough floor. When his head bumped into the wall, he rose and sidled along until he reached the corner. It was only a few more steps to the door, which he angrily threw open.

The work lights set up in the tunnel blinded him, which pissed him off even more. When he could see again, he strode down the tunnel toward the double doors.

"Jesus H. Christ, Mark! It's fucking dark—" He froze when he burst into the control room and found it empty. "What the hell? Yo, Mark, where the hell are you?" he yelled.

Looking around the cluttered room, Gino was about to storm back into the tunnel when he saw a faint glow coming from where the double doors leading deeper into the mountain stood open. Grabbing a flashlight from the worktable, he followed the glow deeper into the mountain.

From the main corridor, a side tunnel branched off, its dark, jagged maw hinting at the haste with which it was cut. When Gino followed the glow into it, he felt the accumulated pain of death pressing down on him. At the end, where the narrow corridor opened into another room, a figure was silhouetted by light reflected off the iron frames set against wet, slime-covered walls. Mark stood as still as a statue, staring into the abyss beyond.

Gino
Friday, April 10th

What the—?" Gino whispered.

He came up to look over Mark's shoulder. The room beyond was lined with racks that looked like bunk beds, but the rusted metal slabs where mattresses should have been and the remnants of bloody sheets belied their true purpose.

"This wasn't a rescue tunnel," Mark said, barely above a whisper. "This was a recovery operation."

"We're under Avon Hill," Gino gulped. Then he turned to Mark, who still stood stock still. "Why'd you come back here?"

Mark shook his head and blinked, his trance broken. "I don't know. I was testing the equipment…" His voice trailed off, then he met Gino's eyes as he remembered. "Then I heard…something—a voice." He squinted. "But it was in my head."

"A voice?" Gino was skeptical. "What'd it say?"

Mark looked away, confusion written on his face. "I…I don't know…I can't remember. In fact, I don't know if it was words at all. I just felt…compelled? Yeah, compelled to come in here. Like they wanted me to see this room."

"They?"

"Did I say 'they?'" He nodded, then pointed toward the racks of cold slabs. "There were a lot of them, all talking with one voice."

Mark shook himself and turned off his light. Then he turned and pushed past Gino and hurried back up the tunnel. Gino scanned the room one last time before following Mark.

When he reached the control room, Mark had already slung his empty backpack.

"Where are you going?"

"Home. Or Lloyd's. Need a drink."

"Is this all set up?"

"Screw that, Man. I'm thinking this was a bad idea."

Mark headed for the entrance.

"Hey, you can't back out now, Dude. We've got a lot invested here, and I'm picking up the Dazed tonight."

Mark stopped, held Gino's gaze for a moment, then his shoulders slumped.

"This ain't gonna end well."

Kathy
Friday, April 10th

Lacey Devine leaned against the car fender, reading the stapled pages. The late-morning sun highlighted the streaks of blonde in her ponytail. Her jeans were tucked into a pair of black Doc Marten boots. A matching leather jacket hung unzipped over a denim chambray blouse. To Kathy, the overall effect was of a city girl trying a little too hard to fit into the local vibe. The denim blouse and blue jeans seemed to be a nod to the overall rural nature of the area, while the leather spoke to the coal-cracker mentality of this part of the state, which, to outsiders, was known disparagingly as 'Pennsyltucky.'

To Kathy, who grew up there but with the cosmopolitan influence of her Indian mother, the look was almost comical. But somehow on Lacey it was…hot.

Lacey looked up as Kathy approached. "This got a lot darker," she said. Kathy stood silently behind her aviator sunglasses. "This rewrite," Lacey continued, "it's very different from what we had before."

"The Writer got an earful from the local 'historians,'" she made air quotes. "Apparently, life around here wasn't as rosy as the rich folks would like to believe."

"It never was anywhere," Lacey mumbled. She reached up and gently removed Kathy's shades. "You look like Hell, by the way."

"And you look *hot* as Hell," Kathy replied with a raised eyebrow. Chuckling, she replaced the sunglasses on her nose.

Before either of them could say anything else, Jan walked up with Jim in tow.

"You've read the new draft?" Jan asked.

"I have. It's quite different. 'Young boys often lost fingers trying to stop runaway mule carts.' Kind of depressing, actually."

Jan nodded. "Yeah, I suppose it is. That's his influence." He hooked a thumb toward Jim. "Lacey, this is Jim Donnelly. He and his wife, Barb, are the local historians. Jim has first-hand—well, second-hand, I suppose—knowledge of the mines and miners."

"My grandfather worked at the Lackawanna Collier for thirty years," Jim said as he shook Lacey's hand. "Listening to his stories is why I became fascinated with the history of this region."

Lacey nodded and smiled, but then Jan said, "Jim will be taking the second tour group. He'll lead the first run-through this morning so you can hear the spiel," he nodded toward the script in her hand. "And answer questions. Please ask whatever interests you, or anything you think the visitors will ask."

Jim looked up from his own copy of the script. "Do I have to stick to this thing?"

"As close as you can. The tours need to be about thirty to thirty-five minutes long, and there is a lot of stuff to cover down there." Jim looked skeptical but nodded, so Jan relented a bit. "I mean, you can embellish where you think you should, but we are time-constrained." Jim nodded again. "Good," Jan said. "Shall we get started?"

Kathy looked around. "No other Board members?"

Jan shook his head. "No, I want to do a couple of practice runs first. Make it as smooth as possible."

"You're worried they won't like the new spiel?"

Jan looked directly at her. "What do you think?"

The four walked in silence to the hoist house, where the mine train waited, suspended by a thick steel cable above the gaping maw of the mine entrance. Jan waved to Charlie, who stood at the controls in the hoist house. Slowly, he turned and let his eyes follow the tracks, which dipped into the mountain at a fifty-degree angle.

He shuddered and heard Kathy mumble, "Yeah."

Jim climbed into the railcar and lay back against the hard steel benches.

"We go down backwards?" Lacey asked a little nervously.

"Too steep to go any other way," Jim responded.

Taking a deep breath, Jan slid into the front seat and took a walkie-talkie off its hook. When Kathy stood without moving, he said, "Aren't you coming?"

Kathy just shook her head and met his eye. "Don't like deep, dark places," she whispered.

Jan nodded and frowned. "Don't blame ya'," he said, then spoke into the radio. "All secured for descent."

Charlie's response wasn't much more than a burst of static, but a moment later, the hoist rumbled to life and, after a few jerks, the train made its slow descent into the pit.

40

Jan
Friday, April 10th

The light of a single electric votive candle flickered in the pitch darkness. It's light danced across the fractal facets of the exposed coal seam, reflecting momentary flashes of brilliance to dazzle their eyes.

The surrounding rock, dull by comparison, glistened in spots where ground water seeped through.

"Once the Nipper, a boy as young as five years old, pulled the door closed, he would snuff out his candle."

Jim clicked off the candle, plunging the ten by twenty-foot chamber into utter darkness. He remained silent for a moment, letting the darkness amplify the drip, drip, drip of the ever-present seepage and the low hum of fans and pumps. Even the smells of damp rock, rotting timbers, and rusting equipment were magnified.

"He had to buy his candles from the Company store with his meager wages. Then he sat in this darkness until a knock came on one of the doors—two raps followed by three for the downhill door, or three raps followed by two for the uphill one. Relighting his candle with a matchstick—also bought at the Company store—" he clicked the candle back on, "—gave himself and the crew of miners just enough light to shuffle into the space, seal the door behind them, then open the other door and shuffle out."

Jim looked from Jan to Lacey, who visibly shivered, then he clicked off the pseudo-flickering candle again.

"Most of the time, he didn't bother with the candle."

A moment later, he turned the overhead light back on, causing them all to shade their eyes.

"My God," Lacey said. "If that kid screwed up, air would be sucked out of the mine and anybody down there would suffocate?"

Jim nodded. "Just one of the many ways people died down here."

Lacey's voice mirrored her enthusiasm. "Are there any ghost stories we could tell the tourists? This is the perfect setting for one."

Jim and Jan looked at each other, then Jan said, "We might do a 'ghost tour' as an added attraction."

"That would sell out every time. It's creepy as Hell down here. And cold."

She rubbed her arms trying to stave off the damp chill.

At that moment, the lights went out.

"OK, Jim, that's not funny," Jan said.

"Shush!" Jim responded. All three fell silent. After a few seconds, he said. "Hear that?"

Jan concentrated, trying to pick up whatever Jim was referring to, but before he could respond, Lacey spoke up.

"I don't hear anything," she whispered.

"Exactly," Jim said, and Jan heard the tension in his voice. "No ventilator hum." He wet his finger and held it up. "No air moving at all."

"The power's out." Jan tried unsuccessfully to keep his voice steady. He pressed the radio's button. "Yo, Charlie! We're in the dark down here."

The radio returned only static.

"Charlie!?! Hey! Answer the damned radio."

"We're too deep," Jim said. "There's no cell signal, either. We need to get to a mine phone."

The radio still returned just static for a moment, then the channel opened, but instead of Charlie's voice at the other end, the three just heard a growl. The sound sent a chill down Jan's spine.

"Charlie! What the hell are you doing? Quit playing around."

Jim, who had clicked on his flashlight when the power went out, pointed it toward the uphill door.

"Don't panic," he said, though there was a tinge of it in his voice. "There's plenty of air down here for the three of us. Let's head for the train. The hoist is on a separate generator, so it should still be running."

Jan flicked on his cellphone's flashlight and shone it on Lacey. She was as white as a ghost.

"My…my battery's dead," she stammered.

"And I don't have a signal down here," Jan answered as he took her hand.

Jim reached the uphill door of the airlock, but froze before opening it. His posture of listening intently held the others in place and held their breath in their lungs.

Into the utter silence of the mine, a whisper intruded. At first, it sounded like the susurration of a breeze drifting up from the depths. As they stood, their bodies and minds frozen in terror, the whisper became a moan that pierced the living through the heart. A moan that became the murmuring of dozens of voices, mumbling indistinctly until they merged together and resolved into a single voice. A voice that issued from deeper down in the dark.

"Get out!"

His terror broken, Jim threw open the door and turned to wave the others through. Still holding Lacey's hand, Jan started for the door also, but came up short when she refused to move.

She stood frozen, still rooted to the spot, her head tilted back and her mouth hanging open. When Jan shone his light on her face, he saw only the whites of her eyes in their sockets. Then, she exhaled in a low voice from deep in her chest, *"Last warning. Stay away!"*

Terror spiked through Jan's bowels, and he had to fight to clench his bladder. He tugged on her hand, but she remained frozen in place, so he grabbed her arm with his other hand, and yanked her into motion.

"Come on, Lacey. Let's get the fuck out of here."

Whether it was his expletive or pulling her off balance, she took a step toward the door. That step broke the spell that held her, and her eyes focused on his.

"Come on," he said more gently. "Let's go."

Ten minutes later, all three stood at the end of the newly refurbished railway. The hoist train sat there, inert.

"Now what?" Jan asked.

Jim shone his light up the steep tunnel. Their depth and the curving of the track kept any light from the surface from penetrating.

Jan walked over to the phone mounted on the wall and spun the crank. A faint ringing echoed up from deeper down, but no answer came from above. Next, he tried the walky-talky, which should have been within range. Also, no answer.

"It's about a half-mile climb," Jim said. "Are you two up to it?"

Lacey, who had recovered enough to be pissed off, responded. "Do we have a choice? What a fucked-up operation this is." Her voice rose in anger. "Why won't Charlie answer the goddamned phone? And what good is the train if there's no one to run it?"

Jim looked at Jan, who spread his hands helplessly. "He's not supposed to leave the Hoist House if there's anyone down here."

"And the phones don't take any power other than the hand crank, so unless the lines were cut, the phone up there should be ringing."

"I heard it ringing down below," Jan said, and Jim nodded.

"So fucking Charlie left us stranded down here?" Lacey practically screamed. Both men shrugged. "Well, let me tell you now, Mr. Scriptwriter, I quit. Find yourself another tour guide." She pointed at Jim. "Get him to do it. He's the know-it-all down here."

With that, she started the climb toward the surface, her Doc Martens slapping against the railroad ties.

41

Jan
Friday, April 10th

When Jan and Jim finally emerged from the mine, Kathy stood with legs spread and her arms crossed.

"What the hell happened down there?" Her tone was accusatory, not at all sympathetic to the exhaustion they felt after their steep, half-mile climb out of the pit.

Jan ignored her and demanded, "Where's Charlie?" as he pushed past her.

But Kathy would have none of that. She grabbed his wrist as he stalked by. "I asked you a ques—"

He shook his hand free so violently that Kathy stared at him in shock. The fury in his eyes drove her a step backward.

"And I asked you. Where the *fuck* is Charlie?"

"I…I don't—"

Jan waved a dismissive hand and stalked toward the Hoist House.

Kathy, open-mouthed, was watching him climb the hill when Jim finally caught his breath and said, "Where's Lacey?"

The question reignited her indignation. But when she turned on Jim and saw his pale, sweaty face, her face softened.

"You should sit down," she said and helped him to a bench in the waiting area. "Lacey's gone," she said once they were settled. "I was in my cruiser—" She nodded to the parking lot down a long set of stairs. "She came flying down there like her hair was on fire. When I asked her what was up, she cursed me, you, and Jan out good, got in her car, and yelled 'I quit!'"

Kathy pulled her phone from her back pocket and frowned at it. "I've been calling her ever since, but she won't pick up."

"So, you didn't see Charlie leave?" Jan called as he returned from the Hoist House.

Kathy shook her head. "Like I said, I was down in my cruiser." When Jan pulled out his phone, she put up a hand. "Stop! Tell me what the hell happened." Before Jan could blow her off again, she added, "Officially." That got his attention. "At the very least, Charlie's absence is a dereliction of his duties—which you and the Board will have to deal with. But at worst, if he's gone missing, that's in my lane."

Jan took a deep breath, then nodded to Jim.

Taking his cue, Jim said, "We were doing the tour run-through. Everything was going well when the lights went out."

"The phone, too," Jan added.

Jim nodded. "Yeah. We tried to call up to Charlie on the intercom phone, but nobody answered. With no power and nobody to run the hoist, we had to climb out in the dark." Jim paused for a breath, then added, "We also heard—" But Jan's sharp look and shake of his head stopped him.

Either because she hadn't heard Jim, or because she was pretending she hadn't, Kathy held up her hand for silence. All they heard was the cawing of a crow.

"The genny's off," she said as she looked toward the Hoist House. "Did you touch anything up there?"

"No. Why?"

"Good. Stay here."

Punching numbers on her phone, she dialed Charlie's wife. When she got confirmation that he hadn't gone home, she called in the Wayne County Evidence Collection Unit.

Her eyes scanned the ground ahead of each step as she headed up the walkway. Without turning her head, she called back over her shoulder, "This area is now a crime scene."

When she was out of earshot, Jim looked at Jan and raised an eyebrow. Jan shook his head.

"She doesn't need to know that her girlfriend channeled a monster down there."

"Girlfriend? Oh, that's why she was so pissed." The two men saw the fear in each other's eyes. "And that wasn't a monster she was possessed by," Jim whispered.

Nodding, Jan muttered in reply, "Yeah, it was a ghost."

"And it was pissed."

42

Kathy
Friday, April 10th

The Board of Directors, Kathy, Sheriff Peterson, Jim, and Barb all sat in the small movie theater in the newly built Mine Tour Visitors Center. They had rearranged the folding chairs into a large circle. The muffled sounds of workers assembling the display cases of artifacts and shelves of souvenirs could be heard through the soundproofed walls.

"What do you mean he's missing?" Mayor Jim asked.

The sheriff shrugged. "He's not answering his phone, his wife hasn't seen him since this morning, and there are no reports of anyone matching his description showing up at Saint Mary's Hospital."

"Did you check all the bars?" the PR woman, Patti, mumbled.

"First places we looked," Kathy responded. "And his car's still out there in the parking lot."

That got a reaction from those present. "He just walked away?" George asked.

"Or, he's still here somewhere," Kathy said. "I have deputies searching the grounds now. It'll be dark soon, though. Tomorrow we'll expand the search to the surrounding woods and backyards, basements, whatever."

"In the meantime," Peterson said, "we'll release a Missing Persons alert to the local media."

"He'll probably turn up sleeping on somebody's couch," Patti sniffed.

Jim and Barb were getting increasingly agitated, and this last comment stirred him to speak. "No. I've known Charlie Lusaitis for fifty years. True, he had a drinking problem in the past—"

"—But he's been sober for most of the last ten years," Barb interrupted.

"Goes to church every Sunday."

"Devoted to his wife and grandkids."

"Wouldn't start up drinkin' again."

"And wouldn't just walk off."

"Somethin' else is goin' on here," Jim finished, and Barb nodded.

Jan, who had been silently observing the interplay, leaned over and put a hand on Barb's arm. "Don't worry. Kathy and her team will find him." He gave Kathy a long look, and she nodded.

"In the meantime," he continued, "we need to make an announcement about the Grand Opening."

"What kind of announcement?" Mayor Luzeski asked.

"Well, a cancellation notice—"

"Why would we cancel?" Patti interrupted. "Just because Charlie Fucking Lusaitis went missing? Anybody can work the hoist."

Jim, Barb, and Jan stared at her in stunned silence. Finally, Jan said, "And because the power mysteriously cut off."

"Because someone mysteriously shut off the generator," Barb finished.

The four stared angrily across the table at each other until George spoke up.

"Charlie didn't have keys to the generator shed." He unclipped a keyring from his belt. "Only I do. And the shed was still padlocked when I got here. The generator wasn't shut down normally. The shutoff valve on the fuel line—which is next to the diesel tank *inside* the shed—was closed. I had a bitch of a time getting the thing restarted."

Patti was obstinate. "Charlie could've shut off the valve and relocked the padlock."

"Charlie knew the right way to shut it down. He wouldn't have—"

"He would've if he was trying to sabotage things," she practically yelled.

Before anyone else could shout their response, Sheriff Peterson slapped his hand on the table and shouted himself, "That's enough!" Cowed, everyone fell silent. "Nobody should be accusing a missing person of anything." He stared at Patti. "Right now, we have to assume that there may have been foul play involved." Patti and the mayor scoffed, but Peterson's voice was firm. "That's our working assumption, right, Detective?"

He looked at Kathy, who nodded solemnly. "That's correct, Chief. Until he's found and we find out exactly what happened to him, the hoist, and the generator."

Peterson nodded, satisfied. "So, no press releases even hinting that Charlie was somehow culpable. Understood?"

Patti's eyes narrowed as she looked at him, then she nodded.

"I also agree with Mr. Sorrensen," the sheriff continued. "Delaying the Grand Opening until this is all sorted out would be prudent. Besides, you don't want the place looking like an active crime scene." He glanced at Kathy, who nodded in return. "I think that would be bad PR."

Patti frowned, but finally nodded as well.

***

An hour later, as darkness fell over the mine entrance, now strung with yellow "Police Line – Do Not Cross" tape, Kathy gathered the deputies.

"Tomorrow, Spaz, I want you and Tom to canvas the neighboring houses to see if anyone saw Charlie this morning. Jeffries, you'll have to organize a crew of Boy Scouts to search the woods," she pointed up the mountainside. "I have a call in for State Police help, but they probably won't get here much before noon." She took a deep breath. "The Sheriff and I will take a team of searchers into the mine."

"Why would he walk down there?" Spaz asked and shuddered at the thought.

"Why would he walk away at all?" Kathy answered. "None of this makes any sense, but our job is to make sense out of it." She looked at her team, most of whom knew Charlie well. "Got it?" They all nodded. "Good. Be here at first light."

43

Kathy
Friday, April 10th

When Kathy got home, Jan was waiting for her with a bottle of bourbon and an extra glass. He poured and handed her the glass. The liquor disappeared in a single gulp.

"How scary was it?" she asked as she held out the glass for a refill.

"Scary. But—" He chuckled. "—dealing with a very pissed off New York actress was worse."

Kathy laughed in return.

"I heard she laid rubber pealing out of the parking lot," Jan said.

"Well, she squealed the tires, at least."

They both fell silent, and Kathy flopped onto the couch while Jan returned to his chair. After a few sips from their glasses, she finally spoke. "What do you think happened?"

Jan was thoughtful for another moment. "There's something I didn't tell the Board, and I'm surprised Jim didn't say anything, either."

Kathy sat up straight. "If it explains—"

"I don't think so," he said. "And with the mood in the meeting, I didn't want to add fuel to the fire."

"Well?"

"We heard…something…down there."

"Something?"

"We heard the voice. All three of us. It was just like Chet Rhingold and the Finley brothers said. It started as a breeze coming up from below, though the airlock doors were both closed. Then it became dozens of whispering voices until they joined into a single one telling us to 'Get out.'"

He shuddered and gulped down the rest of his drink.

"The others heard it too this time?"

Jan nodded. "I'm sure they did, given their reactions. We didn't talk about it, though." He eyed his empty glass, then reached for the bottle. "That's not all."

"Oh?" Kathy raised an eyebrow as she passed him her own empty glass for a refill.

"Your girlfriend. She…she seemed to—I don't know—*channel*—the creepy voice. Her eyes were rolled back, and a man's voice gave us its 'Final Warning.'"

"Like you said that Chet guy did?"

"Like Chet *did*."

"And Jim heard it too?"

Jan nodded. "I think so. He led the way, and we just got the fuck out of there."

Kathy thought for a moment. "Maybe Charlie—"

"The lights had just gone out. He couldn't have gotten down there on foot in time."

"A speaker, like a PA?"

Jan shrugged. "Didn't sound like it, but who knows?"

"Something else to search for tomorrow."

"So, you're going down tomorrow?"

Kathy nodded. "Me and the Sheriff, and a couple others."

Jan contemplated the liquor in his glass for a moment. "I'm going with you."

She shook her head. "I don't think that's a good idea."

"You need someone who was down there to navigate and…"

"Jim already volunteered. Barb didn't want him to, but he said the same thing you did." She eyed him over her glass. "About the voices too."

Surprised, Jan looked up from his own glass. "Then I'm going too."

Kathy didn't bother to argue anymore.

44

Jan

Saturday, April 11th

Jan was nowhere to be found when Kathy left the next morning. He was already up and out, since his phone had awakened him at 2:32 AM. The caller ID read Amanda's number.

"Jan?" she said before he had the phone to his ear. Her tone brought him instantly awake.

"Yeah? What's up?"

"It's Billy."

He felt a twinge of satisfaction. "You mean 'Jude?'"

There was a pause, then, "Yeah, He wouldn't respond to 'Jude,' so I tried 'Billy,' which worked."

She rushed on before Jan could say, *I told ya so.*

"Anyway, he's very…agitated. Ever since yesterday afternoon. Now he keeps calling for you."

Jan rubbed a hand down his face. "Wait. He's calling for me?"

"Well, he keeps saying 'Burned Man.' I'm pretty sure he means you. He started whispering that yesterday. Then, he said it out loud. Now he's practically shouting it every couple minutes." She paused to catch her breath, and Jan distinctly heard the boy's anguished voice cry out, "Burned Man."

"I'll be right over."

Ending the call, he sat on the edge of the bed, staring at the phone. He recognized his reaction for what it was: a protective instinct aimed not at the boy, but rather at Amanda. The boy was an unknown quantity, who never should have been left alone with her. Who knew what he was capable of? Letting her take him into her home seemed now, in the dead of night, to be an incredibly stupid decision. It was her decision, yes, but he had agreed with it, so if anything happened to her, he was at least partially responsible. If anything happened to her…

He stood and reached for his pants.

***

"It's open," she called.

Jan pushed the door open and stepped through. The house was a many-times remodeled company house, built over a hundred years before for a miner's family. It had started as a carbon copy of every other house on its street: a living room in the front, dining room and kitchen in the back, two tiny bedrooms and a bath tucked down a side hallway.

Amanda sat on a couch, her arms wrapped around the boy, who huddled against her like he craved her warmth, despite the coziness of the flames in the gas fireplace.

The boy, Billy, raised his head and reached out when Jan closed the door.

"Burned Man."

His plaintive voice was a well-aimed arrow that cut straight through to Jan's heart.

He barely felt the pain of stretched scars as he knelt before the entwined pair. But when the boy grabbed his shirt, a jolt of energy like an electric shock poured through him. Amanda must have felt it, too, because her arms stiffened and she drew a sharp breath.

Jan tried to pull away, but the boy's grip held him in place with a strength well beyond what his scrawny frame should have been able to muster. Their eyes locked, then Billy's rolled upwards revealing only the white of his sclera. His lips parted, and the voice that had been haunting Jan's dreams flew out of his open mouth.

"Final warning," the voice said, though the boy's lips never moved. "Stay out of my mine." It rose in pitch and volume until its final statement echoed in the small room, "Or else!"

A second jolt of energy sent Jan sprawling backwards onto the floor. The boy, Billy, slumped, unconscious, into Amanda's arms, and Amanda herself shuddered and released the breath she had been holding.

Staring at Jan lying on the floor, anger boiled out of her. "What did you do to him?"

Confused, Jan rubbed the scars on his wrists, as those and every other mark that branded his body burned anew. At first, he thought Amanda addressed the boy, but when he saw the fury in her eyes directed at himself, he felt his own anger rising.

"I didn't do anything! Didn't you hear what he said? He threatened me, then threw me over backwards."

"What are you talking about?" But her features took on their own confused look as if she was processing what she had just witnessed. "You…you never touched him, did you?"

Jan shook his head as the realization that Amanda probably hadn't heard the voice come out of the boy at all, let alone its warning, hit him.

"You didn't hear him say anything?" he asked, trying to keep his voice calm.

Amanda looked down at the boy still cuddled in her arms, but now snoring lightly. She shook her head.

"Shit. Not again," Jan muttered as he climbed to his feet, then sat next to them on the sofa. "He warned me off. Told me to stay out of *his* mine." His voice dropped to a whisper. "Just like Chet did."

"What the hell are you talking about?" Anger, mixed with a bit of panic, colored her voice.

Realizing he didn't have the energy or the words to explain himself, he just said, "Never mind. I thought I heard him say something when he…when I lost my balance."

He looked at Amanda cradling the boy—Billy—in her arms and tentatively slipped his arm around her shoulders. To his relief, she leaned onto his shoulder, silently welcoming his embrace.

45

Jan

Saturday, April 11th

Jan pulled into the mine's parking lot just as Kathy walked down the stairs from the Visitor Center.

"Where were you?" she fired at him.

"Out." His tone told her he was in no mood for her attitude. "Where are you going?"

"Come on. You need to come too."

"Wait. Where? And why?"

"To Amanda's. I want to try to get a *real* name from the kid. To help our search for his parents."

Jan shook his head. "Billy. He told me his name is Billy, remember?."

He saw her disbelieving look, but didn't feel like arguing.

"Anyway, I just came from there. He's asleep now, and I'm betting Amanda won't let you disturb him. He's been up all night." Jan took out his phone. "I'll have her call you when he wakes up."

Kathy eyed him with a hint of a smile. "So, she's in your phone now." It wasn't a question. He just rolled his eyes in response, and she gestured to the car. "Well, get in, anyway."

"Why?" he asked, but reached for the door handle. "Where are we going? And what about the mine search?"

"You already missed that. I'm hungry, and you look like you desperately need coffee."

"You got that right," he said as he slid into the front seat. "And you're buyin'."

***

It turned out Jan was hungry as well. Carleigh, the diner's pretty young waitress, cleared their plates and headed for the kitchen. Her dirty-blonde ponytail poked out through the back of her Rail Riders baseball cap and swished back and forth as she walked away.

"I don't know how she does it," Kathy murmured.

"Does what?"

"Four kids and she still looks like that."

"Four kids!" Jan fought to keep his voice to a whisper. "She's what, twenty?"

Kathy snorted. "Try pushin' thirty. Still looks twenty, though, doesn't she?" Carleigh caught her eye when she came out of the kitchen and Kathy held up her coffee mug.

A couple of full mugs, smiles, and "Thank-yous" later, Carleigh was walking away again.

"You just wanted another look at her ass."

Kathy yanked her gaze back to Jan as Carleigh went behind the diner's counter. She didn't bother to answer. Instead, she turned the conversation back to Billy.

"So, this boy, Billy—that's weird that Amanda started calling him that—what?" Jan looked for a moment like he was about to say something, then just shook his head, so Kathy continued. "Billy kept yelling 'Burned Man,' so Amanda called you over to calm him down?" Jan nodded. "Tell me again what happened when you got there?"

Jan relayed, for the third time, the incident of supernatural ventriloquism, the electric-like shocks that still made his scars ache, and the fact that Amanda didn't hear or feel any of it.

Kathy thought for a full minute while they both sipped their coffee.

"It wasn't PTSD this time, was it?"

Jan's face hardened. "It's never been PTSD. The symptoms are all wrong, and there was nothing to trigger any of the—" He counted on his fingers. "—now three incidents." He shook his head. "No, this is really happening—again."

Kathy put on her skeptical cop expression. "Well, who knows what might trigger an episode? You've been stressed over this mine thing. I know it's a financial stretch—"

"No." He shook his head violently. "You and I both know this shit can happen. That ghosts can possess people and take over their bodies. We've both seen it happen, for God's sake."

"Hey, keep it down. Yeah, I've seen that happen, too. But what are the chances it would happen again? And to someone you know, again?"

Jan's laugh wasn't at all funny. "In this freakin' town? Very high." He took a deep breath to calm himself. "Look, a lot of bad shit went down in and around these mines, and at the Avon Hill mine most of all. It's no wonder there are some pretty pissed off spirits floating around."

Kathy nodded. "Yeah, I've heard stories growing up. Dead husbands just left on widows' doorsteps. Sometimes with an eviction notice pinned to the body if there were no boys old enough to take the dad's place."

"And that's not the worst of it."

"I don't know. That's pretty bad."

Jan leaned in and glanced left and right. "There were a lot of rumors flying around that the Avon Hill Mine disaster wasn't an accident or an 'act of God,' as the official inquest claimed." Kathy still looked skeptical, so he continued. "There was conflicting testimony from mining engineers over how the fire started. All the ones who were being paid, either directly or indirectly, by a mining company claimed it was because the miners incorrectly fired up the ventilation furnace. That sparks set the cribbing in the single shaft on fire. But others—"

Kathy held up her hand to stop him. "Wait. What are you talking about?"

Jan caught his breath. "I've been doing a lot of research. Reading old newspapers and magazine articles. Jim even had a copy of the inquest transcript in his archives."

"Of course he did."

Jan chuckled as well. "OK, so here's the story. The Avon Hill Mine was the last mine in Pennsylvania, maybe the last one in the country, to still have only a single shaft to access the mine. The mine safety laws passed in the mid-nineteenth century were intended to reduce the likelihood of what happened at Avon Hill from happening. But through legal and political maneuvering, Avon Hill kept getting extensions and grandfathered exemptions. For decades! So, in 1873, it still had a single shaft, and a breaker to process the coal built directly above that shaft."

"You're saying there was only one way in and out of the mine?"

"Exactly. That was common practice in the eighteenth and nineteenth centuries until those safety laws were passed."

"OK, but how would a fire start in the shaft? And why was there a furnace in the mine? I thought it's a constant temperature that far underground."

Jan rubbed his hands together. He didn't get to lecture very often, and he took advantage of having a captive audience.

"First, the furnace wasn't for making the miners comfortable. It was for keeping them alive. Coal-fired furnaces were used, up until the advent of electric fans, to ventilate the mines. Mining, especially coal mining, releases all kinds of nasty stuff into the air." Jan ticked them off on his fingers. "Coal dust, explosive methane gas—what they called 'firedamp', carbon monoxide—or 'whitedamp', and carbon dioxide—'blackdamp'. They can all kill you, just in different ways. So, to keep everybody below ground alive, they needed a constant flow of fresh air in and the bad air out."

He took another sip of coffee before continuing.

"That was the furnace's job. The furnace heated the air in its firebox, which rose up a chimney to the surface. That caused a pressure differential, which pulled fresh air down into the mine. That pressure differential, and the resulting fresh air, was regulated by a series of airlocks that were operated by boys, called 'nippers,' some as young as five or six years old."

Kathy nodded. "Jim explained that this morning. I can't imagine kids that young working in the dark."

Jan nodded ruefully. "Since there was only one shaft into the mine, it had to be divided into three sections: the main section for the hoist that carried miners and coal up and down to the various levels, the up-flow chimney for the hot air and soot from the furnace to rise to the surface, and the down-flow section for the fresh air to flow downward. It was an ingenious setup, actually, that worked for centuries both here and in Great Britain. The problems came, of course, when that single shaft was blocked, or the hoist broke down, or, as happened at Avon Hill, there was a fire."

Kathy was intrigued, despite herself. "How did the fire start?"

"Well, that's the big question. It's well documented that the miners were on strike, protesting the very fact that the mine had been violating those safety laws for decades. No one disputes that. Where the controversy arises, though, is what happened next. The miners' nascent union, the Workingmen's Benevolent Association—which was probably a front for the Molly Maguires—"

"Wait, wasn't that a movie? My dad loved it."

Jan nodded, smiling. "A very glossed-over version of events. The Mollies were blamed for several beatings and even some murders. A dozen alleged members were hanged as a result. Anyway, they were on strike, occupying the mine's entrance, picketing and blocking scabs from working there. They had been camped out there for weeks, and the Company was losing millions. Then, suddenly, the Company caved. Seemingly gave in to all the miners' demands. They said they would start digging another shaft if the miners ended the strike."

"They never dug the second shaft, did they?"

Jan slowly shook his head. "Nope. The mine reopened the next day. The fire started first thing that morning."

"And the miners claimed the fire was started? Deliberately?"

"Not just the miners. Some very well-respected engineers and investigators from the government. Anyone, in fact, who wasn't a paid stooge for the mining companies."

Kathy was intrigued. "Why would somebody start a fire?"

"Great question. At the inquest, the mining company blamed it on inexperience restarting the furnace after it had been idle for so long. But the man in charge of the furnace had twenty years on the job."

"OK, if it wasn't an accident, why would someone start it deliberately?"

Jan made a face when he sipped his cold coffee. "Actually, there were a lot of suspects. Other mine owners who had raised their prices because Avon Hill wasn't producing. Other miners, too. The miners at Avon Hill were primarily Irish. Other towns around were mainly German or Polish, and some Welsh. None of them got along with the others, and some of them were the scabs that the Avon Hill strikers drove away—with clubs and sometimes with bullets."

Carleigh appeared as if by magic with two fresh mugs. The look she and Kathy exchanged was steamy.

"Isn't she married?" Jan whispered.

"Not anymore," Kathy answered without taking her eyes off Carleigh's retreating back.

"Sheesh! You need a girlfriend."

Kathy's head slowly turned to face him. "I was working on that when your stupid mine scared her off."

"Whatever. Do you want to hear this story or not?"

She twirled her extended middle finger, telling him to keep going.

Jan rolled his eyes. "Anyway, the most likely candidate was the Pinkertons, acting on the mine owners' behest. There had been several incidents all during the strike. Beatings, and even some shootings. On both sides. Surviving family members, who had brought food to the camp every night during the strike, said that on several occasions, the Pinkerton 'bulls' drove them off at gunpoint."

"But why would the owners destroy their source of income?"

"Look at it from their perspective. They would have to…" He ticked his points off on his fingers. "…dig another shaft, build a new breaker somewhere close by, reroute train tracks to haul the coal away, and shutdown the mine while the old breaker was torn down and moved. What does that sound like?"

Kathy thought a moment. "Sounds like a whole new mine."

"Exactly. If you have to shut down Avon Hill and start a new mine, why not get rid of some troublemakers in the process?"

"That's pretty harsh."

"Harsher than leaving dead husbands wrapped in canvas bags on their widows' front porches? And billing them for the bag?"

Kathy shuddered, and Jan continued.

"The men had no intention of going into the mine again until the safety violations were addressed—which meant shutting the mine down for months while another shaft was dug and the breaker building where the coal was sorted and washed was rebuilt somewhere other than directly on top of the shaft."

"So why did they end the strike based just on the company's promises?"

Jan spread his hands, then Kathy nodded. "I get it. They had family members to feed. And house and clothe."

Jan sipped his fresh coffee and nodded. "Jim found coal company records that show they made a series of large payments to the Pinkerton Agency during the strike and shortly thereafter."

"So, the families think maybe the Pinkertons started the fire?" Kathy asked, and Jan nodded. "It all comes down to how the fire got started."

Jan touched his finger to the tip of his nose. "Exactly. The company said, and the inquest officially agreed, that the miners had incorrectly started the furnace, which hadn't been used for weeks during the strike. It's true that restarting one of those things was very tricky and dangerous. The official findings were that the miners screwed it up, and sparks from the furnace set fire to the wood that lined the up-flow chimney. That fire, fed by the rising air and a high-concentration of combustible gases from the improperly started furnace, quickly spread up the shaft and set the breaker building on fire."

"So, they blamed the victims who couldn't defend themselves," Kathy said, and Jan nodded. "How very convenient."

"But," Jan held up a finger, "the problem with that conclusion is that both the furnace operator and his assistant—who had been running the damned thing for twenty years—were among the miners down the hole. They knew exactly how to restart the furnace because they had done it many times."

Kathy sat back in the booth and shook her head. "Or, the Pinkerton thugs set the fire, maybe to smoke them out."

"Or to teach the newly formed mining unions and the Molly Maguires a lesson. Especially if the owners were going to have to shut down to dig another shaft and move the breaker, anyway."

"A hundred and ten lives is a pretty hard lesson."

Jan nodded, then shrugged. "It was a hard time."

Kathy's shoulders slumped. "I really wish you hadn't told me all of this."

Jan was taken aback. "Why?"

Kathy sat up straight and looked him in the eye. "Because there is no statute of limitations on murder," she whispered.

46

Mollie
April 8th, 1873

Tim Kelly fidgeted under his mother's attention. She smoothed his oversized work jacket for the dozenth time, then checked his work pail again.

"Keep this jacket on. It gets cold down in…there." Jack had retrieved it from the charity bin earlier that morning. "And horde the candle in your pail. It should last a week, at least. The dark's nothing to be afraid of."

Tim nodded, wide eyed, and she had to turn away to hide the tears welling in her eyes. "I'll do enough fearin' for the both of us," she whispered.

"Ah, Ma," Jack, Jr. said as he bounded down the stairs. "Quit your fussin'. He'll do fine." Jack tugged Tim's too-large hat down over his eyes. "Nipper's the simplest job in the world. You hear two knocks, then three, you open the uphill door. Three knocks, then two, and you open the downhill one. Once the crew's inside, you close it up, run to the other one and open it up."

He leaned down to meet Tim's eyes. "Just make sure you close them tight when they're gone. That's *very* important. Keeps the air movin' right so we all get fresh." He stood up straight and gave Tim a reassuring smile. "That's all there is to it. Most o' the time, you'll just be sittin' in the dark. Easy as pie."

Tim, his eyes still wide, nodded. His big brother Jack was his hero. If he said it was easy, then Tim had to believe it, although his heart was still pounding like it had been all night, and his belly told him he shouldn't have eaten that second flapjack for breakfast. Especially since breakfast came two hours earlier than when he went to school. But there he stood, with the sun barely up, ready to go to work. Their twelve-hour shift started at six o'clock, which scrambled his sense of time. He said so.

"Be glad it's not the night shift," Mollie replied, but Jack just laughed.

"Day or night makes no difference a mile underground," Jack told them. "Down there, it's always night. Only clock that matters down there is the shift clock. Time goes quicker if you don't think about it, though. Do your job—the job that's got to be done *now*. Then, you do the next one. Simple as that."

Mollie Kelly wiped her eyes with the back of her hand. She stepped into the house's tiny kitchen and returned with two small parcels wrapped in paper.

"Here's your lunches." She handed one to Jack and placed the other in Tim's pail. "It's meat and cheese wrapped around a pickle." She lowered her eyes. "We've no bread 'til payday."

Jack didn't ask what kind of meat. Instead, he gave his mom a hug. "Thanks, Ma. I'll look after Tim. I promise."

Nodding, she kissed him on his forehead and knelt down to Tim's eye level. "Give your Mom a hug on your first day of work."

He flung his arms around her neck, and they clung to each other until the five-minute whistle sounded.

"Gotta go," Jack said, taking Tim by the hand.

"Listen to your brother," Mollie said as she gave him another hug. "And be safe."

As they trotted down the sidewalk, Tim looked back once at Mollie standing in the doorway. She lifted her hand from her belly to give a weak wave and watched her sons, for the first—and last—time, run down the street together to their fate.

47

Mollie & Tim
April 8th, 1873

Mollie blamed her upset stomach that morning on the baby—Amanda's great-great-grandmother— kicking in her belly. But if pressed, she would have admitted it was concern for her little boy, Tim.

Her mind raced with images—conjured purely by her imagination, since she had never been inside the mine—of her boy whimpering in pitch blackness, trying to be brave. She saw him riding down into the steep shaft in the mine car hanging by its cable. The rough talk of the older men teaching him words no eight-year-old had any right to know. The first whiff of coal dust tickling his nose and making him sneeze. Then, the dwindling light becoming the purest black. She saw it all, heard every squeal of the metal wheels on the rails, smelled the unwashed bodies crowded into the car, and felt Tim's rising fear. She saw, smelled, and felt it all. And she wept.

Tim

Mom's fear as they left the house was contagious. But so was Jack's excitement. As they jogged down the access road toward the line of men and boys waiting their turn to ride down, Jack gave Tim his best advice.

"You're gonna hear some stuff you've never heard before—words and such that men say when there's just men around. Don't ask what they mean and don't *ever* repeat them when Mom's around. Or any ladies, for that matter. Got it?"

Tim nodded.

"Now, be ready for some kiddin' around, this being your first day and all. It'll be good natured—mostly. So just nod and smile when they poke fun at ya'. And most important, do exactly what the bosses tell you to do, exactly *when* they tell you to. Some of 'em don't like havin' kids working down below, so they'll look for any excuse to send ya' home. Okay?"

Tim nodded again. His mind was full of questions, but he didn't trust his voice to come out as anything other than a squeak. Jack, remembering his first day, nodded his understanding of Tim's plight.

"Good. That's right. Do what they tell ya' and only ask questions if you don't understand what they mean."

They joined the queue waiting for the lift, and Jack introduced Tim around. The mood was jovial, everyone glad to be earning a day's pay after their strike.

"They'll have 'im nipperin', I suppose?" Matt O'Reilly, who was a year older than Jack and nephew of the former owner of Jack's work shirt, asked.

Jack nodded, stomping his feet against the early morning chill. "I already talked to our shift boss. He'll be the nipper in Tunnel Sixteen. Joey Stinson is movin' up top to be a breaker boy, on account of his lungs not handlin' the dust."

Tim had no idea what Jack was talking about, but following his brother's advice, he said nothing. Soon, his ears were burning from those words Jack told him about, although he had at least a vague idea of what most of them meant. Such was the rough-edged culture of the coal region in Northeastern Pennsylvania.

When their turn finally came, the brothers squeezed into the lift car with at least thirty other miners. Pressed between Jack behind him and Matt in front, he heard more, and some new swear words in English, Gaelic, and even Polish.

Someone two rows in front called out, "Hey, watch where ya' put your hands, *buachill*."

Guffaws broke out, and Jack responded with, "Don't pretend ya' don't like it," which raised the volume of laughter as the lift swung around a curve and the light faded.

"Only if it's yer momma—" All laughter abruptly cut off. Jack Sr.'s death was still too raw. After a whispered admonition from one of the other miners, the first one said, "Oh, sorry, Jack. Didn't know that was you."

Tim squeezed his eyes shut to fight the tears as Jack's hand gripped his shoulder. When he opened them again, the darkness was so complete he thought he was blind.

His shoulders tighten in fear under Jack's hand.

"We'll be in the work lights soon, Little Man," his brother whispered in his ear.

Despite his big brother's reassurances, Tim felt the darkness pressing on his chest harder than Matt's back in front of him.

"Breathe, Tim," Jack whispered, and Tim couldn't remember the last breath he had taken.

Letting the spent air out and sucking in fresh helped, but only for a moment. A strange scent and a bitter taste in the back of his throat made Tim cough. Breathing through his nose to avoid another cough only worsened his situation. The coal dust in the air assailed his sinuses and before he could stop it, a magnificent sneeze shook his whole body and left him shuddering as a string of three more came unstoppably.

Laughter broke out among the other miners, and got louder when Matt said over his shoulder, "You didn't get any on me, did ya?"

Jack patted Tim's shoulder to let him know it was a joke, and quietly said, "Take shallow breaths until you get used to it." A little louder, he said, "We've all been through it."

Several miners mumbled "Aye" and "'at's right", which made Tim feel a little better, at least. Soon enough, as Jack had said, the track flattened out, and they rolled into a lighted area filled with the men and boys who had already descended.

"What's up?" Jack asked one of those waiting.

"Vent'lation furnace," came the response. "It's been dead since the strike. Gotta get it restarted."

Jack pointed down a side tunnel from which came the sound of men shoveling coal into the furnace's maw. Curses in three different languages drifted out on top of the clang of shovels.

"If they're shovelin' coal, they got the wood starter fire goin'," he said.

A voice called from the furnace room, "There it goes."

"Damn right," another fireman said in response.

Heads started nodding among the waiting miners as the furnace sucked stale air in and sent it up the chimney side of the shaft they had just descended. The rising hot air started a siphon that pulled fresh air down another section of the same shaft that was separated from the chimney by a wooden wall.

"You'll be working tunnels thirteen, fourteen, and fifteen today," the foreman called out. "Use the cross tunnels sixteen, seventeen, and eighteen. Everybody, be 'specially careful today, and you nippers, make sure you're on the ball today. All the damps, but especially blackdamp and firedamp, have probably built up below. Make sure you test for it before making any sparks. Got it?"

Mumbled agreement rippled through the miners.

"Alright. Get your asses to work!"

A cheer of "Huzzah!" echoed through the tunnels as the men and boys went to their designated work areas.

Jack, with a hand on Tim's shoulders, walked him down tunnel fourteen to the head of tunnel sixteen.

"Now, you know what to do, right?"

Tim nodded. He had been rehearsing in his head what Jack had told him. "Two knocks, then three, open the uphill door. Three knocks, then two, means open the downhill one. When everyone is in, close the door and open the opposite one. When they're all out, double check that both doors are closed tight." He looked at Jack expectantly. "Right?"

His big brother gave him a wide, proud grin. "You got it, Little Man." He guided Tim to a stool in the corner of the airlock. "See ya at dinner break. Save your lunch 'til I get back." With that, he disappeared down tunnel fourteen.

Tim closed and double checked both doors, shutting off not only the flow of air, but the meager lantern light as well. Sitting on a three-legged stool in the pitch blackness, his lower lip quivered while he listened intently for any knocks on his doors.

48

Kathy

Saturday, April 11th

Lacey sat, arms crossed high across her chest, at the tiny kitchen table in Kathy's apartment.

"Is this an official conversation?"

Kathy tilted her head. "For now."

Lacey looked around the shabby apartment. "Then why are we here and not at the police station?"

Kathy wanted to say, *For later*, but, given the stern look on Lacey's face, she decided to be more diplomatic. "To save you the embarrassment of walking the gauntlet of reporters."

"Reporters? Gauntlet?"

Kathy chuckled. "Okay, just one reporter. From one of the Scranton TV stations."

Lacey raised an eyebrow, which Kathy saw as a chink in her cold exterior until she said, "Kathy, I'm an actress. I *crave* TV cameras."

She let the rebuke hang in the air for a beat, then smiled. Kathy let out the breath she was holding and laughed.

"Good point. Next time, I'll call in every TV station around."

They both laughed, then Lacey said, "Next time? Are you expecting more trouble? And why is the county sheriff investigating a blackout in a mine?"

Kathy sobered and laid her phone on the table. Clicking the voice recording app, she recited the standard opening of time, date, and Lacey's name. Then she said, "It's more than just a blackout. Charlie, the guy who was supposed to be operating the lift, is missing. I need to know what you saw and heard."

"Not much, really. We rode down—that part went smoothly. That guy, Jim…"

"Jim Donnelly."

"Yeah, him. He was showing us around—"

"Us? Who all was there?"

"Me, Jim…Donnelly, and the writer guy, Jan…something."

Kathy chuckled to herself. "Jan Sorrensen."

"Right. Anyway, we were working through the tour. Jim was explaining how everything worked—you know, so I could answer questions like I knew what I was talking about." They both smiled. "Jan, the writer guy, was taking occasional notes. Tweaking the script, I guess. Anyway, we were in the airlock place when the lights went out. The radio didn't work. Neither did the phone, and there was no air moving."

Lacey's voice rose in pitch, and her eyes grew wider and wider. Her knee started pumping up and down.

Kathy put her hand on Lacey's knee. "Calm down. Then you climbed out by yourself?" She didn't wait for a reply. "You got out safe."

She reached for her phone, but Lacey grabbed her hand.

"That's not all of it." She shook her head as if to banish the memory, but then said, "I kind of blacked out. Standing there. I didn't fall, or anything, but I think…well, I stopped thinking, actually. I'm not sure for how long, but the guys said I was…speaking with a man's voice. Real menacing, like." She shook her head again. "I don't know. Ask them. I was out of it."

"Oh, I will," Kathy promised as she took Lacey's shaking hands in hers. "Anything else?"

Lacey shook her head, but then nodded to the phone. Taking her cue, Kathy paused the recording.

Keeping her eyes down, Lacey whispered, "I'm scared, Kathy. Ever since I got back in fuckin' Dundee, I've felt…I don't know. Fuzzy. Disconnected. Like there's someone or something trying to crawl back into my head." She met Kathy's eyes with tears streaming down her cheeks. "Help me. Please."

Kathy pulled Lacey into her arms, her tears wetting her t-shirt. All thoughts of seduction melted away, transforming instead into the compassion that was at the core of her being—the need to protect those she cared about. The warmth of her embrace hid the cold steel of her determination. While whispering calming platitudes to Lacey, she was at the same time, planning interviews with Jan and Jim.

Lacey had other ideas, though. She looked up at Kathy and, with a hand on the back of her neck, pulled her down until their lips met. Lacey's fear and Kathy's anger were a volatile mix that ignited into a flaming passion. Without conscious thought, they stumbled from the kitchen into the tiny bedroom, their lips never parting.

***

An hour later, Lacey dozed while Kathy drew hearts in the sweat on her breasts. The sex was a pleasant and necessary interlude, but already her mind was racing with questions. Questions and fears that something unexplainable was happening again to someone close to her. Lacey's blackout matched Jan's description of the incident, and his late-night

169

interaction with the boy, Billy, who supposedly had growled warnings that only Jan could hear.

As Lacey's breathing deepened and her lips twitched, Kathy whispered almost silently, "Who are you?"

At first, nothing happened, but when she repeated her question, Lacey's eyes flicked back and forth beneath her closed lids, and her lips parted. After the third try, Lacey's head turned to face her, and her eyes flew open. Whatever stared out at her from those eyes wasn't her lover. And when a voice sounding like it came from the depths of Hell said, "We are Death," Kathy recoiled.

A moment later, ashamed of her reaction, she pulled Lacey into her arms and demanded, cold steel in her voice, "No, you're not. You're my *Lacey*."

A shudder ran through Lacey's body, and she let out a whimper as her eyes cleared.

"What a horrible dream," she mumbled as her tears flowed freely again.

Kathy squeezed Lacey tighter. "Tell me about it," she whispered.

Lacey shook her head, but quietly said, "Fire. Smoke. So many souls crying out. Crying out in a single voice."

Her own voice cracked, and the sobbing started. As Kathy squeezed her tighter and stroked her hair, she knew in her bones she would need all of her strength—and Jan's—to save her lover, and maybe the entire town of Dundee.

49

Mark

Saturday, April 11ᵗʰ

Mark Luzeski shone the flashlight on the rough ground as he led the couple through the tunnel door and into the mine.

"Nobody even knows this access tunnel is here," he said, his voice low and conspiratorial. "So, your privacy is guaranteed."

The young woman, Lauren Tanner, giggled and squeezed her date's hand. Mark chose these two for the DASD Experience's trial run because he'd known them since high school, and he knew they would put on a good show for the hidden cameras. Lauren was clearly into the whole "dark, secret tunnel thing," as she put it. On the other hand, Jimmy Youells, former football team captain and current college student, seemed a little hesitant. Mark was sure that Lauren's *enthusiasm* would win him over, though.

With a flourish, he pushed open the door to the first sensory deprivation room. Lauren practically dragged Jimmy in by the hand. The only furnishing in the room was a king-size air mattress covered in a black sheet.

"The DASD Experience is best enjoyed without the distractions of the senses of vision, hearing, or touch." He flipped a switch next to the door, and small lights at the ceiling dimly lit the room. "When I leave, you will be alone in this soundproof room. The lighting will turn off in thirty seconds, after which you will be in complete darkness." He extended his hand, which held two pills. A bottle of water hung between two of his fingers. "A hit of Dazed will enhance the experience by clearing your mind and letting you concentrate on your innermost thoughts."

Jimmy looked down at the air mattress. "Won't we feel that?"

"And our clothes," Lauren added, then giggled.

Mark pointed his flashlight at two hooks on the wall. "You can hang your clothes there…if you want. The special mattress simulates zero-G, so you'll feel like you're floating. The lights will come back on in thirty minutes."

He turned to go, but before he had even left the room, Lauren pulled her tank top over her head. Closing the door behind him, he hurried to where Gino waited in the control room. A big monitor showed Lauren and Jimmy, already naked, lying down on the mattress. A moment later, the lights turned off, and the cameras switched to night vision mode.

Lauren murmured, "It really is dark," which came through the speakers clearly.

"Are you recording?" Mark asked.

"Ever since you left the room."

The split screen of the monitor showed the view from each of the four cameras in the room. Gino stared at the screen, but Mark sniffed the air and made a face.

"What's that smell?"

Gino shrugged. "Probably a dead rat back in the tunnel somewhere."

"Must be an awfully big rat."

Without taking his eyes off the screen, Gino said, "You didn't lock the tunnel door when you left last time."

Mark stared at the screen, also, as Lauren's hand slid across Jimmy's chest.

"What do you mean? I locked up. I'm sure of it."

"Nope. Padlock wasn't even there…"

Gino fell silent as Lauren straddled her boyfriend and slid her body down his.

"That didn't take long," Mark murmured.

50

Gino
Saturday, April 11ʰ

Jeez, he's a friggin' Marathon Man," Gino muttered after Lauren moaned out her third orgasm.

Without stopping his ministrations, Jimmy leaned back and caressed Lauren's neck. Almost lovingly, he cupped her throat in his hand. After a moment, Lauren's eyes got wide, and she nodded her excitement.

"That's pretty kinky," Mark said and zoomed in with the overhead camera.

The view showed Jimmy's fingers digging into the sides of Lauren's neck while the taut skin between his thumb and forefinger pressed down on her windpipe. A guttural sound, almost a growl, rumbled in his throat.

Gino shifted the focus to Lauren's face. "I think she's kinda into it."

They watched as her eyes got even wider and the flush of her face glowed in the night vision. When her eyes rolled back and her head thrashed back and forth, Mark said, "There's number four."

"I don't think so." Gino zoomed the camera out, which showed Jimmy with both hands around Lauren's neck and leaning his full weight on her throat. Her whole body thrashed back and forth, and her fists weakly beat at his sides. His growl became a full-throated howl.

"Holy shit!"

Mark grabbed the police flashlight from its hook and ran from the control room. Gino followed after grabbing a foot-long heavy-duty Phillips head screwdriver.

After fumbling with the door latch for a few seconds, Mark threw open the door to the sensory deprivation room. The powerful beam of the tactical flashlight revealed Lauren lying half-on and half-off the mattress. She wasn't moving.

Gino ran past him toward her, but Jimmy, naked, burst from behind the door and tackled him to the hard floor. Wrenching the screwdriver from Gino's hand, Jimmy hesitated only an instant before thrusting it almost completely through Gino's neck. With an evil cackle that froze Mark for a moment, Jimmy reveled in the fountain of blood spraying from Gino's severed carotid artery.

Breaking free from the momentary paralysis of disbelief, Mark swung the heavy flashlight with all his might at the back of Jimmy's head. But through some supernatural sense, Jimmy anticipated the assault and shifted his position just enough to take the blow on the shoulder instead. Ricocheting off Jimmy's shoulder, the blow connected with his temple.

Roaring with rage, Jimmy—or what had possessed Jimmy— jumped to his feet and swung his weapon like a short sword, ripping through Mark's shirt and slicing a gouge deep into his chest.

The adrenaline flooding his system let Mark ignore the pain, and his two-handed return swing smashed the big head of the flashlight into the Jimmy-thing's face, stunning him.

The crunch of broken bones fueled Mark's rage, and the sight of his still-dying best friend and the once-beautiful lifeless body of Lauren turned Mark's world red. Without a conscious thought, he slammed the bloody flashlight onto Jimmy's head again, sending him to his knees. He swung again, knocking Jimmy face-forward onto the rocky floor. Overcome, Mark fell into a killing frenzy while a new voice inside his head whispered, "Yes!" with each devastating blow.

When the cracking of skull bones had given way to squishy sounds, he fell to his knees, exhausted.

Through it all, the beam of the heavy-duty flashlight never wavered, and when Mark finally let it fall, its low-angled light illuminated the macabre scene. Lauren, naked, sprawled across the air mattress. Jimmy, also naked, was an unrecognizable, crumpled corpse. Worst of all, Gino lay with blank eyes wide and hands still clutching his throat. His face was frozen in terror as he had tried to hold back his streaming lifeblood.

With the post-adrenaline crash came the searing pain from his chest wound. His own shirt was soaked with blood, and as he struggled to his feet, the drop in blood pressure almost made him pass out. Leaning against the wall for support, that voice inside his head began whispering again. The words were indistinct, but Mark knew their meaning: *"Take me with you."*

Panicked by the feeling that his thoughts were no longer his own, he pushed the voice down and stumbled through the door, up the tunnel, and out into the cool night air.

He didn't notice Lauren's chest slowly rising and falling.

51

Kathy
Sunday, April 12th

Kathy paced back and forth in the hospital chapel like a lioness in a zoo cage. She had just taken Mark Luzeski's statement while he lay under guard in his hospital bed. Now she waited for her boss to get off his phone call.

"What a fuckshow," Sheriff Peterson muttered as he reentered their improvised conference room.

He still held his cell phone in a death grip. Kathy stopped her pacing while Peterson took a deep breath and faced her.

"Send Officer Samuels home."

Kathy raised a questioning eyebrow, but remained silent. Peterson wiped a hand across his face.

"We've got nothing on him. Not enough to warrant a full-time guard, at least."

Kathy finally spoke. "What? We've got two dead college students, another lying in a coma down the hall, an illegal 'sensory deprivation' operation—whatever the hell that is—and some kind of 'Dazed' drug that we don't even know what it is. That seems like plenty to me."

Peterson held up his hands to stop Kathy's rant, then ticked his points off on his fingers.

"It's pretty obvious that Jimmy Youells killed the Kapaletti kid and almost killed the girl. Mark, there," he nodded toward the hallway, "was clearly acting in self-defense. In fact, you could argue that he saved her."

"'Pretty obvious' and 'clearly'? You're jumping to conclusions."

"Kathy, you've seen the video of the whole thing. The autopsies will confirm what's on the recording, I'm sure."

"What about the drugs? This 'Dazed' stuff?"

Peterson shook his head. "You heard Jimmy. He claims it's just some CBD supplements he bought online. Forensics will have to confirm that, of course. Even so, it doesn't warrant a round-the-clock guard. Basically, all we've got on him is a trespassing charge, and even that is a stretch, since his father—"

"Is part owner of the mine, right? That's who was on the phone, wasn't it?"

Peterson's grimace was almost painful to watch. "His lawyer, actually."

"Jesus H. Christ. Already?"

"That's not the half of it. The same lawyer is representing the Kapaletti family. Seems they're both suing Jimmy Youells's parents."

"Oh, crap. Having an outside lawyer involved is gonna totally screw up our investigation. Besides, the Youellses don't have a pot to piss in."

"Somebody's got to pay. At least from their perspective."

"Isn't losing their son payment enough?"

"Apparently not."

They both stood fuming for a full minute. Finally, Sheriff Peterson spoke up.

"Their ambulance chaser is going to want the video. Make sure we keep the original."

"It's already in evidence. And I've squirreled away another digitally notarized copy. If the original gets…altered, we'll know it."

Peterson raised an eyebrow at this violation of procedures, but then nodded. "Probably a good idea."

Kathy's eyes flew open when she remembered the other victim.

"The woman, Lauren, is Spaz's niece, right? How's he holding up?"

"He's with his brother and sister-in-law." Peterson took a deep breath. "He's going to want in on the investigation."

Kathy started to protest, then nodded. If it was her niece, she'd want to be all over it as well. "I'll keep him busy."

"Good."

Kathy turned to leave, but Peterson stopped her with a hand on her arm. "Kaveetha," Peterson almost never used her real name. "Tread—"

"—Lightly?" Kathy interrupted, then snorted.

"I know you better than that. I was going to say 'carefully.' There's been too much weird shit floating around this town lately, and some powerful forces have their own agendas."

She knew he meant the Mine Tour board, but she suspected the forces at work were more powerful and less natural than a bunch of rich, entitled assholes.

52

Jan
Sunday, April 12th

Amanda picked up a dish towel and started drying the plates and glasses Jan had already stacked to drain.

She nudged him. "Thanks for your help."

He returned her smile. "It's the least I could do. That dinner was delicious."

Amanda turned away, trying to hide her blushing. "It was my mom's recipe."

"Well, hats off to your mom."

"She'd appreciate hearing that, if…"

Jan raised an eyebrow when she didn't finish, but Amanda just shook her head. "She's been gone a long time, but my father rarely complimented her—or me. On anything. Neither did my ex-husband, for that matter. I guess the Lee women aren't very good at picking men."

"Oh, I don't know. I think your skills just may be improving."

Jan kept washing, but watched her reaction out of the corner of his eye. Amanda gave him a skeptical look until he couldn't help grinning. After a moment, they both started laughing.

"Don't hurt your shoulder patting yourself on the back," she said, still laughing.

Jan turned to face her. "I'm sure you'd fix me up I did."

Amanda looped the towel around his neck and pulled him closer. "Maybe I'll injure you myself."

"Why? Just so you can—'

Before he could finish his comeback, she used the towel to pull his head down to hers and met his lips with her own. Hesitating only a moment, Jan slid his arms around her waist and pulled her to him. The kiss lingered longer than either had intended, though neither wanted it to end.

Finally, Amanda loosened her grip on the towel, and they both leaned back.

"Wow," she whispered.

Jan leaned his forehead on hers. "Thank you. I've wanted to do that for—"

Again, she didn't let him finish. This time, they let the tips of their tongues find each other. He took her low moan as permission to explore further, which she eagerly reciprocated.

When they again parted breathlessly, Jan whispered, "I still can't…"

Amanda simply pressed a finger to his lips and smiled. "Maybe not yet. I think we need a new treatment plan, though." She laid her head against his chest. "With more…hands-on exercises."

Jan kissed her ear and whispered, "Teach me."

Her throaty growl let him know Lesson One was about to begin.

***

Well, that was…different, Jan thought as he watched a naked Amanda pad across the bedroom floor.

"I remembered I had something to show you," she said as she bent down to open the lowest drawer of her dresser.

"You can show me that view any time."

"Oh, shush." She fumbled through the contents of the drawer for a minute, then pulled something from it and held it in the air. "Found it!"

Turning back around, she struck a pose, and Jan smiled appreciatively. She was what his father would have called a "handsome woman." Especially since she was pulling fifty years along behind her. He patted the bed next to him, and she slid in under the covers.

"What's this?" he asked when she handed him what she had found.

"It's a diary, or more specifically a journal. I thought it might help with the mine project. It's been passed down daughter to daughter for generations. I only have sons, so…"

Jan carefully opened the pages and looked at the dates.

"This was around the time of the fire," he said. "Who wrote this?"

"My great-great-grandmother, I think."

Jan read from the first page. "'This is the daily journal of Mrs. John Kelly, nee Miss Mollie Kennedy. Volume Thirteen, March 1872 to'—there's no end date."

He flipped to the blank pages at the end and paged forward until he came to the last entry.

"'December Twenty-Third, in the year of Our Lord 1873.'" He looked up at Amanda in shock. "That's just a few weeks after the mine fire."

Amanda nodded pointedly at the book, so Jan read the last entry aloud.

This is my final entry. The life I knew, the life that I have diligently chronicled in my poor way, is over. Today I buried my two sons, Jack Jr. and poor young Timothy, next to their father. The house where I raised them, where I bore them, and even where Jack Sr. and I made them, has already been rented to another pair of naïve lovebirds. The Company wasted no time pushing me and the baby growing inside me out into the cold.

Part of me is relieved, I think, that they have made my decisions for me these last few weeks. My grief, and worse, my rage would have ensured foolishness on my part had I had any choice whatsoever in what has happened to me.

I thank God, if there is in fact one out there somewhere, that my sister Elizabeth's youngest, John Joseph, married his sweetheart and moved out, leaving an empty room for me. I just wish they weren't the two who moved into that house of sorrow. There was joy there also, but having them start their lives together in the same house where I lived through so much pain fills me with a deep sense of foreboding.

Indeed, everywhere I turn in this patch town, where almost every man is either out

of work or traveling half-way to Scranton
just for a few hours of meager wages, I see
discontent and strife. John Joseph has joined
the accursed Mollie Maguires already. He
denies it, but I know what goes on in the
back room of Tellip's Bar. If it is a secret, it
is not a very well-kept one.

The inquest investigating our deadly fire
is nothing more than a whitewash. The
miners blame the owners and their Pinkerton
goons, and the engineers—every one of
them on the owners' payroll—say it was the
men's fault.

So the survivors, who are barely
working, meet in secret, drinking their
whiskey, and talking about revenge. I fear
the trouble brewing in Tellip's and other
back rooms in the coal region will boil over
into open conflict.

I dare not share my fears with my dear
sister, however. She has enough worries of
her own.

Anyway, as I wrote above, my old life is
over, and so, I commend this narrative of it
to the dustbin.

"Her sister rescued it from the trash and kept it hidden until
Mollie passed away, when she presented it to that baby Mollie
was carrying. My great-great-grandmother, Rose."

"She lost two sons in the fire?"

Amanda nodded and pointed at the book. "It's all in there."

53

Mollie & Tim
April 8th, 1873

ollie was hanging out the wash when the commotion started. At first, the raised voices were indistinct, but their urgency was apparent, nonetheless. The alarm spread like wildfire up the street—its source, the mine's pit.

Her formless fear turned to terror when she heard the shouts of *Fire!*

Dropping the clothes basket in the backyard, she hurried through the house, each step faster and more urgent than the last. The six steps it took to pass from the back door to the front seemed like an eternity. At last, she threw open the front door.

A stream of women, most with young children in tow, were hurrying down the street toward the mine.

"What's happening?" she called to her cousin, Nancy Whitesell, as she passed, a baby on her hip and leading a toddler by the hand.

Nancy looked up at the sky above the mine's breaker. "Look!" is all she said.

A plume of smoke, black as night, billowed high into the sky. Its lower region was already lit by a red glow.

Seeing her worst fear coming true—and that of every other wife, mother, and child in the patch town—nearly stopped her heart. Without even grabbing a shawl against the early Fall chill, she bolted down her front steps and joined the crowd, running as fast as her pregnancy-swollen belly allowed.

Tim

Alarm bells woke Tim from a fitful nap. Disoriented, he tried to count the poundings on the airlock door. Knowing that something was wrong, but not knowing what, he leaped from his stool and unlatched and yanked open the downhill door.

A flood of miners rushed in and straight across the room to the other door. Without waiting for Tim to do his job, one of the panicky miners threw open the uphill door as well.

This break in protocol allowed a blast of hot air to burst through from above, which was followed immediately by a wall of smoke. The man who had opened the door staggered back as Tim pushed his way through the crowd and tried to slam the uphill door shut again. The force of the heated air and smoke was stronger than what his eight-year-old body could muster, though.

After desperate seconds barely holding his own, Jack's strong hands joined his. Together, the brothers forced the portal closed, and Tim slammed the latch closed.

Coughing in the smoke-filled space, the men fell back through the downhill door into Tunnel Sixteen. The crush of bodies separated Jack from Tim, and gripped by panic, the confused boy retreated from the melee.

After a moment of frantic searching and yelling his name, Jack found Tim cowering in his corner and dragged him bodily into the downhill tunnel. Together, they pulled the second door closed, effectively cutting the miners off from both the wall of smoke and their immediate means of escape.

54

Mollie
April 8th, 1873

Old Man Powell passed Mollie, driving the fire wagon as fast as Casey, his old horse, could drag it. His one remaining arm beat a fast cadence with a willow switch against the poor nag's backside while he held the reins between his toothless gums. The leather distorted his words, but Mollie heard him clearly as he raced past.

"Motherless whores."

In another dozen running steps, Mollie saw what Powell's higher vantage point had revealed.

A line of Pinkerton guards stood, shotguns held at the ready, in a row across the access road.

"Let me through!" Powell bellowed as he raced headlong toward their picket line. Casey didn't share his enthusiasm, however. A blast into the air from the head Pinkerton's shotgun brought her to a skidding stop, and no measure of encouragement from Powell could get her moving again as long as the gun's muzzle was pointed at her.

"Damn you," Powell growled. "My boy Pete's down that hole."

"And mine!" came another panicked voice.

"And Jimmie."

"And Stevie."

Mollie, winded from her run down the hill, couldn't even catch her breath enough to call out the names of her precious boys.

"Stay back!" the head bull roared.

"No," Powell barked back. "We've got to fight this damned fire—"

"I've got my orders," the Pinkerton cut him off, although with less self-assurance. "I—I can't let ya through." He lowered his weapon and wiped his mouth with the back of his hand. "Not without orders—"

"Damn your orders," Powell shouted as he delivered a merciless blow of his willow switch to Rosie's hindquarters.

Caught by surprise, the horse leaped forward, nearly trampling the Pinkerton before he could jump sideways. The other guards were just as surprised, which gave Powell time to rush through their line toward the breaker, which by now was fully engaged.

Before the head bull could yell, "Stand down," one of the more zealous guards sent a load of buckshot into the retreating wagon. The spray of pellets only served to render the meager water tank it carried useless as its precious cargo gushed out, leaving a wet trail behind the wagon.

Powell's efforts were doubly in vain since, as the leaking fire wagon approached the burning structure, a series of screeches and booming cracks, loud as thunder, issued from the interior just moments before the whole five stories of the breaker collapsed like a house of cards into the pit it squatted above.

As a wall of smoke, ash, and embers engulfed the stunned onlookers, their collective wail of grief echoed around the valley.

55

Billy
Sunday, April 12th

Billy tossed his head from side to side, his small body entangled in the bed's sheet and blanket. His whimpers were lost in the moans and sounds of passion coming from the bedroom next door.

The recurring nightmare was becoming more and more real and more terrifying. As always, it started with him and Mommy singing the wheels-on-the-bus song. Her face was half-turned to where he sat in his car seat in the middle of the backseat. The dashboard lights lit only the other side of her face, casting her silhouette into sharp contrast with the fog-shrouded night lit by the car's headlights.

She kept interrupting their song with a sharp word aimed at Daddy, followed by his equally short angry response.

"Face it. We're lost." Her tone grew angrier and harsher each time she repeated the accusation.

"I'm following the damned GPS," Daddy growled back. "I can't help it if it doesn't know where the fuck we are!"

"Language!" She turned fully around to see if Billy had picked up on the curse word. "Go back to the main road and find a gas station or something where we can ask a *human* for directions."

Daddy's response was too low for Billy to hear, but he knew it was laced with more bad words. Mommy turned back to him with her fake smile.

"The wheels on the bus go round and round."

Billy joined in, his high-pitched singing surprisingly better in the dream than it was in real life.

This is where the dream ended the first night he slept at Miss Amanda's house. But over the last few nights, more of it crept into the scene playing out in his sleeping unconscious. Still asleep, he rolled over in the bed, further tangling the bedclothes around himself. His subconscious knew what was coming next.

The voices in the front seat became more strident, although the actual words were lost in a rising fog of noise that seeped in from the torrents of rain pelting the car. The indistinct argument grew in both volume and fury until Mommy and Daddy were shouting face-to-face.

That's when Billy saw the face through the windshield.

It was the only time that what he came to know as the Whispery Voice let itself be seen. And Billy suspected only he could see it. Nevertheless, when he screamed and Daddy turned back to the road ahead of them, he must have seen *something*, a deer, perhaps, because he yanked the wheel hard to the left, pointing the car away from the bridge that suddenly appeared where the road should have been.

"That's enough, Little Man," the Whispery Voice said, soothing and wiping the nightmare from Billy's mind.

Billy knew the nightmare wasn't what had really happened, but with each replay of it, his memories of that night faded away to be replaced by the story the Whispery Voice wanted him to remember to shift blame away from him…and it.

With a start, Billy sat up in bed, his heart pounding and his breath coming in gasps.

"It's just a nightmare."

The Whispery Voice was so soothing, and Billy settled back into the soft pillows. But before sleep could reclaim him, he heard voices coming from the room next door. The few words he could make out brought the Whispery Voice to the forefront.

"The life I knew, the life that I have diligently chronicled in my poor way, is over." Jan's voice was low, but distinct as he read from the journal.

"Mom," the Whispery Voice murmured, its voice filled with awe.

Billy could only watch and listen passively as the Whispery Voice hung on Jan's every word. When he finished, sobs racked Billy's mind as the Whispery Voice receded, but hovered just below the boy's awareness.

56

Billy
Sunday, April 12th

Billy lay awake, wishing for dreamless sleep, but afraid of the nightmare returning. Instead, he listened to the murmured conversation next door until their words were replaced by soft snores.

He tentatively felt for the Whispery Voice in the back of his mind, but it had receded even further from his consciousness. Alone and scared, he slipped out of bed and crept into the hallway.

A nightlight in the bathroom cast a greenish glow onto the old, worn hardwood floor. Billy wiggled his bare feet against the smooth boards, feeling the traces of the many souls who had trod there over the house's hundred-year history. Their lonely residue did nothing to soothe the ache of loneliness in his gut.

When he was younger, if he couldn't sleep, he often climbed into bed with Mommy and Daddy. The warmth of Mommy's embrace always sent him back to the Land of Nod. But this wasn't his house. The people sleeping behind the door weren't Mommy and Daddy. Somehow, deep inside, he knew he would never see them again. His loneliness deepened.

So, he stood there, paralyzed between sleep and wakefulness, between memory and fantasy. Without thinking, and maybe with a gentle push from the voice that lurked below, he stumbled forward to Miss Amanda's room.

The door was unnaturally quiet as Billy slowly eased it open. Amanda and the Burned Man lay together under a thin blanket. Amanda lay on her side, her head nestled in the crook of the man's shoulder. Her bare arm was cast casually across his chest.

Billy crossed silently to her side of the bed but, with no room to squeeze into, he laid a hand on her shoulder and froze.

A voice drifted into Billy's mind through his hand resting on Amanda. Its beseeching couldn't be denied, and the Whispery Voice rushed forward, taking control without demanding or even asking for permission. A second, younger presence followed the Whispery Voice, rushing forward and only glancing at Billy in passing.

Billy was swept aside like a dried leaf in a windstorm. As the Whispery Voice and the other, younger presence looked out through Billy's eyes, Amanda rolled away from Jan to face him. But he didn't see Miss Amanda lying there. Rather, he saw the face of her great-great-great-grandmother, their—Jack and Tim's—mother, Mollie Kelly.

Mollie, fully in control of her descendent's sleeping body, gathered her boys into her arms.

Their communion was brief but heartfelt.

"Mom! Mommy!" The boys' ghostly voices called to her through Amanda's dreams.

"Jack. Timmy. What is this? Where are we?"

"Not 'where,' Mom. When."

All that the Whispery Voice—Jack and Tim—had learned over the past few days poured into Mollie's ghostly presence. It did not evoke the response they had hoped for.

"Possession? You have possessed the mind of this poor boy? This child that you have orphaned! Is this what you have

become? A demon bent on revenge." The horror and revulsion in her tone cut Jack and Tim to their cores. *"Get thee gone, Demon!"*

In an instant, Molly was gone, and Amanda opened her eyes still embracing the boy.

"Billy? Are you alright?"

Rejected by their mother, the ghostly presences fled into the furthest reaches of Billy's mind, far from his awareness. Confused and more frightened than he was when he awoke in the sinking car, Billy clung to Amanda like he was drowning.

57

Kathy
Monday, April 13th

Kathy paced—no, stalked—back and forth in Sheriff Peterson's office.

"I think it's a very bad idea," she said for the fourth or fifth time.

"Look, if I'm on this investigation, I need to see *all* of the evidence," Spaz countered.

Peterson looked at Kathy. "He's got a point." He raised his hands to stop her sixth protest, then turned to Spaz. "You have to understand, Jonah, it's pretty hard to watch someone—some people—get killed or almost killed. And it doesn't paint your niece in a very favorable—"

"Oh, for Christ's sake," Kathy interrupted. "She's naked, Spaz. And fucking her boyfriend. Do you really want to watch that?"

Spaz swallowed hard. "I…I told her parents I'd find out everything to try…to try to explain…"

"There is no good explanation for what happened in that mine," Peterson said. "But they do have a right to know."

He spun his laptop around and nodded to Kathy. Frowning, she pulled up the recording, then stepped back. Spaz pulled his chair closer and hunched over the screen as if he was trying to block the view of the others.

At the ten-minute mark, when Jimmy Youells reached for Lauren's neck, Spaz's face blanched. When Lauren's eyes rolled backwards, Spaz's whole body heaved in sympathy. Kathy, standing at the ready, grabbed the Sheriff's wastebasket just in time. She held her breath and turned her head while Spaz vomited his lunch into it.

When he finished and lifted his head, the scene showed the final carnage, which brought up his breakfast as well.

"You okay?" Kathy's tone was soothing. It wasn't the first time she'd helped a friend that way. "Here, take this." She handed him the wastebasket. "And go clean yourself up. After you've talked to your brother and sister-in-law, I'll have an assignment for you." Spaz took the trash can and held it at arm's length.

Peterson caught his eye. "I'm sure I don't have to tell you to be gentle with them. They don't need to know all of the details."

Without another word, Spaz headed for the Men's room.

When he had left, Kathy rewound the recording to the point where Jimmy was choking Lauren and zoomed the view in on Youells's face.

"What's up?" Peterson asked.

"He's mumbling something," she replied as she turned the volume up all the way.

The words were garbled, but after three passes, they had pieced together, "Come, Revenge, come…Come to me, filthy spawn…Pay for your families' guilt."

"What the hell?" Peterson shook his head.

"He wasn't trying to kill Lauren," Kathy said. "He was luring Kapaletti and Luzeski into a trap."

Peterson nodded thoughtfully. "That's why he was hiding behind the door when they entered the room."

He and Kathy stared at each other with their mouths hanging open.

Finally, he said, "What's the business about 'filthy spawn' and 'your families' guilt?'"

Kathy thought for a moment as a piece of the puzzle dropped into place. When she had processed the revelation, she nodded.

"The current mine owners are the descendants of the robber barons who owned it way back when it was active." She looked at Peterson, determination on her face. "A lot of people—miners and their families—suffered because of them."

Peterson nodded. "And a lot of them died. I've heard the stories. My great-to-the-something grandfather and uncles worked down there. Things got really bad after the fire. The Mollies came up from underground—literally—and caused a lot of trouble. It was pretty much open warfare between them and the Pinkertons."

"The 'Mollies?' You mean the Mollie Maguires?"

He nodded again. "And it was a lot more violent back then than the movie showed." He thought for a moment, then looked Kathy in the eye. "I haven't heard the rumors in many years, but when I was a kid, my Granddad insisted the Mollies were still alive and well. Every time there was an industrial accident, he would say, 'The Mollies strike again.'"

"You think there's a connection to this? That Youells was somehow affiliated with them, or something?"

Peterson shrugged. "It's worth checking out."

"Something good for Spaz to do. He's plugged into the blue-collar side of the county. Maybe he can dig up some dirt—if the Mollies still exist."

Kathy turned to go when her phone buzzed. After a quick look at the message, she turned to Peterson.

"They found Charlie."

58

Kathy
Monday, April 13th

Oh, God." It was Kathy's turn to be sick, but she bit down hard and swallowed. "What…" she barely managed to get out.

"What ate his face?" Coroner Kevin Disque, the town's local mortician, asked without a hint of ghoulishness. "It was probably rats that did the most damage." He nodded to the tunnel behind him that led into the dark mine. "There's got to be a whole colony of the little buggers back in there."

His casual tone made Kathy's skin crawl.

"Most of the damage?" she asked.

The coroner bent over and pointed at Charlie's throat. "This is what killed him, I'd bet. We'll have to do an autopsy, of course. But I'd put money on 'exsanguination due to ripping wounds to the throat and neck.'"

The flesh of Charlie's throat was ripped and torn, exposing severed arteries and veins. His trachea was almost ripped free of its connective tissue.

"Holy shit. What would do that? Not rats."

Kevin shook his head and pointed at Charlie's hands, which were flung out to his sides. They were covered in dried blood, and bits of skin and cartilage hung from their fingernails.

Kathy had to swallow her gorge again. "Jesus Christ," she muttered when she could breathe again. "He did this to himself?"

The coroner shrugged. "Looks like it. I'll know more when I get him on the table and we compare that—" he pointed to Charlie's hand then to his throat "—to that."

Kathy looked around the tunnel lit by the forensic crew's work lights. Then she turned to the other source of illumination further up the slope, where the DASD murders had taken place.

"How'd you find him way down here?"

"We were processing the scene up there. After we removed the bodies, the decomp smell kept getting stronger. I just followed my nose."

Kevin's sly smile made Kathy feel sicker than either the sight or smell of Charlie.

Disgusted, Kathy turned to leave, but he called after her, "Don't you want to see the weirdest part?"

Stopping, she slowly turned back to the grinning mortician. "Excuse me?"

Nodding, Kevin pulled back Charlie's torn shirt. There, clawed into his chest was the word "BULL."

"What the—?"

"Told ya."

Taking out her phone, Kathy snapped a picture.

"I've already taken about a hundred." The dismissiveness in his voice was finally too much for her.

"They better not show up on the internet," she growled. "This was a person, And a friend of mine. With a wife and family. Show some respect."

Disque scoffed. "And a long history of drug and alcohol abuse."

"You think this was because of drugs?"

"Ever hear of anything else that would cause somebody to rip their own throat out?" He shrugged. "The toxicology report will tell us for sure."

"Send it out to the State Police," she said.

"I'm perfectly capable of—"

Her stare stopped his protest as if she had slapped a hand across his mouth.

"I need an *objective* and *unbiased* assessment."

Without waiting for another objection, she turned on her heel and stormed up the tunnel.

You've no idea, she thought when the words "Dike bitch" followed her.

Jan

Monday, April 13th

The board members of the Lost Miners Coal Mine Tour shuffled silently into the Miners Bank conference room. Most kept their eyes downcast, only exchanging a quick glance, or at most a curt nod before taking their seats.

Jan, though, looked at each of the other members in turn, trying to gauge what their reaction would be to his proposal. He didn't like what he saw.

Finally, after a few moments of awkward silence, Mayor Luzeski rapped his knuckles on the table, calling the meeting to order.

"Ahem, let's get started—"

"Just a minute, Jim," Patti Trieste interrupted. The head of PR scanned the room. "I think we should take a moment of silence for the young people, including George's nephew Gino, who lost their lives, and those, like your son, Mark, who were injured in the recent incident."

Everyone but Jan nodded enthusiastically.

'The incident?' Is that what we're calling an attempted mass murder now?

"And for the quick recovery of Mark, Jim. He's the hero in this story," she continued, offering a wan smile.

"Thank you for that, Patti. I thank God that Mark should make a full recovery, and pray that Sheriff Peterson will fully exonerate him quickly."

Heads nodded, then bowed around the table, amid murmurs of "Amen" and "Indeed." Jan looked stoically from one face to the next. His expectation of how the board would handle *the incident*—to sweep it under the proverbial carpet—was coming true before his eyes.

After a few heartbeats of silence, George Kapaletti, the group's engineer, spoke for the first time.

"My nephew, Gino, was a good kid. He could be…headstrong at times, but all-in-all a good kid."

"Quite the entrepreneur," Patti offered. "Mark, too," she added, nodding to the mayor.

"Yes," George murmured. "If a little misguided in their ambitions."

Mayor Luzcski grunted and cleared his throat again. "Yes, anyway, let's get started." Then, turning to Patti, he asked, "What should we do next?"

She gave him a broad smile. "I've already begun some…damage control. Through my contacts at WSCR, I've arranged for an independent video journalist to do a video piece on the mine and how we are honoring the memory of those miners who lost their lives down there."

"Exploiting the memory, you mean," Jan muttered.

Patti pointedly ignored his comment. "The reporter I got assigned to the piece is very familiar with our operation—Lacey Devine."

Jan snorted. "You got Lacey to come back? She quit as a tour guide because the mine freaked her out so much."

Momentarily flustered, Patti quickly recovered. "I thought she quit because of other commitments."

"That may be the excuse she gave, but she was with me when the power went out, and believe me, she totally freaked."

"Hmmm. Perhaps she wasn't the best choice…"

"I have a different proposal," Jan said a little too loudly for the small room. "I propose that we shut the whole thing down. If not permanently, at least until next year. The town—"

"That's ridiculous," Buddy Lewis, the CEO of Miners Bank, practically shouted. "We have millions invested in this venture."

"And we're almost ready to open," George added.

Jan shook his head, standing his ground. "When it comes to net worth, I have a lot more invested in this than any of you. But I still think it's incredibly disrespectful to open so soon after '*The Incident,*' as you so delicately put it, Patti."

Mayor Luzeski glared at Jan. "I don't see the connection between the unfortunate events of yesterday and our operation. That tunnel where Mark and Gino were…doing business…isn't even part of the mine. Nobody even knew it was there, or what it was used for."

"You're wrong," Jan countered. "That tunnel was dug to recover the bodies of the men and boys who died in the fire of 1873. The very 'Lost Miners' we've co-opted for the name of our attraction."

The mayor looked to his engineer, George, who nodded. "He's right. The tunnel connects to the room in the mine where the bulk of the miners' bodies were found. It was also intended to be an escape route, if ever needed again. It doesn't appear on any charts because the mine never reopened after the fire."

A thoughtful silence fell over the group as the mayor continued to glare at Jan. Finally, Patti spoke up.

"Does our tour go down to that room where the bodies were found?"

"No," George said. "That is three or four levels deeper down. Why?"

Patti shrugged. "I'm just spit-balling here, but what if we offered a 'Deep Immersion Tour' that went down there and led out through the 'newly discovered' escape tunnel?"

"That's an intriguing idea," the mayor said. "It's pretty macabre. Maybe as a Halloween attraction."

"So you don't think we've exploited those poor dead souls enough already?" Jan fumed. "We should tramp gawkers through what ought to be hallowed ground? On Halloween, no less?"

"May I remind you," Banker Lewis said, "that this is a for-profit endeavor. We should consider and exploit every opportunity to be profitable."

"At the expense of the town's collective grief?"

"What grief?" the mayor exploded. "That fire was tragic, but it happened over a hundred and fifty years ago! Nobody remembers—"

"Oh, Mayor, that's where you are dead wrong," Jan growled. "The working people in this town—your constituents—trace their roots even further back." He pulled Mollie's journal out of his satchel. "There's a collective memory, passed down from generation to generation, among the people in this town that your new proposals, and this tour in general, shit all over."

Gasps escaped the other board members, and Mayor Luzeski rapped his knuckles, gavel-like, on the table.

"That's enough! If you can't maintain proper decorum, Mister Sorrensen, I'll have to ask you to leave the meeting."

Jan slowly rose to his feet and scanned every face in the room. Seeing no support from any of the other board members, he raised his chin and looked down his nose at the mayor.

"You don't have to ask, Mr. Mayor."

Without another word, he strode out of the room.

60

Kathy
Monday, April 13th

The letter came when Jan and Kathy were having a drink with Jim and Barb Donnelly. Only Kathy noticed the young man, with a satchel slung cross-body, enter the Towne Tavern and whisper something to the bartender, Lloyd. When Lloyd pointed to their table, Kathy held up a hand to stop their conversation.

"Uh, oh," she said.

Seeing her attention elsewhere, the others looked up and followed her gaze. By the time the twenty-something messenger had crossed to their booth in the back of the barroom, his cheeks were flushed. Kathy couldn't decide if it was from exertion or from embarrassment. It turned out to be neither.

He stopped at the end of their table and reached into his satchel.

"Mr. Sorrensen," he said, meeting Jan's eyes for the first time. "My boss at the bank, Mr. Lewis, sent me to deliver this letter to you."

His little speech was clearly memorized, so Kathy's investigative instincts kicked in.

"How did you find us—Mr. Sorrensen—here?"

The young man's mouth worked like a landed trout's. "I, ah. I just assumed…"

Jan took the interrogative baton. "You just assumed I'd be sitting in a drinking establishment at—" He glanced at the clock behind the bar. "—Five-twenty in the evening?"

"Not a bad assumption," Kathy muttered.

The messenger looked to Jim and Barb for help, but Barb stared him down with one raised eyebrow, and Jim just pressed his lips into a wry smile.

"I, ah, I…" the fellow stammered.

Jan finally broke down and barked a laugh. "Give me what you have for me."

He nodded with relief. "If you could sign this receipt first."

He held out a clipboard, which Jan scanned quickly, then signed. When he handed it back, the messenger handed over a sealed envelope with Jan's full name typed on the front.

"Thank you," Jan said, dismissing the young man and pulling reading glasses out of his breast pocket.

But instead of leaving, the messenger stood there, shifting his weight from one foot to the other. Jan looked at him over the rim of his readers.

"Is there something else? Are you expecting a tip?"

"Yes, er, no—no tip, sir. But—"

He reached into his satchel again and pulled out a paperback copy of Jan's *The Mackey House Ghost*, which he held out. A pen was clipped to the wrinkled and cracked cover.

"Could I get— Ah, would you sign your book, Mr. Sorrensen? Can you sign it to 'Stevie'?"

Jim snorted a laugh, and Kathy rolled her eyes, but Jan smiled and took the book from Stevie. With a flourish, he signed the title page and handed it back.

"Always willing to help out a fan."

Only Kathy caught the barest hint of sarcasm.

"Thanks!" Stevie gushed, then turned and practically ran out of the tavern.

"Ah, the perils of being a best-selling author," Jim said.

His sarcasm was lost on Jan, though, as he slid his butter knife under the flap of the envelope and sliced it open. He held the letter close in the dim light for a moment, then nodded several times.

"Bastards."

"Let me guess, you got kicked out of the Rich People's Club," Kathy said.

Jan eyed her over the edge of the single sheet of paper. "Were you reading over my shoulder? Yeah, it's a 'Tender Offer.' With a not-so-subtle reminder that the partnership agreement we all signed says a member can be voted off the island by a two-thirds majority. And I'm quoting now, 'with a remuneration commensurate with their percentage of ownership shares relative to the partnership's liquid assets.'"

"What the heck does that mean?" Jim asked.

"It means I would get bupkus," Jan spat. "There are no 'liquid assets.' Just a lot of sunk cash."

Kathy cut to the chase, as she always did. "What's the tender offer?"

Jan gave her a half-smile. "Well, that's the thing. It's very…lucrative."

"Like how 'lucrative?'"

"Like three times my initial investment."

"Holy crap," Jim said with a smile as he raised his beer mug. "That's a nice ROI."

Barb was having none of it, though. "They're trying to buy your silence. I bet there'll be a pretty ironclad NDA that comes with the check."

Jan nodded. "No doubt."

"So what are you going to do?" Kathy asked, her steely gaze locked with his.

Without looking away, he said, "It's tough walking away from this much. And I really want to be done with this whole affair. But…there are other considerations, aren't there?"

It wasn't really a question. Kathy nodded in agreement while they held each other's gaze.

Barb had finally had enough. "Cut the bullshit."

Jim nodded. "We have a pretty good idea what's going on here."

"It's happening again, isn't it?"

Kathy and Jan just looked at them with wide eyes.

"Come on," Jim said. "We aren't stupid. The official story of how you got those scars, Jan, is flimsy at best. Besides, I'm the one who gave you the whole backstory on Mackey House. The rumors and eyewitness accounts that it was haunted go back generations."

"Writing a novel about it was genius, though," Barb added. "The fact that it became a best-seller cemented in everyone's mind that the story was just fiction."

"Which propped up the flimsy official story."

The husband-and-wife historians fell silent and stared at Jan, who stared back silently. Finally, Jim sighed in frustration and turned to Kathy, who was keeping her eyes on the mug of beer in front of her.

"Don't forget, Kath, that I was down in that pit when something—someone?—took possession of your girlfriend, Lacey. That wasn't her that told us to get out of there. It was something not of this Earth. Or at least, not *still* of this Earth."

Jan and Kathy looked sidelong at each other, then Jan shrugged and Kathy nodded.

Jan met Jim and Barb's eyes in turn. "Whatever it is, has its hooks into the kid, Billy, too. It's warned me off through him a couple of times now."

Barb nodded her acceptance of that news. "We have a pretty good idea of what *it* is. It's Jim's idea, actually."

Kathy spread her hands. "I'm all ears."

Jim took a deep breath. "Assuming your novel tracks pretty closely to what actually happened to Sandy in Mackey House— your house, Kathy. I still can't believe you bought the place, by the way. Anyway, from your account, Jan, and from the research I've done since reading your book, we can assume that a ghost, spirit, or whatever has to be pretty pissed off about what happened to them when they were alive to be able to manifest itself and actually possess a person." He took another breath. "And there can't be too many spirits who are more pissed off than those Avon Hill miners. Especially if it was the mine owners who set the fire."

"Was it, though?" Jan asked, hoping to redirect the conversation. "The inquest—"

"The inquest was a total whitewash." Barb's voice dripped venom.

"Maybe, but all the evidence of a conspiracy among the mine owners was circumstantial, at best."

"As was the owners' evidence," Jim fumed. He took a calming breath. "Sorry. The wounds of that day go very deep in my family."

"And mine," Barb added. "And a whole lot of this town's working folks, too. That's why the Mollie Maguires were so strong in this region."

"I've read that it was them and their violence that kept the mine from reopening. That left a lot of families out in the cold."

"The mine owners refused to make even minor safety improvements." Jim's raised voice made Lloyd look up from his phone. "The place was—is—still a deathtrap."

She patted her husband's arm. "There was plenty of blame to go around for that. I just hope there's a reckoning someday."

"Which may be exactly what this new ghost wants," Jan said by way of getting the discussion back on track.

"But why now?" Kathy asked.

Jim nodded at Jan, but it was Barb who answered. "You boys decided to open the mine back up—not as a memorial, but as a friggin' tourist attraction."

"I didn't know any of this—" Jan protested, but Barb waved him to silence.

"I'm not blaming you, or any of your cronies, for that matter. The question is, what are you going to do now?"

"Gee, thanks for that. I get that we must have disturbed the miners' ghosts, which explains their possession of Lacey in the mine."

"And Jimmy Youells's."

"And Charlie's."

Jan shook his head. "But that doesn't explain Billy's possession. He's never been near the mine. And ghosts are usually bound to the location of their death."

It was Kathy's turn to shake her head. "That's not really true. I picked up Billy right outside the main shaft entrance."

"You think that's where he got…infected, possessed?"

"I don't know. He was already weird, right? After all, he had already escaped from Wayne State."

"And lived in the woods for several days," Jim added.

"Then why Billy?" Barb asked. "Why not the mother or father?"

Jim shrugged. "Target of opportunity?"

"We don't even know where the mother and father are," Kathy said.

So, Barb asked again. "Still, why an eight-year-old boy?"

Jan, who had been silent through much of this exchange, suddenly raised his head. "An eight-year-old boy? Yes, an eight-year-old boy. Of course." He met the eyes of each of the other three in turn. Then, with a knowing nod, he said, "I think I know who our ghost is—or was."

Before anyone could respond, his phone buzzed with a text message from Amanda.

Help. Billy's freaking out.

61

Hestia
Monday, April 13th

Fearful of an overwhelming deluge of sensations, Hestia slowly peeked into the world outside of her stasis state, starting with the clatter of the hospital's day room. At first, she could make no sense of the ambient sounds present in any gathering of the living—the squeak of a lunch cart's wheels, the scraping of worn chair legs on terrazzo tile, the murmurings and occasional ravings of the mentally disturbed.

Awash in the sounds of human activity, she felt adrift with nothing to grab hold of—nothing solid to center and anchor herself. With anxiety mounting, she began to raise her defenses again, to flee behind her shield wall back into her comfortable, wasting isolation.

But as her window onto the world was closing, a new sound intruded as Samson the orderly turned up the volume on the day room television.

"The Wayne County Sheriff's Department has closed the case on the disturbing deaths that took place this past week within the Avon Hill Mine."

Hestia found her anchor. The local news reporter's voice was a lifeline that she latched onto and held fast.

"The official finding is that the two incidents were unrelated. The first to be discovered was the brutal murder of Eugene (Gino) Kapaletti at the hands of one James Youells and the subsequent justified killing of Youells by Mayor Luzeski's son, Mark. Mark Luzeski is being credited with saving the life of Ms. Lauren Tanner, who, according to authorities, was rendered unconscious by Mr. Youells and is currently in the hospital recuperating. Why the young people were gathered in a previously unknown access tunnel into the mine is still unknown, according to Sheriff Peterson."

The reporter's voice wrapped itself around Hestia's mind as if she was listening to a kindred spirit. Or at least someone who might be sensitive to her plight. She found the voice, and the mind behind it, comforting, and Hestia knew that, somehow, they would meet.

"The circumstances around the second incident at the mine, which is slated to open as a tourist attraction—The Lost Miners Coal Mine Tour—are still unclear. One Charles Stimson was found dead deeper within the mine's access tunnel. A tunnel that was dug after the mine disaster in 1873 that killed over one hundred miners, some as young as eight years old. Tests have confirmed that Mr. Stimson died before the Youells attack, although his body wasn't found until that attack was being investigated. There are more questions to be answered, but for now, the Stimson death has been ruled a suicide." The reporter paused ever so slightly, and Hestia heard the disapproval in her voice when she said, "According to Mayor Luzeski, who is one of the principal owners of the mine and the tour company, the mine tour attraction is still scheduled to open to the public this weekend."

The reporter paused, then concluded, "This is Lacey Devine of the *That's Devine* podcast on assignment for WSCR News 8."

Hestia felt the flame inside her roil at this last pronouncement. The memory of the Ghost's touch rippled through her, making her body shudder in its wheelchair. Without understanding, Hestia knew both of these killings were Ghost's doing, And, perhaps because of a residual connection between them, a name bubbled up into her consciousness.

"Jack," she murmured through long-unused lips.

"Jack," she said again, then louder, "Redemption," before retreating back into the comfort of her catatonia.

***

Samson squinted at the shell of Sandy Adams. Her shudder had drawn his attention away from the TV. Did she actually say something? As he leaned over her shoulder, he clearly heard her utter the next two words—"Jack" and "Redemption"—words that made no sense, but were a breakthrough nonetheless.

Glancing at the clock to note the time, he texted the facility's social worker.

> *Patient Adams exhibited enhanced cognition, physically reacting to the television news report and speaking twice. Her first word was indecipherable, but she spoke clearly, saying two words: "Jack" and "Redemption", before returning to her previous catatonic state.*

> *How would you like me to*
> *proceed?*

The reply was quick to come.

> *Monitor her closely. If she says*
> *anything else, I'll have to call*
> *that Deputy Jensen.*

Samson smiled to himself as he pulled a chair up next to Hestia and turned her from facing the window looking onto the lawn toward the television.

"Come on, Sandy. Give me some more."

But she remained silent, staring blankly forward.

62

Kathy
Tuesday, April 14th

Sheriff Peterson shuffled the crime scene photos around on his desk without really looking at them.

"I'm too old for this shit," he muttered. Then, looking at Kathy and Spaz, who sat in the guest chairs in front of his desk, he said, "Thoughts?"

Spaz wiped his mouth with the back of his hand. His face was pale, and there was still a sheen of sweat on his forehead from his sprint to the bathroom. He just shook his head.

Kathy, with a rare gesture of solidarity, patted him on the arm. The faint smell of decomposition that clung to her clothes turned him even paler. He got unsteadily to his feet and backed into a corner of the small office. Taking a cue from him, Kathy sniffed the collar of her shirt and wrinkled her nose.

"Sorry. I'll go home and change when we're done here."

"Good," Peterson grunted. He spread his hands over the sheets of the Preliminary Coroner's Report scattered across his desk. "Tell me what this all means."

"Disque is pretty sure he did the damage to himself, given the gore covering his hands and embedded under his fingernails."

"That's…"

"Yeah. The question is 'Why?' of course."

She rifled through the report until she found the page she was looking for. Holding it up, she said, "Preliminary toxicology. No alcohol. No drugs, per se. But high levels of…stuff I can't pronounce that *could* have had a psychedelic response. I insisted he send samples to the State Police to get another opinion."

"That'll take weeks. They're notoriously backed up."

Kathy shrugged. "I made a call." When she didn't continue, Peterson raised his eyebrows questioningly. With a sigh, she said, "I called my dad. Asked him to put a rush order on it."

Kathy's dad was a senior commander with the Pennsylvania State Police.

Peterson nodded appreciatively and rocked his chair back. "It's about time you learned to use whatever leverage you've got."

"Leverage? Not over my dad, Captain Straightlaced."

"Leverage can take many forms, including a father's love for his…difficult daughter."

"Oh, please! He and I—"

At that moment, both Kathy and Spaz's phones buzzed with an incoming text. Spaz got to his first.

"Lauren's semi-conscious," he blurted. He came halfway out of his chair.

"Good." Kathy gave him a smile. "Why don't you go take her statement?"

Nodding, Spaz bolted from the office, nearly tipping the chair over in his haste.

When the door swung shut, Sheriff Peterson gathered up the coroner's report and slid the papers into its manila folder.

"There's some weird shit going down in that mine," he said.

"*Too much* weird shit," Kathy echoed.

"What are you going to do about it?" Peterson's voice was challenging.

"Don't you mean 'we'? You're the sheriff, after all. I'm just a—"

"Enough bullshit. This is *your* case, Detective." He pulled a single sheet of paper from a desk drawer and slid it across to Kathy. "Besides, I've already filed this with the mayor's office."

She glanced at the subject line, which read, "Intent to Retire." Then she sat back and looked up at him.

"So, you're finally pulling the ripcord? Well, congrats, I guess. When?"

"Soon. Couple of months, I think." He reached over and tapped the paper. "Read the last paragraph."

She met his gaze before leaning forward again.

"It says, "It is my heartfelt recommendation that Detective Kaveetha Jensen be named Interim Sheriff—" She nodded without looking up. "—until the next election cycle."

She gave him a wan smile. "Thanks, Boss. Think they'll go for it?"

Peterson returned a steely gaze. "That depends."

"On?"

"On how you handle the investigation of the weird shit surrounding this mine. Remember that Mayor Luzeski is a major stakeholder—"

"Are you telling me to—"

Peterson held up a hand to stop her. "I'm not telling you to do anything. The way I see it, there's something fishy going on out there. So fishy it smells worse than you do right now."

There wasn't even a hint of humor in his voice, and Kathy didn't smile.

He leaned forward with his elbows on his desk and continued. "So, you have two choices. You can 'go along to get along,' as they say, and sweep whatever stinks so bad under the carpet. Or you can find out what stinks and put it in your back pocket for leverage. Real leverage. Election leverage."

Kathy met his steady stare with one of her own. Finally, without breaking eye contact, she said, "If I sweep it under the carpet, it'll just keep stinking worse and worse. And if I 'stick in my back pocket,' I'll end up stinking worst of all." She paused and licked her lips. "Or I can take the third option."

Peterson raised an eyebrow, and the beginnings of a smirk curled his lip.

"I can take the third option," Kathy repeated, "which is to figure out what's stinking up the place, and then do my job and get rid of whatever it is once and for all."

"Even if that's a career-limiting choice?"

"Even if it's a career-*ending* choice."

Peterson's smirk became a full-blown grin. "I expected nothing less."

What he didn't know, but what Kathy was increasingly beginning to suspect, was that the stench wasn't human-born, but was coming from something much, much more dangerous.

63

Kathy
Tuesday, April 14th

Kathy met Spaz outside Lauren's hospital room. "How is she?" she asked. Spaz just shook his head. "Did you get a statement?"

"No, she's not really awake. She just keeps mumbling about fire, and flames, and smoke. She doesn't respond to any questions. There wasn't a fire in that place, was there?"

"Not for a hundred and fifty years. Okay. Let me take a shot."

Kathy walked toward Lauren's door with Spaz following. When she got there, she turned and placed a hand on his chest.

"Alone. She might respond better to a non-family-member." Before he could respond, she added, "A female non-family-member."

As she turned away, he grabbed her arm.

"I've seen you interrogate people, *Detective*. She's in a very fragile state. Be careful. Please."

Kathy stiffened and looked down at the hand gripping her arm, then relaxing, she patted it and met his eyes.

"Don't worry. She's not in any trouble. I'll be gentle."

Seeing him nod, Kathy pushed open the door and stepped through it.

As the door closed behind her, she scanned the room. It was a typical low-attention hospital room. The color of the pale teal walls was probably supposed to feel warm, but instead Kathy felt the opposite. In fact, everything about the room, including the Venetian blind-covered window, the ancient TV hung from the ceiling, and the insistent beeping of the monitors, screamed cold, clinical efficiency to her.

Lauren lay on the hospital bed with her arms at her sides on top of the thin blanket that covered her legs and torso. Her head was propped up on two pillows, which framed her freshly brushed blond hair fanning out around her face. Her eyes were closed, but her lips moved slightly in an incessant mumbling. The bruises on her neck from Tommy's fingers were still angry shades of purple and yellow.

Lauren's parents, Steve and Janice Tanner, flanked her bed, leaning forward in the uncomfortable guest chairs. They looked up at Kathy's entrance, and after her initial scan of the room, Kathy forced a smile.

"Hello," she said, looking first at the dad, Steve Tanner, then settling on Spaz's sister, Janice. "I'm Detective Jensen with the Sheriff's Office. I'm investigating the assault on your daughter."

Steve Tanner stood, and Kathy shook each of their offered hands.

"Jonah, ah, Officer Spatz, said you'd be coming. Jonah's my brother."

"Yes, I know, Mrs. Tanner. Spa—Jonah and I are working together on Lauren's case. Tell me, has she said anything about what happened?"

Both parents shook their heads. "She hasn't really *said* anything," Janice said. "She just keeps mumbling things that don't make any sense."

"What have you heard her say?"

Steve spoke up. "She keeps repeating, 'Fire, fire, fire. Smoke. Smoke and flames.' Over and over again."

Janice asked, "There wasn't any fire…down there…was there?" Kathy shook her head. "Then why is she fixated on a fire?"

The references to fire and smoke reinforced Kathy's suspicions, but she needed to be alone with Lauren to be sure.

"Would you mind if I talked to Lauren alone?" Steve and Janice looked at each other. "I'll be gentle, I promise. She's not in any trouble. None at all. I would just like to know if her assailant, Mr. Youells, said anything to her." Lauren's parents exchanged worried looks. "I promise, if she gets upset, I'll stop and let her rest."

Finally, Steve nodded, and Janice followed suit. Kathy opened the door and spoke to Spaz who was nervously pacing in the hall.

"Jonah, would you take your sister and brother-in-law to get a coffee or something?"

As the parents filed out of the room, she added, "I'll just be a few minutes."

When they had left, Kathy crossed to Lauren and leaned down with her ear to the young woman's lips. The words were just whispers, but distinct.

"Fire, fire. Smoke. Flames." Lauren took a shallow breath. "Fire, fire, fire." Her voice seemed to rise on the last word. "Smoke. Flames."

Before she repeated her mantra, Kathy laid a hand on her shoulder.

"Lauren."

"Fire, fire—"

"Lauren, I know what fire you mean."

"Fire. Smoke—"

"And I know the smoke must have been choking."

"Flames."

"And the flames were terrifying. I understand that. But how do you know that? How do *you* know about the fire, smoke, and flames?"

Lauren's mantra faltered, and her eyes flicked side-to-side beneath their lids.

"How do you know?" Kathy repeated.

Lauren mumbled something that Kathy didn't catch, so she leaned down again with her ear so close she could feel the young woman's faint breaths.

"Tell me again, Lauren. How do you know?"

This time, her voice took on an inner strength. "I saw it." Her voice grew stronger still. "I saw it through his eyes!"

The last words came out almost as a shriek, and the bedside monitor's beeping became a continuous alarm as Lauren's heart rate spiked. Kathy held Lauren as she shook with sobs.

By the time a nurse rushed in, Lauren's heart rate had subsided, the alarm had stopped, and she lay there crying quietly. Kathy held her hand and got a strong squeeze in return.

As the nurse fussed over her, Lauren's eyes flicked open, then closed again. "Thank you," she whispered.

64

Jan

Tuesday, April 14th

The scene when Jan burst through Amanda's front door was chaotic.

Amanda cowered in the corner of the tiny living room's couch while Billy stood atop the matching easy chair. His eyes flashed red when he saw Jan come through the door, and his demonic laughter froze Jan in his tracks.

Red eyes! Oh, shit. Jan thought, remembering the terror of the night his lover, Sandy, possessed by another malevolent ghost, tried to immolate him. *Has it gone that far?*

The eyes flashed red again, and more malevolent laughter, which seemed to be born more out of terror than mirth, echoed around the room.

"He won't stop laughing like that!"

Amanda's shout broke Jan out of his terror-filled memories. He ran the three steps to her and gathered her into his arms. Without turning his back on Billy, he shielded her from the boy and searched for some kind of weapon. Spying the poker leaning against the lit fireplace, he reached for it, but Amanda would have none of that.

She pushed him away. "Don't you dare. Not in my house," she spat.

Her reaction broke her out of her own fugue. Sliding across the cushions to kneel on the floor, she reached a hand out towards the boy. "It's okay, Billy. Nobody's going to hurt you."

His face seemed to clear a little, and the fire in his eyes dimmed as she cooed soothingly.

But then a ring on her outstretched finger caught the firelight and, screaming, Billy slapped her hand away. As Amanda fell backwards, the red fire returned manyfold to his eyes, and the possessed boy leaned forward to let loose another bout of terrified laughter.

In Jan's unconscious, puzzle pieces clicked into place. *Red eyes. Flickering like fire. Dimmed when Amanda knelt in front of him. Reflected firelight flashing off her ring. The fireplace!*

Jan, acting purely on instinct, leaped into action. But this time, instead of grabbing a weapon, or jumping to protect Amanda, he reached for the fireplace and turned off the gas.

The effect was immediate. Billy's threatening posture collapsed into itself, and he slid down to huddle in the corner of the overstuffed chair. His hellish laughter became a little boy's heart-wrenching whimpering cries and nothing like the horrific sounds he had been spewing a moment before.

Amanda, seeing the transformation, climbed onto the chair and gathered the boy into her arms. After murmuring reassurances to him, she looked up at Jan.

"How did you know?"

Jan just shrugged. "I didn't. Something just clicked in my head."

But to himself, he thought, *If I'm right about what is possessing the poor child, the ghost in him is terrified of fire. Makes sense, given what killed him.*

He gave a little laugh. "I think we should forgo cozy evenings in front of the fireplace from now on."

Amanda returned his laugh. "I think you're right."

She looked down at Billy, who was already snoring lightly in an exhausted sleep.

"Help me put him to bed."

***

Ten minutes later, Amanda and Jan sat at her kitchen table, sipping mugs of steaming coffee.

"Why would the fire set him off like that?" Amanda asked. "He must have had some trauma involving fire. Have they located his parents yet?"

Jan shook his head. He knew why Billy—or, rather, whatever was lodged inside Billy—was so terrified of fire, but he had no idea how to tell Amanda his suspicions without her thinking he was nuts. Still, she had a right to know, given she had invited the angry ghost into her house.

If I could convince her of our—mine, Kathy's, Barb's, and Jim's—suspicions, she would send Billy back to Wayne State Hospital where they could keep him safely secured.

An image of Billy growing up in a padded cell flashed through his mind, and he shook the image away.

We must break the possession. Then he pictured Sandy sitting by the window in her catatonic state. *Without breaking his mind.* And his hands reflexively gripped the scars on his wrists. *And without scarring anyone for life—at least not physically.*

Taking a deep breath, he started to explain. "I think I know why, but it's going to take some explaining, and you're not going to believe me. At first, anyway. But you need to know the truth."

Amanda looked at him skeptically. "I'm not sure how to process that."

He laughed a little. "Don't try. Not yet, anyway. Think of what I'm going to say as a story I'm telling you. It ought to sound familiar, actually."

Over the next twenty minutes, Jan told her how, after he and Sandy, the previous owner of Mackey House, had become lovers, Sandy was possessed by the ghost of Flora, a chambermaid who had died in a fire back when the property was a hotel in the 1920s.

Flora's anger-fueled desire for retribution resulted in the murder of Sandy's husband and the burn scars that covered much of Jan's body. Sandy herself was left in a catatonic state, locked away in Wayne State Behavioral Hospital.

When he was done with his tale, and despite his best efforts, Amanda just looked at him with a bemused expression.

"So, you're trying to tell me that the plot of your novel is true?" Her tone practically dripped skepticism.

"Not just the plot," Jan said. "Pretty much all of it, dialog and everything. As best as I can remember it, anyway."

Amanda's expression told him she thought he was either crazy or trying to pull her leg. She shrugged dismissively. "Whatever. What does that have to do with Billy? Are you trying to tell me this Flora ghost is back?"

"Oh, no. I'm pretty sure she's gone for good."

"Then—?"

"There are one hundred and twenty-four other poor souls who are probably pretty pissed off about what happened to them down in that mine." He paused to gauge her reaction, which was still solidly disbelieving. He nodded toward the fireplace. "All of whom would probably be pretty terrified of fire."

He could tell Amanda was having none of his argument. She sat, arms folded across her chest and a scowl on her face. He tried one last time.

"Look, I know you don't believe me. Hell, I wouldn't believe me if I hadn't lived it." He held out his arms, palms up. "And had the scars to prove it." He dropped his arms and lowered his voice. "But it's all true. Whether you believe me or not."

Amanda slowly shook her head. "I thought…" She stopped to gather her thoughts. "I thought you were a level-headed, if somewhat nerdy, guy. Maybe with a little too much taste for the macabre, but regardless, a nice guy. I didn't think your…incident…had affected you so much that you would come to believe such a crazy story was true."

"I know it sounds crazy, but—"

"It doesn't just *sound* crazy, Jan. It *is* crazy." She took a deep breath, then dropped her bombshell. "I can't…with Billy…I can't deal with two mentally damaged people in my life right now. I'm sorry, but I have to prioritize Billy's well-being over helping you. And I do want to help you, I do. I just can't handle both."

Jan, stunned by what he was hearing, simply said, "Are you breaking up with me?"

Even to his own ears, he sounded like a jilted teenager.

Amanda nodded decisively. "Yes. At least for now. Seek out some help, Jan. Get your head straight, and then, maybe… I don't know. We'll see."

As if he were walking through a bad dream, Jan simply stood and walked out of the house without another word.

65

Kathy
Tuesday, April 14th

The drive home that night from the bar seemed to take forever. Kathy could barely keep her eyes open as she wound her way along the mountain roads to Mackey House. So when she got there, she didn't recognize the car that was parked in the grove of trees that had served as a parking lot when the place was a bed-and-breakfast.

As she turned off the street, she could see a head, silhouetted by the bluish glow of a cell phone, in the driver's seat. Jan's car wasn't in the driveway, so she pulled all the way up to the old garage. Unconsciously, her hand found the semi-automatic on her hip as she slid, crouching, out of the car.

Her visitor was already standing alongside their car when Kathy stopped at her Interceptor's rear fender. The motion sensor lights mounted on the garage illuminated the driveway and sidewalk leading to the front porch, but left the parking area in shadow.

Using the bulk of the SUV as cover, she unsnapped the restraining strap on her holster and called out, "Who's there?"

The breath she was holding broke free when a familiar voice called back, "Jesus Christ, Kathy. I didn't think you were mad enough to shoot me."

"Lacey?"

Sure enough, Lacey stepped from the shadows into the glare of the floodlights. Kathy met her in the middle of the driveway and, after a moment of awkwardness, the two sometime lovers embraced.

"What are you doing here?" Kathy asked as she pulled back from their lingering hug. Before Lacey could answer, though, she continued, "Not now. Tell me inside."

Her head swiveled, searching the shadows without knowing why.

"Ah, okay. What's gotten into you?"

Kathy grunted. "Don't know. Just feels…creepy."

"Spidey sense?" Lacey said with a lilt in her voice. When Kathy didn't react, though, she added, "This old place sure looks creepy. And I've heard stories…"

"I bet you have. Come on, let's go inside."

Once they were settled in the house's front parlor, Kathy poured them both two fingers of bourbon from Jan's personal stash and sat down next to Lacey on the sofa.

Clinking glasses, Kathy said, "Okay. Tell me. Why did you come back after bolting so…"

"Abruptly? Yeah, sorry about that. I guess I was really spooked. I'm not sure what happened in the mine, exactly. All I know is that by the time I had hiked out, I was bound and determined to get the hell out of Dodge."

"Without so much as a text goodbye."

Lacey looked momentarily chagrined, but then her expression became more determined.

"You don't know what it was like down there. It was like…"

"Like you lost time? Like you blacked out standing up, and when you came back, the others were staring at you?"

"How? How do you know that?"

Kathy chuckled. "Lacey, I'm a *detective*, remember? And my housemate was down there with you."

Lacey nodded, but eyed Kathy speculatively. "That's not all of it, though, right? This has happened to somebody else, hasn't it?"

Kathy's tone turned wary. "A lot has happened in that mine since you left. Which brings me back to the question. Why are you back?"

Lacey took a swig of her bourbon. "I'm on assignment."

Kathy's expression said, *Go on.*

"On assignment from one of the local TV stations to report on the murders, attempted murders, and apparent suicide that have happened while I was gone."

Kathy sat back, putting emotional as well as physical distance between them.

"How'd you get that gig?" But before Lacey could answer, Kathy continued. "So, this is an official visit? You know I can't give you anything without authorization."

Lacey held up a hand. "I'm not here to pump you for information. And anything you tell me will be strictly off-the-record. No 'unnamed sources' quotes, I promise. Everything will be on deep background, which means I won't report anything you tell me without independently verifying it. Okay?"

"How long did you practice that little speech?"

Her half-smile softened the blow of her words, and Lacey chuckled.

"They teach it to you in Journalism 101."

Kathy leaned forward again. "Okay, but we play it this way. You ask questions and I either nod—" She nodded her head up and down. "—shake my head, or shrug. Deal?"

Lacey gave it a moment's thought, then nodded. "I can live with that." She leaned in even closer and grinned slyly. "First question: Do you forgive me for bolting without saying goodbye?"

Taken aback by the question, Kathy smiled and nodded.

Lacey's sly grin grew wider. "Good. Second question: Can I spend the night?"

Nodding enthusiastically, Kathy downed her bourbon, stood up, and offered Lacey her hand.

***

Lacey rested her head on Kathy's bare chest. The two lay intertwined on Kathy's antique four-poster bed, cuddling between Egyptian cotton sheets under a lacy down comforter. This bed, Kathy's only girlie-girl possession, was her sanctuary—her escape from her real world of murder, mayhem, and ghosts. Based on Lacey's reaction, she loved the space as well.

A cloud crossed in front of the crescent moon, plunging their cozy nest into near-total darkness.

I could get used to this, Kathy thought as she felt herself drifting into sleep. *Wait. Am I falling for her?*

The thought felt comfortable. Being with another strong woman let her relax and let down her emotional shields.

Well, alright, then.

235

Lacey's wriggling of her naked body even more tightly against Kathy raised the heat beneath the heavy bedding. Kathy basked in the warmth and the all-too-infrequent sexual afterglow. Her eyes were heavy, and she was welcoming the arrival of a deep sleep when she heard Lacey's barely audible voice.

"You know, I didn't seek out this assignment. I've never been hired by a TV station before. But the station's news director told me I was specifically asked for by the mine tour's board. I've had a lot of—actually mostly—sleepless nights since I was here last. So, I figured if I could get to the bottom of what's going on, maybe I'd get some closure."

Kathy, having only half-paid attention, simply moaned an "Uh, huh" response.

What Lacey said next brought her fully awake, though.

"Do you think all of these events are related?"

Kathy's eyes snapped open. *Not now. I just want a good night's sleep for once.* But then, *A deal's a deal.*

She nodded.

"Don't freak out over this next one," Lacey whispered. "Do you think they could be, maybe, ah, supernatural?"

Kathy stiffened and held her head perfectly still.

Feeling her reaction, Lacey shifted and laid her head on the other pillow facing Kathy. They could barely make out each other's expressions in the dim light.

"Don't think I'm crazy," she said. "I firmly believe in ghosts, spirits, or whatever. I have to, since I grew up in a haunted house."

Kathy just raised an eyebrow in response, but she felt her heart pounding.

"I grew up in my Grandma's house," Lacey continued. "She was a widow, but my grandfather was still around, or at least his ghost was. You could hear him walking across the floor and sometimes see a light floating around that Grandma called his 'specter light.' So, please don't think I'm crazy, and I won't think you're crazy, either, if you confirm my suspicion."

There was a long pause while Lacey held her breath, and Kathy considered her options. Finally, trusting her lover's word, she gave a single, curt nod.

"Thought so." Lacey snuggled closer to Kathy again and laid her head in the crook of her shoulder. Kissing her ear, she whispered, "We'll discuss it in the morning."

All thoughts of sleep disappeared as their lips found each other in the dark.

66

Jan
Tuesday, April 14th

Jan and Kathy sat in the Mackey House dining room sipping coffee. His insistence to Amanda that his novel's story was real, and that Billy was probably possessed by a ghost from the Avon Hill mine fire, combined with her active resistance to both ideas, had resulted in their first argument. When she had made it clear that he wouldn't be sharing her bed then, or for the foreseeable future, he had slunk home.

When he arrived and saw the strange car, he assumed Kathy had a "sleepover guest." So, he was surprised to find her in the kitchen making a pot of coffee.

Nodding toward her owner's apartment door, he asked, "Who…?"

Reluctantly, Kathy murmured, "Lacey."

He couldn't keep the smile off his face when he said, keeping his voice low, "Sorry I missed her. I saw her on the news yesterday."

Kathy, who had watched Lacey's report on her blog while she slept soundly in the next room, poured them both steaming mugs. They pushed through the swinging door to the dining room.

"She came to interview me." She held up her hand to stop his protest. "I didn't give her anything she hadn't already figured out. I think she mainly wanted to confirm her own suspicions—

which were pretty much spot-on, by the way. She's very…sensitive."

"I bet she is!" Jan's barking laughter earned him a swat on the shoulder.

"You know what I mean. She still feels some residue of her blackout in the mine. That's what brought her back."

"Not your bubbly personality?"

Kathy gave him a cold look before saying, "What brought you home tonight? I thought you'd be staying at Amanda's."

"Touche. Lacey may be a believer, but Amanda certainly is not."

Kathy gasped. "You told her?" He nodded. "*What* did you tell her?"

"I told her about Sandy and Flora, and that the book was more memoir than fiction. It didn't go well."

"So, the bloom is off the rose, eh?" Her tone was a mixture of sarcasm and sympathy.

Jan eyed her over his coffee mug, then changed the subject. His next statement was a little tentative.

"I think I'm going to take the tender offer."

Kathy thought for a moment. "You should wait them out. They may raise the offer even higher."

Shaking his head more decisively, he said, "No, I don't think so." He took another sip. "Look, their offer is more than generous, and besides, what are the possible outcomes? One—" He raised his index finger. "—the mine is infested with pissed-off ghosts, and bad shit keeps happening until even the high-and-mighty Mayor Douchebag has had enough and the mine closes for good. Two—" He raised a second finger. "—I convince the board to abandon the project, which ain't gonna happen. Or three—" He didn't bother to raise a third finger this time. "—you convince Sheriff Peterson to shut it down."

"That's not gonna happen, either. Peterson's on his final glide path to retirement. He's not going to jeopardize that by pissing off the powers that be around here."

Jan raised an eyebrow at this news. "So, who's replacing him?" Kathy's sheepish grin gave him his answer. "You? Well, congratulations…I guess." He raised his mug in salute. "Maybe you could…"

She shook her head vigorously. "No way. I've been warned off. Told not to make any waves if I want the job." Her face clouded for a moment. "Or to keep *this* job, probably."

Jan could tell the situation didn't sit well with Kathy. "How do you feel about that?" he prodded.

"Not happy. But legally, there's nothing I can do, anyway. Gino's murderer is dead, and I can't even get Mark on trespassing, since you guys own the friggin' mine."

"What about the drugs—this 'Dazed' stuff?"

She shook her head. "Mark claims, and preliminary analysis confirms that it is just a bunch of herbs and supplements, and a ground-up gummy or two. Nothing worth pursuing, especially since he's the mayor's son."

"What about Charlie? Those pictures you showed me were pretty damned horrific. Something ripped his throat out, for God's sake."

Shaking her head again, she said, "With all the gore on his hands and under his fingernails, he clearly did it to himself."

Jan made a disgusted face. "But why? What *possessed* him to do that?"

Kathy shrugged. "The coroner says he was high on something."

"'Coroner?'" Jan scoffed. "He's a hack undertaker. Besides, Charlie's been clean for years."

"Regardless, he's the authority around here. Although I did have him send samples off to the State Police for them to analyze. If they confirm his findings, then case closed."

"And if they don't?"

Kathy just shrugged and sipped her coffee. "If you want to shut the place down so badly, you can't take the payoff."

"Buyout."

"Huh?"

"It's a buyout, not a payoff."

"Oh, please, we both know that's bullshit. Oh—"

Although he didn't want to admit it, he knew she was right. The board was just trying to buy his silence. The look on her face wasn't the satisfied smirk he expected, though.

"What…?"

She shook her head. "Nothing." But the *oh-come-on!* expression on his face made her nod. "Okay. I didn't show you all of the crime scene photos." She pulled out her phone and fiddled with it for a moment. "Here." She held it out to him. "I haven't figured out why he would do this."

The photo showed the deep, bloody gouges in Charlie's chest that spelled "B U L L."

Jan gasped, but before he found his voice, Kathy said, "Now I'm thinking that he might have been writing 'BULLSHIT,' but didn't finish."

Jan shook his head almost violently. "No. No, he meant exactly what he wrote: 'BULL.'"

"I don't get it."

Jan reached into his satchel and pulled out the book he had meant to return to Amanda, but hadn't when they argued.

"In Mollie Kelly's journal, she calls the Pinkerton guards, 'bulls.' I bet Charlie's ancestor was one of the Pinkerton guards who kept the townsfolk from fighting the fire. And who may have set it to begin with."

"That's a stretch, don't you think?"

"Maybe, but it's easy enough to check." He pulled out his phone and typed a text to Jim Donnelly.

"If Charlie is descended from a Pinkerton bull, the ghosts in that mine would be especially pissed off at him."

Kathy pursed her lips, still unconvinced, and was about to continue arguing the point when Jan's phone chimed. Instead, she said, "That was fast."

"Aha!" Jan crowed. "According to Jim, Charlie's great-grandfather was the Pinkerton guard in charge during the fire." He scrolled further down the message. "He was shot in the back one night. One of the Mollie Maguires was hanged for his murder." He looked up and met Kathy's eyes. "Talk about bad blood."

Kathy looked down and shook her head. "This is all speculation—"

Jan, furious, slammed his mug down onto the table and pulled the sleeves of his shirt up to his elbows, exposing the deep scars on his arms.

"*These* aren't speculations. We both know what can happen when you disturb angry ghosts." He let that sink in for a few heartbeats. "I can't just sit back until this—or something worse—happens to somebody else."

Kathy nodded. Slowly at first, then with increasing conviction.

"Then you can't take the buyout," she said firmly.

"I just said—"

"I know, but if you sell your share, you'll have no influence at all, no leverage."

Jan shook his head. "You don't understand, Kath. I don't have any leverage—or any influence at all—now. I'm just the outsider naysayer who will either be bought off or somehow else gotten rid of."

"You think they'd go that far?"

Jan snorted. "You saw what they offered me for my measly five percent stake. They stand to lose a lot more."

Finally convinced, she nodded. "Then you had better take the payoff and cash the check before we shut it down." Grinning, she said, "At least that way, you'll be able to get your own place."

He held up his mug, and she clinked it with hers.

"Or that sweet RV I've been drooling over," he said.

"Can you live in it?" Her mocking tone had an undercurrent of seriousness that he knew reflected both of their growing dissatisfaction with their living arrangement.

"While I'm on the road. Maybe I'll take a road trip all summer. You know, I can write from anywhere."

Kathy nodded appreciatively. "Anything that'll get you out of my house." Her phone buzzed and she fished it from the back pocket of her jeans. "Holy shit."

"What now?"

"I think somebody found Billy's parents."

67

Amanda

Tuesday, April 14th

The argument with Jan left Amanda confused. He had seemed so even-keeled, so level-headed. Then he told her everything in his novel actually happened, and that he thinks poor little Billy is possessed? And by her own ancestor? Talk about going off the rails.

Still, there were aspects of his story that made a kind of weird sense in a way, if you looked at it from a skewed angle, or upside down. In hindsight, she didn't know why she got so angry, and definitely not why she practically threw him out of the house. She may have overreacted as much as he did. As she got ready for bed—alone and lonely—she resolved to call him in the morning to patch things up.

The next twenty minutes tossing and turning in bed were a mental whirlwind as fantasies of adopting Billy, and a future with Jan swirled around in her mind. Her racing thoughts eventually gave way to a fitful sleep.

Far from restful, her dream was full of confused images of miners and their widowed wives and orphaned children. Their anguished families watched helplessly as the men and boys walked past in a straggling line. As they passed, the tears of their loved ones wet her own cheeks.

Tangled in the bedclothes, she moaned in dismay as one of the nameless faces in particular, leading a child by the hand to their deaths, shouted unintelligible, yet fully understandable, rage-filled curses and vengeful vows at her.

The dream became a full-fledged nightmare as the miners all turned to face her, and one by one, their faces merged into the angriest of them all, who glared at her while squeezing his brother's hand.

Ready to scream, Amanda suddenly felt a calming presence on the edges of her dream awareness. The faint pink glow that surrounded the presence reminded her of summer afternoons spent at her grandmother's when she was a little girl. The halo of love and warmth surrounding this new presence drove the harrowing images to the edges of her awareness, then finally into the darkness beyond.

"Hello, my dear." The voice of the presence soothed away Amanda's fears and slowed her pounding heart. *"I am your great-great-great-grandmother, Mollie."*

Mo—Mollie? Amanda whispered in her dream. *I have your diary. Your story is so sad.*

Mollie's image smiled and gathered Amanda's dream self into a warm embrace.

"It is true. My life was hard and filled with sorrows, but also with much joy. You must remember that and cling to the joy of life when those angry spirits come around."

Amanda leaned back and looked into Mollie's smiling face. *So, they are real? Real spirits?*

"Of course they are, Child. Just as I am."

Amanda buried herself in Mollie's arms again. *They were so...terrifying. But you drove them away. Thank you!* She squeezed Mollie's presence tightly. *I'm afraid they'll come back. Please stay with me. Protect me.*

A small gasp escaped Mollie. *"Are you inviting me in? To share your dreams when you are asleep?"*

Yes. Please.

Mollie hugged her even tighter and whispered, *"I will, my child."*

Who were those angry miners? And the angriest of them all, the two holding hands?

"Ah, you know the answer to that. You have read about them in my journal, have you not?"

Yes. Jack and Tim, your sons. Seeing them in my dreams must be so painful for you.

"Oh no, Amanda. What pains me is seeing them so angry and hateful."

They have reason to be, don't they?

"True, but after so long..."

Poor Tim! The same age as my Billy. He must be the angriest of all.

"No, that is not Tim's nature. He is a loving, caring boy. It is his brother, Jack, who is fueling his anger. Jack is using Tim as a channel through your Billy to reach the real world. His rage and hate have consumed his soul and are now eating away at Tim's too."

Mollie's sobs cut Amanda to the core. The dream no longer felt like a dream. Fully lucid, in that moment, Amanda believed. She believed in ghosts, both malevolent and beneficent. She believed everything Jan had told her, including in Billy's possession. And most of all, she believed she needed Mollie's help to stop Jack and to save Billy's mind...and Tim's soul.

That thought and her conviction strengthened Mollie's presence tenfold.

"Then we shall work together. Starting now."

Amanda watched as Mollie summoned Tim's spirit to her. He walked into their circle of light from the darkness beyond. His steps were hesitant at first, but he broke into a sprint when he saw his mother's spirit. The ghost of Jack emerged from the darkness beyond as well, but lingered on the edge of Amanda's awareness.

Seeing her oldest son, Mollie murmured, *"I can't reach him...yet."* And with a wave of her hand, she sent him back into the darkness.

"Mommy!" The joyful word burst from Tim as he ran into her embrace.

"Ah, my beautiful boy. Oh, how I have missed you." But after a moment of pure joy, Mollie's glowing, loving presence transformed into that of a stern mother. *"You need to stop helping your brother exact his revenge. What you are doing is evil."*

Tim's own presence stiffened under her scolding. *"It is also my revenge, Mother. I died in that hole, too. You can't understand what it was like."* On the last words, his voice became a plaintive wail.

"Then help us understand. Tell us your story." Mollie paused for a second. *"Remember when you were playing with our dog, and Rusty fell into an old test shaft? You wouldn't tell us what happened for two whole days."* Tim nodded reluctantly. *"But remember how much better you felt after you told us what happened."*

"I remember. You told me it wasn't my fault, and I felt better."

"Yes, and nothing that happened in that mine was your fault either. So tell us, and you will feel better."

Tim stepped back from Mollie's embrace and began.

68

Tim
April 8ᵗʰ, 1873

Jack led Tim away from the airlock and deeper into Tunnel Sixteen. The dim light of his Davy headlamp barely lit the rough ground, and only for a few steps in front of him. Tim, being dragged along by his brother's tight grip, stumbled again and again, seeing nothing of the rough tunnel floor.

"Come on, Tim. Climb onto my back. We've got to find a way out."

Squatting down, Jack let Tim climb onto his back. Together, they ran hunched over into the blackness.

Jack was finally gasping for air when they reached the airlock leading to Tunnel Fifteen.

"We can loop back through here," Jack gasped as Tim climbed down.

Tunnel Fifteen would lead them back to Main Street, the corridor from which the numbered tunnels branched off, and which they could follow back up to the mine's only shaft to the surface.

Jack knocked three times, then twice more, following protocol. When no response came and the door remained closed, he pounded on it with his free hand. Still no response. Shaking the doorhandle only produced a rattle from the inside latch.

Pulling Tim forward, he said, "Help me. It's latched from the inside, which means the nipper, Jimmy Simon, is still in there."

Tim knew Jimmy well. The Simons lived two blocks down from the Kellys. Jimmy was a year older than Tim, but they had formed a friendship over catching frogs in the creek behind their houses.

Together, they pushed against the heavy door, but to no avail. Then Tim, remembering how his own door fit into its frame, dropped to his knees and rammed his shoulder into the door's bottom corner, opening a small gap between it and the doorframe.

Smoke billowed out of the opening, engulfing Tim's face and head.

"Shite!" Jack shouted and grabbed Tim by the collar of his coat and hauled him back from the door.

The door slammed shut again, cutting off the flow of smoke, but Tim sat on the tunnel floor coughing uncontrollably, his lungs trying to rid themselves of the smoke and poisonous damps.

"Come on, Little Man. We gotta be movin'. There's no hope for Jimmy if he's still in there."

With throat burning and coughing still wracking his small body, Tim climbed to his feet and clutched his brother's hand. Together, they descended deeper down Tunnel Sixteen.

Stumbling along by the light of Jack's lamp, Tim felt his head growing heavy, and each step became a struggle. In a few more steps, he dropped Jack's hand as the world seemed to spin around his head. All he wanted to do was lie down and sleep.

"Blackdamp," Jack mumbled, as his headlamp flickered and nearly died.

Plunged into pitch blackness, the dizziness Tim felt grew even worse. Overcome, he dropped to his knees, plunging him even deeper into the heavier-than-air carbon dioxide— blackdamp.

"Don' ya give up on me, Little Man," Jack said as he scooped Tim up and tucked him under his arm. "Side tunnel's just ahead."

Bouncing along in Jack's firm embrace, Tim thought he was dreaming when he saw a faint glow up ahead. Sure enough, after a few more steps, Jack lifted him up onto a shelf of rock about shoulder-high.

"Crawl ahead." His brother's voice was weak.

Scrambling upward toward the light, which Tim hoped was more real than a dream, he heard Jack grunting as he struggled to climb up into the steep side tunnel that followed a seam of coal deeper into the mountain. Turning around in the tight space, he reached out and found the collar of Jack's jacket. Remembering how his brother had plucked him from the billowing smoke, he crawled backward, dragging his big brother with all his might. Jack's scrambling boots finally found purchase, and he plunged forward into Tim's embrace.

"Thanks, Little Man. I wouldna' made it without ya." Tim reluctantly let Jack pry his arms from around his brother's neck. "Come on," Jack said, trying to sound hopeful. "Let's join the others."

This time with Tim in the lead, the two brothers crawled thirty feet up the tunnel into a room formed from the tapped-out coal seam. Dozens of other miners huddled in the unused room, a level above the active section of the mine. The seams on this level had been emptied of their hard coal a generation before.

"Welcome," said one of the miners hiding there.

"Huh. Less air for us," grunted another further back in the shadows.

"Enough o' that," barked the first. "We're all brothers down 'ere."

A chorus of "Aye" came from some of the others.

"Just means we'll all die together," grumbled the one in the back.

"Then so be it!"

Before the argument could continue, a deep rumbling echoed through the confined space, followed by an ominous whooshing sound and a blast of foul air rushing up the tunnel they had just crawled through. Holding his breath along with the others, Tim swallowed to pop his ears as the pressure of the air changed.

"There goes the breaker," someone whispered.

"Sure 'nough."

Jack looked around at the despondent men and two other boys, one older and one younger than Tim.

"Tunnel Eight leads back up to Main Street, right?"

Headlamps waggled back and forth and Tim heard the tapping sound of hammer on rock.

"Blocked," came a voice from the dark. "This here cave-in took my Grandpa twenty years ago."

A sullen silence fell over the group, as each man and boy knew their only means of escape was up the mine's single shaft, but they were trapped by deadly gas below and thousands of tons of rock above. Besides, the rumbling and air pressure change surely meant that the main shaft was now blocked as well.

After several minutes of silence, with only the sound of the group breathing the limited supply of air, a voice finally whispered, "Well, 'at's it then.".

More "Aye"s were followed by another's voice. "Any paper?"

"I've some."

"I've a pencil," said another.

As scraps of paper and a few pencils were handed out, the men wrote out their dying messages to their loved ones. When each finished and handed the pencil to the next, they extinguished their headlamps.

When only Jack's light remained lit, he scribbled "Goodbye, Ma," and handed the paper and pencil to Tim. Terrified, Tim couldn't picture the A-B-Cs he had learned in school. Then he remembered the Christmas card he had made in school the previous year, and a serene calm settled over him as he thought of his Mom.

In the near-perfect darkness, he printed as carefully as he could, "I lov you Momy."

Jack slipped an arm around Tim's shoulders and reached up to his headlamp's valve, but Tim stopped his arm.

"I don't want to die in the dark," he whispered.

"Don't worry, Little Man. It'll be just like goin' to sleep."

Letting go of Jack's arm, Tim wrapped his brother in a bear hug as the darkness consumed them.

69

Amanda
Tuesday, April 14th

T he spirit of Mollie Kelly gathered her son's ghost into her arms.

"Oh, my poor little boy."

Her voice was full of sorrow, but Tim would have none of it.

"I'm not your 'poor little boy' anymore, Mother." His ghostly eyes glowed like hot coals deep in a bonfire. *"I've waited over a hundred and fifty years, reliving over and over that one day I spent in that hellhole. The hellhole you sent me to."*

Mollie's heartbroken gasp fueled Tim's rage.

"And how quickly you forgot about Jack and me. By the time they pulled our bodies out of the pit and laid them on our front porch, you were gone. Moved out. Moved on."

Tim's ethereal voice dripped with emotional pain.

"I had no choice," Mollie protested. *"The Company wanted its rent, and I had none to give them. I did not* choose *to move in with your Aunt Elizabeth, but I had to protect your sister, Rose. I had to ensure the baby I carried would have a better life. A life better than one filled with tragedy and pain. A life better than mine."*

Mollie's speech seemed to have little effect on Tim, although his eyes' fiery red glow dimmed a bit.

"And now you're in league with my dear sister's spawn." He aimed his glowing glare at Amanda's dream self. *"Why? To stop Jack's—our—revenge?"*

Mollie's presence in Amanda's dream, which had faded to translucency under Tim's onslaught, grew more solid as she gathered her strength.

"Yes. I have come back from the beyond to stop your madness. These people you are punishing know nothing about their ancestors' crimes. Just as you know nothing about the lives that came before yours."

"Don't try to convince me, Mother, that the Owners' spawn are blameless. Look at their lives against the life of one of your own. They still own the town and everyone in it. They still make the rules, and break them whenever they wish."

Amanda bristled at his last claim, and she finally found her voice.

"That's not true. Yes, they may have more money than me. They may eat in fancy restaurants, and take trips to far-off places, but I could do all of that, too. I've been to college. I have advanced degrees and a career that lets me live comfortably in a house I own. They are no better than I am."

Tim's snicker was spine-chilling. *"And yet, despite our warnings and our—Jack's—killings, they will still disturb our unhallowed tomb. They'll use it, just like their ancestors did, to exploit us, or our memories at least, simply to make more money!"*

The deep red glow spread from his eyes to the rest of his presence. Amanda's dream-self felt his rage as a burning heat.

"And you lie with one of them, like a common whore."

Mollie's reaction was so fast that neither Tim nor Amanda saw it coming. Her slap across his face stunned him into silence, and her next words, simple though they were, quenched the fire of anger within him.

"Shame on you."

Into the stunned silence, Amanda whispered, "Jan is a good man. A brave man. A gentle man, despite the pain and struggles he has endured. And he is not afraid of the likes of you or your brother. Although I believe it is your brother who is the real danger. I believe you are simply his tool. His *channel* into the world of the living. Am I wrong? Aren't you just a channel?"

Tim's presence collapsed into itself, and he was an eight-year-old boy again.

"No, you're not wrong. But I have been so lonely. The rage that has driven Jack to madness is like a disease. A disease that has infected all of us. That is how he has gathered all of the others into his essence. His power is the combined strength of all the lost miners…except me."

"Because he needs you to reach into our world."

Tim's spirit nodded, and a sob escaped him.

"It's just so dark and lonely. Seeing nothing. Hearing only Jack's spewed hate. Seeing the world through this boy, through Billy's eyes…hearing others' voices…touching the real world after so long. It's so exhilarating."

"But that is Billy's life," Mollie said soothingly. *"Not yours."*

Tim bristled. *"No, you're right. But what right does he have to it? After all, he killed his parents."*

Amanda was shocked into silence by Tim's revelation, but Mollie reached out to her son. *"That wasn't him, though, was it?*

That was you—or Jack." She took both of Tim's hands in hers. *"Timothy Jonathan Kelly, I can show you how to end your loneliness. I can show you how to move on from the netherworld you have been trapped in. But you must let me. You must let me help you."*

Tim's eyes brightened with hope, a hopefulness he had never known. But then he turned to look back into the darkness beyond Amanda's awareness as if he heard an irresistible voice calling his name.

Without another word, he turned away from them and drifted away.

Mollie's plaintive voice called as he faded from view. *"Please remember what I have said."*

But Tim's essence was already gone.

As the rest of Amanda's dream faded, she heard Mollie's whispered plea, *"And you, Amanda, remember this dream. And me."*

Her eyes flickered open, and for a moment she lay in bed, still disconnected from her body. But then she felt the warmth of another. A small, eight-year-old boy snuggled up close to her. Rolling over to face Billy, she gathered him into her arms as she had seen Mollie do to her Tim. And she knew what she must do.

70

Jan

Wednesday, April 15th

Somehow, Jan was getting used to his phone buzzing in the middle of the night. It was Amanda. His voice was groggy when he picked up.

"Hey, what's up?"

"Ah, sorry it's so late, but I really need you with me now."

"Now?"

"Now."

Fifteen minutes later, Amanda opened the front door as Jan was walking up the porch steps. She was dressed in her nightgown and a fuzzy robe and slippers.

Not a booty call, he thought as she pulled him into a hug.

"Thanks for coming. I know it's late."

He thought of the sun brightening the eastern horizon. *More like early.*

"Sure. What's wrong? Is it Billy? Is he—"

"No," she said, trying to calm Jan down. "He's sleeping quietly. At least for now."

She led him into the small living room, and they sat together on the sofa. She took his hands in hers and folded them in her lap.

"I want to ask you something, and I need you to be perfectly honest. No covering up what really happened. Just the truth. Trust me, I will believe what you tell me."

Jan eyed her skeptically. He figured he knew what she was going to ask, and he tried to gauge whether she really would believe him if he told her the truth.

If we're going to make a life together, I can't keep a secret like that from her, now can I?

He nodded. "What do you want to know?"

Still holding his hands in one of hers, she slid his sleeves up his arms. With the lightest of touches, she traced the tracks of raised white flesh that ran from his wrists to his elbows. Her touch made the whole network of healed-but-not-healed tissue—on his chest, belly, thighs, and groin—tingle like an electric shock.

"Tell me—truthfully—how you got these scars."

Still skeptical, he was quiet for a moment. Then, "Are you sure you want to know? It'll be hard to hear, and you may not like what I have to say."

She took a deep breath and nodded. "At this point, I'll believe anything." He still stared at her until she got the meaning of his last words. "Oh. Don't worry. No judgements."

Yeah, right, he thought. *I can't stop judging myself.*

***

The Mackey House Bed and Breakfast had been Jan's go-to spot when he needed to get away on a writing retreat. After his divorce and losing his job, the idyllic setting in the Pocono Mountains and the friendship of the B&B's owners, Sandy and Dan, had been his salvation. It was at Mackey House that he wrote his first best-seller.

But after an horrific murder-suicide in the house, Dan quit the business and his marriage to Sandy. His sudden and mysterious disappearance had left both Jan and Kathy, a local Sheriff's deputy, suspicious.

As Jan extended his stay, Sandy's behavior became more and more erratic and erotic, fueling a physical relationship between the two that was, at times, both pleasurable and painful.

His infatuation with Sandy progressed over his stay from light flirting to the kinkiest sex he had ever experienced. One moment, she seemed to be a damsel-in-distress, whose husband had split, leaving her with a business to run, guests to take care of, and a big old house to maintain. A single flirtatious word or touch, however, could transform her, in the next moment, into a tigress who seemed to enjoy inflicting pain as much as receiving pleasure.

Then there was the ghost. A malevolent spirit who, his research uncovered, was the remnant of a chambermaid named Flora who had died in the fire when the original inn on the site had burned to the ground. The inn's owner, Sandy's ancestor, then built a stately home on the ruins of the inn. He was soon terrorized, however, by the ghost of Flora, until he was eventually able to capture and lock her inside a statue.

That statue graced the Mackey House's front lawn for a century until one night Flora escaped her prison and, bent on revenge, took possession of a guest staying at the bed-and-breakfast. The possession resulted in the extremely brutal murder-suicide that Sandy blamed for her husband leaving.

Fueled by rage, Flora found in Sandy the fulfillment of her need to possess a vehicle for her retribution.

Jan, reluctantly partnering with Kathy, who was investigating the disappearance of Sandy's husband, tried to rid Sandy of Flora's possession. In the process, though, Jan was trapped in a death chamber and assaulted by Flora-Sandy. The ghost's burning touch restrained him while Sandy mercilessly tried to immolate him through sex.

Rescued on the brink of death by Kathy, who banished the ghost of Flora to some unknown Beyond, Jan was left with terrible scars, both emotional and physical. Sandy was left a catatonic shell.

***

Amanda suppressed a sob and wiped a tear from her cheek. "I…I didn't know."

Jan shook his head. "You believe me?" Amanda nodded. "Kathy and I have never told anyone else. You're the first."

"She saved your life. No wonder you two are so close." Her voice was tinged with a little jealousy.

His relationship with Kathy, a well-known and open lesbian, had been the topic of much speculation among the town's gossips. Especially after she purchased Mackey House, he moved in, and she became his caregiver until he was back on his feet.

And the fact that he stayed in the house, even after his novelization of those horrific events had become a worldwide best-seller, kept those gossiping tongues wagging. His blossoming relationship with Amanda, rather than damping down the rumor mill, only seemed to add grist to the grind.

"She did save me." He looked down at his still-tinging scars. "She could have gotten there a little sooner, though…"

His gallows humor, and Amanda's chuckling reaction, broke the tension a little. When he looked up and met Amanda's eyes, he saw a fear in them he had never witnessed before.

"Why did you need me to tell you all this? And why do you believe it?"

She took a deep breath, then blurted, "I think…I *know* I'm being possessed, and Billy is, too."

71

Jan
Wednesday, April 15th

Jan's lack of reaction disappointed Amanda a little. "You don't seem surprised."

"I'm not. Not in Billy's case, anyway. I've seen his possessing spirit come through more than once." He released her hands, which he had been holding through his whole recitation. "Why do you think *you're* being possessed, too?"

Amanda looked confused and unsure of herself. "Tonight I had a dream, though it was more than a dream. More like a visitation. My great-great-great-grandmother came to me."

"Mollie Kelly? The woman who wrote the journal?"

"Yes. It's her sons, Jack and Tim, who are possessing Billy. Or at least Tim is. It's all so confusing."

Her breath was ragged, so Jan held her hands again.

"Tell me everything you can remember about the dream."

***

When Amanda finished her retelling of the dream, Jan sat thinking for a full minute. Finally, Amanda couldn't stay quiet any longer.

"Well? Do you think I'm crazy?"

"Oh God, no. I believe you. Everything you said makes sense. Mollie seems like a benevolent spirit, not one to be afraid of. Especially since she tried to guilt Tim into rejecting his brother's influence and leaving Billy alone."

He thought for a few more moments, then looked Amanda in the eye.

"Would you be willing to bring Mollie back? But while you're awake this time?"

She looked momentarily terrified at the prospect, but after a moment, she reluctantly nodded.

"How will you bring her back? And what will you say to her?"

"The 'how' is complicated. I've done a lot of research trying to understand what happened to me. Once she's with you, though, we can try to convince her to take her sons with her back to wherever she came from."

"Will I…still be here? And will I remember?"

Jan nodded. "You remember the dream, right? And you were asleep then. You'll be awake this time."

Amanda's face clouded. "What if she doesn't want to leave?"

Jan nodded. "It's risky, but she voluntarily left you in your dream, right? Plus, I believe you're strong-willed enough to hold your own, especially awake."

She took a breath, then nodded. "Okay, how do we do this?"

"First," he pushed her shoulders back against the couch cushions, "you need to get comfortable." She leaned back, but he saw the tension in her shoulders. "Take a deep breath and hold it…now let it out. Good. Now close your eyes. Good."

She was still stiff.

"Let's try a relaxation technique. Listen to the sound of my voice and imagine you are sitting in a beach chair. Your toes are in the sand. Gentle waves are lapping at the shore. Hear them? Hear them whispering in their soothing voices. Feel the gentle breeze caressing your face."

Jan paused and looked at his lover, afraid that it might be the last time it was *her* that he was looking at. Rather than express his fear, he resumed his hypnotic monologue, seeing the tension in her body slowly lessen. As she became more and more relaxed, he leaned his phone against a lamp on the end table and started recording.

"Now, you see a figure standing down the beach. You can't make out any features on the figure's silhouette, but you know who you *want* it to be." He paused again, but only long enough for Amada to envision the new arrival. "You *want* it to be your great-great-great-grandmother, Mollie. You want it to be her with all your heart, and as she walks toward you, you see her features appear on the blank silhouette. As she gets closer, you not only see her clearly, you feel her presence, just like you did in your dream."

He took a breath before testing her.

"Do you feel her?" Amanda nodded. "Tell me, is she with you now?" Amanda's lips moved, but no sound came out. "Tell me, Amanda. Is Mollie with you?"

Weakly, she whispered, "Yes. She's here."

"That's wonderful, Amanda. Now, keep control of your body, but let her speak through you. Can you do that?"

Amanda nodded and her eyes flickered open, but instead of her throaty alto, she spoke in a higher-pitched voice.

"I'm here." Then, "Amanda, my child, you have nothing to fear from me."

Jan breathed a sigh of relief, then said, "Welcome, Mollie. We wish to speak with you. I suspect you know why."

"She knows," Amanda spoke in her normal voice.

Then, Mollie spoke. "You wish to rid the boy Billy of the hold Jack and Tim have over him. I do, also. I wish to lead my boys' spirits out of that pit they are bound to and on to the next world."

"Do you think you can do that?" Amanda asked.

Mollie's voice replied, "Tim, yes. I believe I can save him. But, Jack…Jack is so filled with hate and rage. I am not sure about Jack."

Jan didn't care about her sons' spirits, only about Billy. "If you can get Tim to move on, will that free Billy?"

Amanda frowned and seemed to struggle to maintain control. Finally, Mollie spoke. "I don't know. Tim is the channel to your Billy, but Jack is the real possessor. It may well be that without Tim's help he will not be able to reach Billy. Or, he may already have enough of a grip on the child's mind—"

Mollie stopped speaking, and Amanda turned her head toward the hallway, as if gazing into the distance.

"Tim is coming," Mollie said.

"So is Billy," Amanda said in her own voice.

Sure enough, Jan stared as a sleep-walking Billy padded down the hallway and into the living room. He climbed up onto Amanda's lap.

"Are you Billy or Tim?" Jan asked.

The child cocked his head to the side, then spoke in a voice that was neither that of an eight-year-old nor the menacing growl Jan had heard him use before.

"Both. The boy is dreaming, but I am alive."

Amanda bristled, and Mollie's voice spat, "No, you are not, Timothy. You have no right to claim this poor child's body."

Mollie's scolding didn't have the effect she was hoping for.

"The mine owners and the Pinkertons had no right to take my life from me. And neither did you. You're the one who sent me down there to die."

Amanda let out a sob that was pure mother's guilt.

"I know!" Mollie cried. "I condemned you to a miner's death, whether it was to happen on your first day, or twenty years on. I bore the burden of that guilt for the rest of my living days, and all the nether-time since. And I will for the rest of eternity. I accept that. But that is still better than seeing your torment trapped here, and the hate that consumes you. Let that go and come with me to a better existence."

The tears streaming down Amanda's cheeks were matched by those brimming from Billy's eyes.

"I want…I want to be with you, Mommy." Tim's voice had become that of a scared child.

"Then, come with me."

"But Jack. I can't leave Jack."

Mollie's voice became hopeful. "Then bring Jack, too. You both can come with me."

But Billy's face clouded, and he shook his head. "He won't. That's not what he wants." Billy-Tim lifted his hands in front of his face and stared at them in wonder. "He wants this."

Amanda's voice was like a face slap. "He can't have that! This is Billy's body, not his."

Jan spoke up, trying to rescue some sense of progress and hoping he was right.

"He can't have Billy without your help, though, right?"

Billy looked at him and nodded. "Jack still needs me. At least for now."

Amanda took up the cause. "So if you tell Jack you're going with your Mom, maybe he'll decide to go, too."

"Rather than spend eternity in that mine alone," Jan added.

Mollie was frantic. "Please, Tim, tell your brother you'll come with me, so he'll come as well. Then we can be a family again."

"He…he won't…he won't like it. But I'll try."

With that, Tim's spirit left, and Billy collapsed into a sleeping child on Amanda's lap.

When it was clear that Tim had left, Jan said, "Well, that's progress, I guess. Thank you, Mollie, for your help."

"It's not over yet," Mollie warned. "Jack was always the stubborn one."

Amanda lifted a hand as Tim had lifted Billy's. "And I can see the attraction…"

"Hey!" Amanda jerked her hand down to her side. "You promised."

Abashed, Mollie said, "I know. Don't worry, blood-of-my-blood, flesh-of-my-flesh. Your body—your life—is yours to live."

Amanda's eyes grew heavy.

"My God, that was exhausting."

"Mollie's gone?" Jan asked.

Amanda nodded. "Yes, she's gone. We don't have to worry about her."

I hope you're right, Jan thought, but said, instead, "Let's get you two to bed."

Mollie taking control of Amanda's arm had shocked him. Somehow, he knew that from now on, he would always be looking for signs of Mollie in Amanda.

72

Kathy
Wednesday, April 15ᵗʰ

Kathy scanned the pictures arrayed in chronological order on Sheriff Peterson's desk. The first ones showed State Police divers in a rain-swollen mountain stream. Next were a couple of shots of a heavy-duty tow truck winching an SUV out of the water.

The next shots were gruesome. They showed two badly decomposed bodies in the front seat. One, which Kathy assumed was a woman based on the length of hair, was still strapped into her seat. The driver, a man, had managed to unbuckle his seatbelt, but the shorted-out electric windows had served as a very effective cage.

The next picture made Kathy gasp.

"A car seat?"

Peterson nodded. "But no kid."

Kathy nodded, in return. "I'm pretty sure we know where the kid is. How'd he get out?"

The sheriff pointed to the last picture.

"The back window was open?"

"It must have been opened before they went off the road."

"Which let the water fill up the car quickly."

"And it settled on the passenger side, which left the open window as an escape hatch for the kid."

"Who had to undo his car seat harness and swim up and over to the bank of the stream. Can an eight-year-old do that?"

Peterson handed her a brochure advertising the Coyote Lodge, an indoor water park about ten miles from where the car was found.

"My granddaughter's seven. She's been swimming since my daughter took her to Mommy-and-Me swim lessons when she was still a baby. Swims like a fish."

"It's almost like the whole thing was planned," Kathy muttered to herself.

"Seriously? You don't believe that, right?"

Kathy shook her head. "No. Just dumb luck, I guess." She tossed the brochure onto the desk. "Do we have a name?"

"Yeah. Their IDs were still readable. Stefen and Letitia Saint-Germain. Visiting from Ohio. Had a week's reservation at Coyote Lodge—which they never showed up for."

"That's why no one noticed they were missing."

"And get this. Their son's name really is William. Quite the coincidence."

Not really, she thought, but kept that thought to herself.

Kathy pulled up the map app on her phone and zoomed in on the location of the accident. Comparing the accident scene photos and the angle of the car's entry into the water to the app's terrain view, her face clouded.

"They were headed the wrong way. The water park is a couple miles in the other direction."

She showed her phone to Peterson and scrolled it along the route to the lodge.

Peterson shrugged. "I've lived here my whole life, and I still get lost on some of these back roads."

Kathy grunted. "You never had to patrol them in the middle of the night, did you?"

Before she had proved her mettle by solving the Mackey House mystery, Kathy had been low-man on the totem pole among the other, misogynistic, deputies.

She picked up a photo of the car's interior. A cell phone was still in its dashboard mount.

"Why weren't they following their GPS?"

Before Peterson could answer, someone knocked on his door, and the deputy on desk duty stuck his head in.

"A Mr. Richard Smith, the fisherman who found the car, just got here, Chief. He's in IR four."

Kathy looked at the sheriff, but didn't have to ask her question.

"Have at it, Detective," Peterson said as she gathered up the photos and other evidence.

She stopped before leaving, though. "Why weren't we called as soon as they found the car?"

"State Game Lands. Not our jurisdiction. It wasn't until the Staties realized there might be a missing kid involved that they thought of our Billy."

And it was probably Dad who made the connection, she thought as she walked through the squad room to Interrogation Room Four.

"Mr. Smith, thank you for coming up here from…" she checked the note the duty officer had handed her. "…Stroudsburg. I won't keep you long. Just a few questions."

Smith huffed a little. "I already gave a statement to the Staties. I don't know anything else."

Kathy gave him her best *so-sorry-for-the-inconvenience* smile.

"Yeah, I know. I have your statement right here." She patted the evidence folder. "The thing is, the car you found seems to be related to a missing-child case—a missing-parents case, actually—that we have here."

"Oh, yeah. The empty car seat in the back. I saw that."

"Right. So, why don't you tell me how you found the wreck."

"Sure. I was fishing my favorite spot—brownies are running now that the weather has warmed up. Anyway, I was up to my ass in the crick—water was high on account of the rain we've been having. I cast my favorite Green Bottle with a fuzzy strike indicator into a pool where they like to hang out. Wouldn't ya know it, it snagged on my first cast. I love that fly, I wasn't about to lose it right off the bat like that, so I walked the line in to the edge of the deep pool. That's when I saw it—the car. My Green Bottle was hooked into the side window's weather stripping."

Still looking at her pad where she was making notes, Kathy asked, "You didn't disturb anything in or on the car, did you?"

Smith shifted uncomfortably in his chair. "Well. I might've unhooked my Green Bottle…"

Kathy chuckled. "I don't blame you. I've caught many a brownie on one of those, although I prefer a blue Hare's Ear this time of year."

Smith's face broke into a big grin. "You fish?"

She let him eye her with a new sense of appreciation. "Of course. I bet I've fished that same stretch of Wolf's Crick a hundred times. Great spot. So, did you call the Staties right away?"

Jim screwed up his face, then nodded. "As soon as I could. Just as soon as I got a signal."

"Oh, right. There's no cell service there."

"No GPS, either, which is why I like that spot. No weekenders mucking up the water."

"Of course." She gave Jim a big smile and held out her hand, which he quickly shook. "Thank you for your help. Now that we know who our foundling's parents are—were—we can get him back to his family."

She stood up, and Smith followed suit.

"Glad to be of help," he gushed as she escorted him to the door.

Sheriff Peterson was waiting for her outside the observation room for IR Four.

"I didn't know you fish."

"Chief, there's a lot about me you don't know," she said as she breezed past him. "Didn't know there's no GPS there, though. At least we know now why the Saint-Germains were lost."

73

Kathy
Wednesday, April 15th

As Kathy walked across the parking lot of Wayne County's only hospital, she had to dodge Jonah Spatz's cruiser as it sped up to the curb.

When Jonah jumped out of the car, Kathy called out, "Yo, Spaz!" and ran up to intercept him.

Startled, Spaz spun around as Kathy approached. "You got the call, too?"

"Yeah, the duty nurse called as soon as Lauren woke up."

He turned to hurry into the building, but Kathy grabbed his arm.

"Spaz, we need to be careful. She's probably still pretty fuzzy, and may not remember much of the attack. Can you keep your cool?"

Spaz looked down at Kathy's restraining hand, then sighed. "Yeah, Kath. I'm just glad she's recovering."

"Okay," she said, but thought, *'Recovering' might be an overstatement.* Out loud, she said, "So, no pressure, right?"

"Yeah, yeah." He turned back to the door. "Come on."

Nodding, Kathy followed him into the building and up to Lauren's room.

Lauren's parents were fussing over their daughter when Spaz and Kathy entered the room. While Spaz and the Tanners exchanged hugs, Kathy stepped up to the bed. Lauren's reaction to her presence was guarded, so Kathy smiled, patted her shoulder, and mouthed the words, "It's okay."

When she got a wan smile in response, she said out loud, "I'm glad to see you're feeling at least a little better, Lauren. I just have a few questions for you, then I'll let you rest with your family. You okay with that?"

Kathy turned and smiled at the Tanners, who gave her curt nods in response. Lauren's face clouded, though, and she glanced at her parents and Spaz hovering at the foot of the bed.

Reading the young woman's signal, Kathy asked, "Would you be more comfortable if we chatted privately?"

Lauren's relief was clear on her face, and she nodded quickly.

Kathy turned to Spaz. "Jonah, you know the drill."

Spaz frowned but nodded. "Come on, Steve and Janice. Let's get some of that horrible hospital coffee."

After he had led them out of the room, Kathy smiled at Lauren. "You're one brave, strong woman, Lauren. I don't think I could have—"

"Oh, come on, Deputy. I've heard stories about you."

"Ah…?"

"Yeah, if you look up bad-ass-woman in the dictionary, it has your picture next to it."

Genuinely stunned by Lauren's comment, Kathy just stared with her mouth open.

"Seriously, Detective. You're a folk hero among every squad of us brats."

Finding her voice, Kathy just said, "I…I don't know what to say. Other than 'thanks,' I guess."

Lauren snorted a laugh. "Thank you for teaching us girls how to stand up to and overcome misogynistic jerks like…" She nodded at the door, then lifted an IV-pierced fist.

Tapping Lauren's fist with her own, Kathy felt a pride she had not felt in a long time. Her years on the force had been mostly lonely and underappreciated—or at least so she thought. To hear that she was inspiring a new generation of young women, and rebellious ones at that, gave her an unfamiliar warmth inside.

Offering Lauren a genuine half-smile, she took out her phone and started the voice recorder app.

"Detective Kaveetha Jensen interviewing Lauren Tanner on April fifteenth at six-thirty-four PM. Miss Tanner, this interview is being recorded, and a transcript of which will be entered into the official record of your case, which may be used in a court of law."

Kathy hit the Pause button and whispered, "Lauren, if you want to tell me anything that you *don't* want in the official record, just do this—" Kathy held up her clenched fist. "—and I'll pause the recording. Got it?"

Lauren nodded and held up her fist before Kathy could even push the Resume button.

"Yeah? What is it?"

"Who'll be able to read the transcript or listen to this?"

"Me, Sheriff Peterson, lawyers, just about anyone officially connected to your case. Including Spaz."

Seeing Lauren's quizzical expression, Kathy chuckled and added, "That's what we call your Uncle Jonah."

Lauren's laughter told Kathy she had scored big time points.

"But don't tell him I told you that." Kathy and Lauren's shared chuckle warmed the space between them. "Tell you what, let's do a quick, formal interview with just the facts, then you can tell me anything else off the record. Okay?"

Lauren nodded, and Kathy hit the Play button.

For the next ten minutes, Kathy pulled a bare-bones account of how Mark Luzeski, the mayor's son, approached her boyfriend about their D-A-S-D, "Dazed Experience," venture.

"He led us through the woods and into this dark tunnel. Then he gave us each a pill of the Dazed stuff—"

"Which was just a bunch of herbs and a ground up gummy," Kathy interjected.

Lauren made a face. "Huh." She held up a fist.

When the recording was paused, Lauren added, "I think there was more in it than that. I got all flushed, and suddenly I was incredibly…" She glanced at the door and whispered, "horny."

Kathy frowned, thinking about how she had just let the locals do the analysis of the Dazed pills. *Got to send one of those pills off to the State Police lab*, she thought.

"Ready?" she asked with her finger poised above the Resume button. Lauren nodded.

"When you were having sex with Mr. Youells, when did it change from…normal?"

Lauren held up a fist, but Kathy shook her head and mouthed, "Sorry."

Shrugging, Lauren said, "It wasn't ever 'normal' with Jimmy. He liked it pretty rough. So, when he grabbed my neck," she rubbed the bruises that were still visible, "I wasn't surprised. But then his grip got tighter and tighter, and I couldn't breathe at all." Lauren's eyes got wide as she pulled up those memories. "I fought him best I could, but he wouldn't let go." The last word rose into a sob.

Kathy spoke in her official voice. "I am pausing the recording to give Ms. Tanner a moment to compose herself," she said and hit Pause.

"Sorry, Lauren, but we need your version of the attack on the record." She didn't mention that the whole incident had been low-light video recorded. "You okay?"

Gathering herself, Lauren nodded, and Kathy hit Resume. Thinking back to the video at the point when Lauren lost consciousness while Jimmy Youells's lips were moving without the recording capturing what he said, Kathy asked, "Do you remember anything else before passing out?"

Kathy reached for the Stop button, not expecting a response from Lauren. So, she was surprised when Lauren nodded and whispered, "Yes."

"Go on."

"Just before I passed out, I remember this voice. A voice that wasn't Jimmy's."

A chill ran down Kathy's spine. "Not Jimmy—er, Mr. Youells's?"

Lauren shook her head, and her face paled. She took quick, shallow breaths, making the Pulse-Ox monitor beep its alarm.

"What was the voice? And what did it say?"

Lauren shivered and gasped out in a strangled voice, "It was a horrible, evil voice. Not Jimmy's at all. In fact, it seemed like someone else was in his body. *Everything* felt…different."

Hyperventilating, she took a few more shallow breaths, and Kathy knew the monitor's alarms, which were squealing loudly, would quickly bring a nurse.

"What did the voice say?"

Taking another half-breath, Lauren whispered, "It said, 'Good job, Whore. You're making the owners' spawn come running.'"

"'Owners's spawn?'" was all Kathy got out before the door burst open and the duty nurse rushed into the room, followed by the Tanners and Spaz.

The nurse hit buttons on the monitor to still the alarms and adjusted the oxygen flow, then she turned to Kathy.

"That's enough, Detective. Ms. Tanner needs to rest." She looked at the Tanners. "You two can stay, but no more talking. Let her sleep." Then she turned to Kathy and Spaz. "You two—out!"

74

Kathy
Wednesday, April 15ᵗʰ

Spaz paced an agitated loop in the back of Sheriff Peterson's office. He'd been fuming ever since he had followed Kathy out of the hospital and back to the station to brief the sheriff. Once the office door closed, though, he couldn't hold back any longer.

"What did you say to her to get her so upset?"

His fists were balled at his sides, and his red face could barely contain his anger as he rushed forward.

"Jonah, I just took her statement—"

He leaned forward, his face only inches from Kathy's. "She was hyperventilating, for Christ's sake."

The violation of her personal space was too much for Kathy. She put a hand flat on his chest and eased him back. "Jesus, Spaz, get it together. She was reliving being raped and almost strangled to death. Of course, she was upset. But you macho men think—"

"That's enough!" Peterson interrupted the argument before it got out of hand—or physical. "Jensen, why did you say 'raped?' She was there with Youells voluntarily and seemed to be a willing participant up 'til…"

Kathy thought quickly, trying to explain without breaking Lauren's trust or sounding like a nutcase.

"Lauren told me, off the record, that the pill Luzeski gave her…affected her strangely."

Peterson raised an eyebrow. "'Off the record?' Is that why the recording is so disjoint?"

Kathy shrugged but stood her ground. "It was a traumatic event for Lauren, and some of the more intimate details don't need to be public knowledge."

Her and Peterson's gazes locked for a moment, then he nodded his assent.

"You said it affected her. How?" Spaz asked. His breath was still coming raggedly, but he seemed more in control.

"Ah, the way she described it sounded like it might be something like a Ruffie, but with a…different…effect."

"Different? How?" Spaz pressed, but Kathy pressed her lips together. There was no way she would reveal that detail to Lauren's family—especially to her uncle, the misogynist who'd been harassing Kathy since the day she started on the force.

Peterson, seeing the tension between the two growing again, interrupted their stare-down after a moment. "Maybe whatever is in the pills had a different reaction in Youells."

"You mean maybe it pushed him over the edge from rough sex to violence?"

Kathy was at first glad for the interruption, but then winced when she realized her gaff. Spaz jumped on her comment.

"Rough sex? What—"

"Spaz! That's part of the off-the-record stuff. Shit. I shouldn't have said anything. But," She looked over at the vomit stain on the floor. "You've already seen the tape." Chagrined, Kathy grabbed Spaz's arm. "Look, you have to keep that confidential. Lauren doesn't want anyone—her parents especially—to know details of what was going on down there. She trusted me with the intimate stuff, and we need her trust, especially if we're going to need her to testify. Got it?"

Spaz was fuming. His lips were drawn into a straight line, but he nodded. His eyes looked like he was thinking about ways to punish all of them: Luzeski, Kapaletti, and Youells—even in death. If that meant doing it through the legal system, so be it. But if that didn't work, he'd figure something else out.

Kathy didn't like what she saw in his face, but decided to let him stew. "I want to send one of the pills to the state lab for analysis."

"Good idea. Get it out of Disque's hands."

Peterson's comment got Spaz's attention. "You think the coroner is covering for Luzeski?"

The Sheriff shrugged. "Mark is the mayor's son. And *Assistant* Coroner is an appointed position."

"Jesus," Spaz muttered. "The power boys have this town locked up tight. Us little guys can't catch a break around here. It's always been that way."

Kathy nodded slowly, the meaning of Youells's cryptic comment as he choked her into unconsciousness clicking into place. *That's what his whole thing is about.*

Spaz was getting angry again. "So what happens next? How is Luzeski going to pay for drugging my niece and almost getting her killed?"

It was the sheriff's turn to get angry. "Hey! I know you're pissed about what happened, or may have happened to your niece, but there's a process we need to follow here. No vigilante stuff. Let the detective do her job. Got it?"

Spaz turned an appraising eye on Kathy, who returned it with all the steadfast determination she could muster. Seemingly satisfied, Spaz nodded, but Kathy could see he just meant, *For now.*

75

Hestia
Wednesday, April 15ᵗʰ

The mental identity known only to herself as Hestia slowly opened her senses to the stimuli reported by her body. For two days, she listened to the sounds of the other patients, the joking banter between the aides and orderlies, and all the other common, ambient sounds within an institution like the Wayne State Hospital. All without giving away her growing awareness.

Knowing that she was being scrutinized by Samson and the woman social worker, Hestia, through an instinctive reticence, kept her gathering consciousness a secret. Along with the awakening of her mind came the awakening of her body—sensations of touch, heat, and cold. Sitting for hours in front of the drafty picture window, the chill of the common room in the early morning pricked at Hestia's comfortable inner world.

Like an itch that needs a scratch, the cool breeze raised gooseflesh on her bare forearms. Not yet able to control her atrophied muscles, she couldn't rub warmth into them or even pull down the sleeves of her dressing gown. Annoyed, she reached inside instead, where she found the reassuring warmth of Flame waiting.

Feeling the heat that infused her limbs, first starting with her fingertips and working all the way to the tips of her slipper-clad toes, Hestia let out a satisfied sigh. A sigh that drew the attention of the ever-present Samson and the unwanted attention of her nemesis.

Although the boy who had been her constant, though uninvited companion was gone—taken away a few days before—the spirit that had possessed the child's body still occasionally reached out with its tendrils to test Hestia's mental shell. This time, it felt a texture it had not encountered before. It was the mental mirror of the gooseflesh on her arms, papillae of awareness tasting the outside world.

"Wake up, my dear. We have much to discuss."

The only response Ghost received was an enveloping mental silence. Unable to penetrate her defenses, it chose a different means of contact.

Just as Hestia was discovering her own body, Ghost was learning to control the boy's. Applying what it had learned, it reached out mentally, simply trying to lift Hestia's arm.

The jolt of heat that gushed from her through the spiritual connection drove Ghost back to the edges of her awareness and made Hestia jerk and stiffen in her chair.

Samson, who had been diligently watching for more signs of Sandy's awakening, hurried over to her when he saw her stiffen. He came up short, though, when he heard Sandy's growl.

"Be gone, *Jack*."

Her command sent Ghost—Jack—back to the netherworld where it lurked.

Samson came up behind Sandy and touched her shoulder. Even through the layers of flannel pajamas and robe, her fading heat made him snatch his hand away in surprise.

Rubbing his burned hand, he said, "My God, Sandy. You're burning up."

He was long past expecting a response, so he was shocked when she slumped in her chair like a half-deflated balloon. Worried that she was feverish, he pulled out his phone and quickly texted Ms. Stupine, the social worker.

> *Patient Adams spoke again,*
> *refring to someone named 'Jack'.*
> *Patient appears to be running a*
> *very high fever. Am taking her to*
> *infirmry.*

His phone buzzed with the response as he spun Sandy's wheelchair around and headed for the mental hospital's infirmary.

> *Will notify sheriff then meet you*
> *there.*

Ten minutes later, as the nurse on duty took Sandy's vitals, the social worker joined Samson.

"I left a message for Deputy Jensen. How is Sandy? Did she say anything else?"

Samson shook his head. "Nothing." He was still unconsciously rubbing his hand.

The nurse cleared her throat. "Well, all her vitals are normal. Specifically, her temp is just ninety-nine-point-one. Well within the normal range. Why did you think she was running a fever?"

Samson looked confused and looked down at his hand. "When I touched her shoulder, it felt like I tried to pick up a hot dish. It's still…tender." He sounded tentative and even a little embarrassed.

"Let me see your hand," the nurse said, and Samson held out his heavily callused right hand. "Looks okay. Any pain?"

After a pause, Samson shook his head. "I guess I overreacted."

"Overreacted?" Ms. Stupine interrupted. "Overreacted to what? Did you just imagine that touching her burned you?"

Very uncomfortable with the implication of his boss's tone, he just shrugged. "I…guess so."

Eyeing him suspiciously, she added, "You didn't imagine her saying something, too, did you?"

Samson shook his head violently. "Definitely not! I know what I heard."

After a few uncomfortable seconds of silence, the nurse nodded. "Why don't you take Ms. Adams to her room? Check on her every hour, okay?" She handed Samson a forehead thermometer. "Here. Just scan her forehead with this from an inch or so away." She demonstrated on the unresponsive Sandy. "See, down to ninety-eight-point-two. Still normal."

Samson dropped the device into his pocket. "Got it, Doc," he said with a sheepish smile. "Sorry to waste your time."

The nurse shrugged. "No problem. It's been a slow day anyway." She eyed the rows of paper cups holding the patients' meds. "Same shi—er, stuff—different day."

Ms. Stupine sniffed her disapproval, spun on her heel, and stalked out of the exam room.

Samson fingered the thermometer in his pocket.

"You said, '*Down* to ninety-eight-point-two.' It was ninety-nine-point-one the first time you took it."

"Did I?" She thought a moment, then shrugged. "People's temperatures can vary slightly minute to minute," she added, though her tone wasn't very convincing.

"By more than a full degree?"

"Ah, not normally."

Samson nodded and tentatively laid a hand on Hestia's shoulder. It was cool to the touch.

"There's nothing *normal* about this one," he said as he patted her shoulder like he would a child, or a pet.

Annoyed, Hestia let a hint of Flame's heat warm his hand. Not enough to burn, but more than enough for him to notice. He didn't react, since the heat faded quickly and the nurse was still watching him closely. But something was going on with the strangest patient he had ever known. Without another word, he wheeled Sandy to her room.

76

Jan

Wednesday, April 15th

Jan's yawn was contagious, and Amanda yawned in sympathy. She looked down at the sleeping child in her lap, then up at Jan.

"Help me put him to bed."

Awkwardly, Jan hoisted Billy into his arms. Holding a sleeping child was a new experience for him, and it wasn't as unpleasant as he had imagined. Feeling Billy's warmth pressed to his chest tickled a long-dormant corner of his heart. Since his divorce, he had buried the notion of raising a family deep in his psyche. But now, hearing the boy's quiet snores next to his ear, his parental nature stirred a bit, if not coming fully awake.

Once he had accepted that the deaths in the mine were the work of a malevolent spirit, he knew that ridding the town of Jack's ghost would have consequences. Consequences that could be devastating to his burgeoning love life. Until that moment, Billy's welfare was, at best, a secondary consideration. Unconsciously, he believed that if, to accomplish that goal, it left Billy as an empty shell, as it had with Sandy, condemned to live out his days at Wayne State Hospital, then so be it.

But holding the living, breathing child in his arms made him face that unspoken conviction. No longer could he think of Billy as a pawn in the coming battle. No, in that moment, he knew that defeating Jack's spirit without also saving this child's mind and body would be nothing short of abject failure.

Jan was also self-aware enough to know that he couldn't live with himself if he failed. His life, though hopefully still with many years to run, was nothing compared to the potential of Billy's.

As he laid Billy back down in his bed and pulled the covers up to his chin, Jan felt his heart quicken with both conviction and trepidation. He swore to do everything in his power to save the child, though he knew it would probably cost him dearly.

Amanda slipped an arm around his waist, and he gathered her into an embrace. Together, they gazed down at the sleeping child for a moment, before Amanda spoke in a whisper.

"Stay with me tonight. Please."

Jan looked at her in the dim light from the hallway. It revealed a face fraught with worry, and whose eyes had grown heavy. Nodding, he led her to her bedroom.

***

Jan sat in the small house's living room in his underwear. A bottle of whiskey sat on the end table next to his chair, and he absent-mindedly swirled a glass containing two fingers of the brown liquor. After an hour of trying not to disturb Amanda, he realized he wasn't going back to sleep, he had padded out there and raided her liquor cabinet instead.

So, he sat in the semi-dark, with just the light of a streetlight three doors down coming through the room's bay window. His mind wandered between Billy, Amanda, the ghosts, and the plot of his next novel. He couldn't shake the pent-up anticipation that had kept him tossing and turning until he finally gave up and sought the familiar refuge of a bottle.

So, he wasn't surprised when a movement at the archway that led to the bedrooms caught his attention.

Billy strode confidently from the dark hall into the dim living room. Except Jan knew immediately that it wasn't Billy or Tim walking with such a swagger. It was Jack.

"Are you going to growl at me this time?" Jan's voice didn't carry even a hint of fear.

Stopping in front of Jan, Jack-Billy put his hands on his hips and rolled his head from side to side.

"Nope." He rubbed his throat. "I'm feeling a lot more comfortable in this body than I did when we first met." His eyes went to the bottle on the table. "Ah, nice."

Grabbing it, he took a swig, then made a face and coughed roughly. "Heh, heh," he chuckled as he wiped the tears from his eyes. "That's what I remember."

Keeping hold of the bottle, he flopped onto the couch.

"You don't look surprised to see me," he said as he took another swig. This time he handled the burn in his throat with a smile.

Jan shrugged. "I'm not. I chatted with your mother and brother, so I figured it was only a matter of time before you made an appearance. Where is Tim, by the way?"

He kept his voice and face neutral, although he worried that Jack had discovered how to control Billy without Tim's help.

"Oh, he's here. Just…in the background." He took another swig. "You know, soon I won't need him to occupy this body."

Jan bristled. "It's not just *a body*, Jack. Billy's a child, a boy the same age as Tim was—"

"Exactly! Tim's life was cut short at eight. Why should this *Billy* have a longer one? At least his body won't be food for the rats like Tim's—and mine—were."

Jack tilted his head back and took a long pull from the bottle.

That's a lot of booze for such a small body, Jan thought. He needed to get some information out of Jack, though, before the alcohol did its work.

"How'd you get so strong all of a sudden? You've been in that hole for what, over a hundred and fifty years?"

Jack's smirk was pure evil. "Oh, me and my mates joined forces over the years. We wouldn't let go and *move on*—" He spat the two words. "—like those other pussies did. No, we sat in the dark down there until the time was right."

"Until we reopened the mine, you mean?"

Jack shook Tim's head. "Nah," he said with a slight slur. "We was waitin' for the right…vehicle to come along."

"Vehicle? You mean a car?"

Jack barked a laugh, and spittle ran down his chin. "No, ya idjet. I mean this." He pounded Billy's tiny fist against his chest.

"He's not just a *vehicle*. He's a boy," Jan couldn't keep the anger out of his voice this time.

Jack snorted and shook his head, then swayed and rolled his eyes. Looking down at the bottle, he smiled. "Huh. Good stuff." Lifting it to his lips, he slurped down what little remained in it.

Seeing how the whiskey was working on him, Jan knew he didn't have much time to get the answers he needed.

"Who are these 'mates' you said you've joined forces with?"

Jack's eyes refused to track Jan as he leaned forward. "I'm talkin' 'bout the Mollies. There was a lot o' us on 'at shif'." His voice was barely understandable. "Took some convincin' but I managed to eat 'em all 'ventually."

"Eat them?"

"Aye. Some came will'nly. Some…didn't. Each gave me stren', though. Now, I cin do th' same ta spawn o' Owners…an' Bulls."

"Did you do that to—" Jan started to say, but before he could say more, Jack-Billy dropped the empty bottle and made a stumbling dash for the bathroom.

When the sound of wretching, toilet flushing, and running water finally ended, the boy came wobbling back.

"Jack?" Jan asked tentatively.

The boy shook his head and flopped down on the couch. "He's passed out."

"Now you're Tim, right? Did you hear what he told me?"

Tim just nodded, and Jan continued. "So you know he'll just 'eat' your soul, too."

Another nod. After a few seconds of silence, Jan spread his hands in exasperation. "Well?"

The tears streaming down Tim-Billy's cheeks were barely visible in the dim light. They dripped onto his Pooh pajamas when he nodded a third time. This time, though, he said, "Doesn't matter. It's what I deserve for helping him."

77

Kathy

Thursday, April 16th

Sheriff Peterson slid the local assistant coroner's report across the coffee-stained and cigarette-burned desk to Kathy. The folder's edge caught on a splintered gouge in the surface.

Got to replace this old thing when this office is mine.

But thoughts of being Sheriff evaporated when she opened the folder. Her brow furrowed as she read its account of Charlie's death, then she violently shook her head.

"Bullshit," she said as she looked Peterson in the eye. He raised his eyebrows in surprise, so she continued. "This says Charlie was high on—" She looked down at the paper again. "—something I've never heard of and can't even pronounce."

"That Dazed stuff?"

She shook her head. "Can't be. This fucking thing says his blood was loaded with a supercharged form of Angel Dust. But I know that's a lie, and that the DASD was just some herbs and a little THC." When Peterson raised a questioning eyebrow, she explained. "My dad texted me this morning. He put a rush on the samples I sent to the Staties' crime lab."

She pulled out her phone and showed the text to the sheriff.

"He says there was no sign of 'any alcohol or drugs' in Charlie's blood. And the DASD stuff was harmless. A little dope is all. The official reports will be coming later today."

Peterson's face clouded. "Remember what I told you about making waves."

"Waves? This deserves a tsunami. They've clearly invented this 'Aryl-something-or-other' to sweep his death under the carpet. And to send me on a wild goose chase trying to track down the source of this mythical shit."

Kathy stood and angrily paced back and forth in front of the old desk. Peterson watched her for a second, then sighed and tilted his head back in frustration.

"Dammit, Kathy. I'm three months away from retirement and a pension that the mayor—whose son is in the middle of this mess—can evaporate."

"I know, but, Chief—"

The sheriff held up both hands in a gesture that meant both *Stop,* and *I surrender*.

"All I ask is that you walk softly. Don't go accusing anybody of anything until you have ironclad proof. And then—and only then—pass the evidence on to your dad, since the State Attorney General will have to be the one filing charges. Got it?"

Kathy met his gaze, then nodded. "Got it."

"And—" Peterson stopped her as she turned to go. "—you realize, of course, that will be the end of your career in this county, right?"

Kathy didn't answer, only looked at him defiantly, so he continued.

"They may file charges against the hack 'Assistant Coroner' and maybe the mayor, too, if Disque squeals, but the others will close ranks. You know how this town works. The AG will never get them all."

"I'll be *persona non grata*."

"At best. The powers-that-be around here haven't been in power for well over a century through benevolence and goodwill. You'll have a big, fat target on your back."

"Shit."

She knew her boss was right. Was clearing Charlie's name, and removing at least that much of a burden from his family worth her career, or, hell, the whole life she had built? They were probably vindictive enough to poison her whole career. And she knew they could.

Would she miss this life, though? She lived in a formerly haunted mansion with Jan, a dear friend, yes, but one who was drifting away into the arms of Amanda. Her Friday afternoons were spent drinking alone since she had no one else to get drunk with. And she knew, though she hated to admit it even to herself, that her thing with Lacey was just a fling of convenience and mutual loneliness.

In contrast to her bleak home life, though, she knew she had skills. Skills that would be valuable to some other small-town police force, or even as a gumshoe-for-hire. That idea, trite as it was, held a certain appeal to her independent nature.

She nodded slowly, then smiled at her boss. "Don't worry, Chief, my investigation will be *slow and thorough*. I'm sure it'll take, oh, I don't know, at least three or four months to complete."

Peterson gave her a wry smile. "It had better." Then he got deadly serious. "Thanks, Kath. I mean it. But you do what you need to. I'll be okay, either way."

With the unspoken feeling of mutual respect hanging in the air, Kathy spun on her heel and left his office.

78

Kathy
Thursday, April 16th

Lacey pushed the spaghetti and jar sauce around on her plate.

"You cooked this?"

"Uh huh," Kathy mumbled around her mouthful.

Lacey pulled out her cellphone. "Stick to *detectiving*. I'm ordering a pizza."

Genuinely hurt, Kathy said, "You don't like it?"

Lacey snorted a laugh. "Kath, I'm English and I can make a better sauce." She held up a forkful and watched as the thin sauce slid off the limp pasta. "Haven't you ever heard of *al dente*?"

Kathy just blinked.

"You know, 'to the tooth?'"

Kathy shrugged and looked down at her plate. The "red sauce" had settled to the bottom of her plate and, as she watched, it separated into a pool of oily something.

"Ick."

"'Ick' is right," Lacey chuckled and hit Send on her phone. After a moment, she got a text reply. "The real dinner will be here in twenty minutes."

Kathy picked up their full plates and headed for the kitchen. "Sorry."

Lacey followed her. "Don't be. You have other redeeming qualities." She squeezed Kathy's ass, making them both laugh.

For the next ten minutes, the two cleaned up the disastrous meal. When the last dish was dried and put away, Kathy took Lacey by the hand and led her into the big house's front parlor.

"Cocktail?" she asked as she opened Jan's liquor cabinet.

"Isn't that…?"

Kathy shrugged. "His is better stocked. Let's see, Blanton's, Red Breast, Sazerac, …"

"He really likes his brown stuff, doesn't he?"

"Yep. But he's got white liquor, too. Ah, here we go." She held up a bottle of tequila with a white label. "George's finest." Kathy poured two shots. "I might be able to scare up a lime, if you need one."

In response, Lacey raised her glass, which Kathy duly clinked with her own.

"Cheers," they said together.

Kathy pounded hers back, but Lacey took a sip, raised her eyebrows, then savored the rest.

"You like it, eh?" Kathy reached for the bottle again. "Another?"

But Lacey shook her head. "Not until after we eat." She checked her phone. "Delivery's still a few minutes away, and I have some questions for you."

"Questions?" Kathy was the one who usually asked the questions. "Um, okay. Shoot."

"This apparent suicide. Charlie…ah—"

"Charlie Lusaitis. Good guy. He'd been sober for, like, ten years."

"So, he really did all that damage to himself?"

Kathy's eyes narrowed. "How do you know—"

Lacey rolled her eyes in response. "I have other sources than you, you know." Then she smiled to soften the blow. "None as cute, though."

Kathy was having none of that, though. "That was supposed to be confidential. Who gave you that?"

Lacey's smile disappeared. "You know I can't reveal my sources."

Kathy felt the heat rising in her neck and cheeks. "Well, the pool of people who had that information is very small. And I bet I know who spilled it." Her eyes bored into Lacey's. "And I'd bet a week's pay that it was our hack of an *assistant coroner.*"

Keeping a poker face, Lacey took a deep breath and said, "I can neither confirm nor deny…you know the drill."

That's a non-denial-denial if I ever heard one, Kathy thought.

Trying to deflect the conversation, she waved her hand dismissively. "Whatever. The case is basically closed. There was some kind of potent drug in Charlie's system—"

"A form of Phencyclidine—PCP—right?"

"Shit. I'll have the bastard's ass."

Enjoying Kathy's discomfort, and hoping for anther tip, Lacey asked, "You said *basically* closed. So the case isn't fully closed?"

Shit. Damned tequila.

"Are we on the record, Lace?"

Lacey's blank look was a wall between them. *Shit. Two can play this game.*

"I, ah, just have one or two things to follow up on. Purely routine."

"Sure. Purely routine. Anything I should know about?"

Thinking back to her conversation with Sheriff Peterson, Kathy knew the last thing she needed was Lacey digging any deeper, so she pressed her lips together and shook her head.

The tension in the room was broken when the doorbell rang. Lacey jumped up to answer it while Kathy carried the bottle and glasses into the dining room, then fetched plates and napkins.

"Dinner is served!" Lacey called faux-cheerfully as she returned with the still-hot pizza.

Kathy held up a full shot glass. "Truce?" Without words, her tone of voice said, *Please don't let our jobs come between us.*

Lacey touched Kathy's cheek and tucked a wayward strand of hair behind her ear. "No worries," she whispered, and her kiss was gentle.

The one Kathy returned was a lot less so. She set the shot glass down, its contents forgotten.

They ate reheated pizza that night.

79

Kathy
Thursday, April 16th

M mm. Good call," Kathy giggled as she slurped up the mozzarella hanging from her third slice.

They sat at the corner of the big dining room table. That table could accommodate up to twelve of the previous owners' bed-and-breakfast guests. Yet, to Kathy and Lacey, still reveling in their afterglow, it felt cozy. The room was only lit by the antique wall sconces, not the matching chandelier that hung over the table. Their yellowish glow lent an air of intimacy to their meal—which suited Kathy's mood perfectly.

"Can't go wrong with pizza," Lacey said around a mouthful.

"Even reheated pizza is still…pizza," Kathy agreed.

"It's the perfect food. Every food group is represented—bread, dairy—" She lifted a slice of pepperoni. "—meat. Even veggies." She waved a spear of bell pepper. "And whatever group mushrooms fit into."

"And fruit. Don't forget the fruit."

"Where's the fruit?" Lacey asked while chewing crust, cheese, pepperoni, and sauce.

"The tomato sauce. Tomatoes are fruit."

"Fruit? No they aren't. They're vegetables."

"Fruit," Kathy insisted, smiling.

Lacey rolled her eyes. "Okay, here we go—"

Kathy egged her on. "They have a skin like an apple and seeds like an orange."

Lacy waved the piece of bell pepper again. "So do these."

Grinning widely, Kathy said, "Yup. Another fruit."

"No friggin' way." Lacey was exasperated until she saw the grin on Kathy's face. "Okay, you say 'tom-*ay*-toe,' I say, 'tom-*ah*-toe.'"

"You say 'potato.' I say, 'No, thanks, I'll have the rice.'"

Lacey stared for a moment, then they both burst out laughing. Leaning forward, she wiped a drop of tomato sauce from the corner of Kathy's mouth. A moment later, they were tasting each other's mouths again.

"Mmm, garlic," Lacey whispered.

Kathy pulled back. "Oh, sorry."

But Lacey's hand on the back of her neck pulled their lips back together.

Lost in the kiss, Kathy suddenly felt Lacey stiffen, and the passion that a moment before had been building again, went cold.

She pulled back to find Lacey's eyes glazed over and her mouth hanging slack.

"Hey, are you okay?" No response. "Lace! Hey, Lacey!"

She shook her lover's shoulder, but to no avail. Standing, she grabbed both of her shoulders and shook her again. Leaning all the way forward, she opened her mouth to shout right into Lacey's face when the episode broke. Lacey's eyes flickered, and she took a deep breath, letting it out a second later in a small sob.

"Oh, my God, Lacey. What the hell was that? Was that some kind of seizure?"

Still groggy, Lacey shook her head and took a few more deep breaths. "I don't know," she said at last. "They've been happening ever since I came back to this friggin' town."

"And you're still driving?" Kathy knew it was the wrong thing to say as soon as she said it.

"That's your response, *Detective*?"

"Sorry. That was stupid of me." Kathy sat back down, but took Lacey's chin in her hand and turned her face so their eyes met. "Who'd you see? Jack?"

The shocked look on Lacey's face told Kathy she had hit pay dirt.

"How—?" Seeing that Kathy was serious, she nodded. "Is that his name? Why now, though?" She looked around the dimly lit dining room, where so many similar events had taken place, fictionally documented in Jan's novel. "Oh, of course. So the stories are true?"

Kathy chuckled. "*That's* your response, *Reporter*?"

Lacey chuckled as well. "Touche. And it's *Investigative Reporter* to you."

Kathy sat back and poured each of them more tequila.

"Jan told me about the episode in the mine. He thinks you were channeling an angry ghost."

"'Angry' doesn't cut it. This guy—Jack, you said?—is really pissed off. He keeps trying to…"

"Take over?" Kathy asked, and Lacey nodded. "But you can fight him off?"

She shrugged. "More like pushing him away. I don't *fit* him well, I think."

Kathy processed this for a moment. "Then why'd he pick you in the mine? Jan and Jim Donnelly were there, too. I'd have thought they'd be a better fit?" *Especially Jan*, she thought, but kept that to herself.

Lacey looked almost embarrassed when she said, "I've always been…sensitive…to the spiritual world."

She waited for a reaction and looked relieved when Kathy reached out and took Lacey's hands in hers.

"I get it. Believe me, I've seen some shit that would make your hair curl."

"So I've heard."

Kathy raised a questioning eyebrow, but Lacey simply said, "Investigative reporter, remember? Your lips tend to get loose when you drink."

Chagrined, Kathy said, "Damn Lloyd. I thought there was a code of honor among bartenders."

"Like a Seal of the Confessional?"

"Yeah, a Seal of the Tavern."

"Hardly. You'd be surprised by what you can pick up by asking the right questions in a bar."

Reminding Lacey that she was a cop, Kathy rubbed her knuckles on her chest as if she was polishing a badge.

"Oh, yeah. I guess you already know that. Still, don't blame Lloyd. It's fairly common knowledge around these parts that something…extraordinary…happened here a while back."

"Great. That'll help my election—" Kathy's face paled at Lacey's smirk. "Shit. Please don't—"

After a moment, Lacey made a lock-and-throw-away-the-key gesture. "It'll cost you, though."

Kathy slipped off her chair and onto Lacey's lap. "What's the fee?" she whispered in her ear. "Does it involve my 'loose lips?'" Somehow, Lacey never got to answer.

***

Lying in bed with Lacey curled up next to her, Kathy couldn't sleep. Her mind kept spinning out possible scenarios of the coming days and the approaching mine tour opening.

What kind of havoc will Jack do once he has access to friggin' tourists? And what if there are more of them? Over a hundred miners died down there, after all. What if more of them wake up?

"Shit," she whispered out loud.

Lacey stirred. "You can't sleep, either?"

"No. Can't stop thinking."

"Me, too. Jack's a bad dude, isn't he? Feels like a smarmy creepizoid."

Kathy shuddered. "Yeah, he's bad. Killed three so far."

"Three? Oh, Charlie, too?"

"Officially, no. Unofficially...?"

"Got it. Off the record," Lacey said, then poked Kathy in the ribs. "Don't want to mess up that election campaign, right?"

"Oh, fuck. You, too? Peterson gave me that same advice. Regardless, we have to figure a way to stop Jack and save this fucking town."

"We?"

"Yeah, me and Jan."

Lacey propped herself up on the pillows. "You don't want my help?"

Kathy swallowed hard. Something told her that was more than a simple question.

"Uh, yeah. I'd love your help, if you're willing."

306

Lacey met her eyes. "If I'm going to be hanging out around here, I don't want some creepy ghost causing trouble."

Seeing the excited glint in Lacey's eyes, Kathy knew she had to convince her how dangerous this could—would probably—be.

"Look, we could really use your help, especially given your, ah, sensitivity. But I'd rather you be safe. This isn't like some movie. And the consequences can be very real."

She reached for her phone on the bedside table and pulled up pictures she had taken of Jan after Sandy-Flora's attack, then more after the wounds had healed but the scars remained. The puss oozing through the bandages covering sixty percent of Jan's arms and torso made Lacey swallow hard. The final picture, taken just a month ago, showed Jan in his underwear, his body a network of white scar tissue and barely healed welts.

"You've read his *Mackey House* book?"

"Sure." Lacey's tone sounded like she knew what was coming next.

"It's pretty much all true."

"Shit." Lacey sank back down under the covers. "And you're willing to risk *that* again?"

"Gotta." Her next statement made Lacey gasp. "And so will Jan."

Lacey nodded toward the phone with its pictures of what saving them from Flora had cost him. "Are you sure?"

"I know him. He'll do whatever it takes." She paused for emphasis. "We couldn't save Sandy last time. He—we—won't let happen to the boy this time."

"Oh, yeah. The boy." Lacey swallowed hard. "I'm in."

"You sure?"

Lacey, who had been lying stiffly next to Kathy, rolled toward her and threw a leg over hers and an arm across her belly.

"I'm sure."

Kathy wrapped her arms around her lover. "Good. We'll talk with Jan tomorrow. Now, get some sleep. I've a feeling it's going to be a rough couple of days."

Jan
Friday, April 17th

Jan sniffed the air as he struggled to work on a plan. He had bolted from Amanda's as soon as the sun came up, despite her offer of coffee and breakfast. Just as the attack that had left him so scarred separated his old life from this one, he felt the coming conflict with Jack as a heavy curtain cutting off his current life and all that went before it from a completely uncertain future.

Sitting in the small living room of his suite of rooms in Mackey House, he tried to put his thoughts into some kind of action plan. Once he was back on his feet after Sandy and Flora's attack, he had moved into these rooms just above where his old life had ended. The irony was not lost on either him or Kathy.

He wrinkled his nose at the scents drifting in from the kitchen.

Bacon. Bacon and eggs? Not again.

He waited for the smells and sounds that usually accompanied Kathy's attempts at breakfast—burned toast, scorched grease, and the scream of the smoke alarm. Instead, the delicious scent of freshly made coffee was added to the milieu. It made his mouth water.

Did she take a cooking class?

Unable to resist, and needing a break from his ineffective writing session anyway, he followed his nose down the central hall to the kitchen.

"When did you learn to cook?" he asked before he noticed Lacey standing at the stove.

"When I was a kid," she responded, wearing an oversized T-shirt he'd seen Kathy in many times.

The scene brought him up short.

"Oh, Lacey, Hi. Well, that explains the lack of the smoke alarm."

Lacey chuckled as she slid perfectly cooked scrambled eggs onto three plates that already held toast and several strips of bacon.

"Bring the coffee if you would, please."

With the ease of a seasoned waitress, which he thought was probably how she paid her way through college, Lacey backed through the swinging door into the dining room. Jan, bemused, followed with three mugs hanging from his fingers and the full pot of coffee.

Kathy sat at the head of the table, a look of hungry anticipation on her face. When she saw Jan, she nodded, then beamed at Lacey, who set a full plate in front of her.

"Wow. This looks—and smells—delicious."

Jan set the coffee mugs down and filled them from the pot.

"No thanks to you."

"Hey," Kathy said around a mouthful. "She banned me from the kitchen."

"You would have started a grease fire!" Lacey countered.

"It wouldn't 'ave been th' firs' time," Jan muttered, his own mouth full. "Oh, my, God, Lacey," he continued once he had swallowed. "This is wonderful. How long will you be staying?"

She and Kathy exchanged a grin, which made Jan smile as well. "Oh! Well, welcome to Mackey House. The kitchen is yours!"

He saluted her with a forkful of eggs in one hand and a strip of bacon in the other.

"It's only while I'm in town." He thought he detected a bit of a blush on her cheeks and neck. "Just to save on hotel—"

Kathy nearly did a spit-take, and Jan barked a laugh himself.

"Sure. Hotel," he said as he smeared his toast with some strawberry preserves that he had picked up at a local farmers' market. "What brings you back to our corrupt little town?"

Curiosity flashed across her face. "Corrupt?" She looked from Jan to Kathy, who just nodded back toward Jan. "Is there something I should know about?"

Jan looked at Kathy. "You didn't tell her about my buyout?"

"Not my place." Kathy mumbled as she shoved another forkful into her mouth.

"Buyout?"

"Yeah. The Bastards of Directors of the Lost Miners Coal Mine Tour, LLC offered me, the only dissenting voice to their big plan, I might add, a payoff to quit the Board."

"Dissenting over what?"

"Whether to open the damned thing given the unexplained shit that's been going on down there." Jan's voice rose in pitch.

"And if you don't take it—the buyout, or payoff, or whatever?"

He snorted disgustedly. "They'll find some other way to get rid of me, I'm sure."

Having cleaned her plate, Kathy said, "I thought you had already decided to take the money and run."

Jan nodded furiously. "That was until what happened last night—" He stopped himself before telling them about meeting Tim, Mollie, and ultimately Jack. But Kathy caught his eye, tilted her head toward Lacey, and nodded.

Still reluctant, though, he continued. "Anyway, this morning, I got the official divestment paperwork, which includes an NDA so I can't disclose why I'm leaving the project or any of my issues with it. Including anything even remotely resembling them appearing in a future fictional story."

"A non-disclosure agreement? You realize I'm a reporter, right?"

"And I'm a *detective*."

Jan gave them both a sly smile. "Well, I haven't signed it yet, and the hack who wrote it made it effective the moment I sign, not when I received it." He spread his hands. "So it's not yet in force."

Lacey barked a laugh, and Kathy rubbed her hands together. "Well played. So, tell us what happened last night."

While looking at Kathy, Jan gave a sideways nod toward Lacey.

Seeing his reluctance, Lacey said, "Strictly off-the-record. Deep background."

"Oh, it's deep," Jan muttered, still looking at Kathy. "And you?"

She gave him an *oh-come-on* look. "If I put any of this shit in an official report, I'd never write another one, because I'd be unemployable."

"And you'd never get elected Sheriff," Lacey said, smirking.

Jan's eyebrows shot up, but all he said was, "Later. But we *will* talk about that later. Anyway, buckle your seatbelts. It's gonna be a bumpy ride."

***

Half an hour and another full pot of coffee later, he finished his recitation of the previous night's events at Amanda's house. Lacey and Kathy had a million questions, which he answered as best he could. But many were simply unanswerable, which led to much speculation and discussion, including Lacey telling him about her sensitivity and resisting Jack's advances.

Finally, their discussion ran down.

"So, the upshot is that we have three ghosts. Mollie, who wants to save her sons from the mine's purgatory—"

"And from doing evil, it sounds like," Kathy chimed in.

"Yeah," he responded hesitatingly. "I'm not convinced that's a particularly strong motivation. I mean, think about it. She lost a husband, two sons, and her whole first life to the mine owners. She has reason to be pissed-off, too."

Kathy and Lacey nodded in agreement.

"So, that's one ghost," Jan continued. "We also have Tim, who Jack is treating as a pawn, and who is Mollie's best chance to redeem. Then there's Jack." He took a deep breath before continuing. "Jack is the real problem."

"He sounds strong," Lacey said. "Given that he has *eaten* the souls of the other Mollie Maguires."

"But you can resist him," Kathy said.

Jan shook his head. "You didn't when we were in the mine."

Lacey shuddered. "If you say so. I don't remember any of it, just coming out of it and seeing you two staring at me."

Kathy reached out a hand to Lacey, who held it tightly. "Then we had better keep you out of there," she said. "He's clearly strongest down there."

Jan's voice was ominous when he said, "Then that's where we need to…finish this. Otherwise, he'll just retreat down there and bide his time until some other sensitive sucker comes along."

"Like another kid or someone in a tour group. Imagine what he could do to a group of twenty tourists in the dark."

Kathy's scenario made the others shudder.

"Which could be as soon as this weekend," Jan said quietly.

"They're going through with the Grand Opening, then?" Kathy asked, and he nodded. "Makes sense. Peterson closed Charlie's case as a suicide—which, technically at least, it was."

"Is there a statute of limitations on demonic possession?" Jan asked, but his attempt at gallows humor fell flat.

Lacey tried to bring the discussion back to reality. "So, what do we do?"

Both women looked to Jan, who looked first at Lacey, then turned to Kathy and held her stare. "First thing I'm going to do is sign the damned forms."

"And deposit the money somewhere other than Miners Bank."

"Got that right."

"And then?"

"I have a plan, but you're not going to like it. And neither is Amanda."

Kathy held his gaze for several heartbeats, then said, "Probably not." But she nodded, at least.

81

Kathy
Friday, April 17ᵗʰ

Kathy was driving her Interceptor with Lacey hanging onto the overdoor handle for dear life. The SUV's deep-throated rumble set her teeth on edge as they raced through the residential streets toward Amanda's house. More than once, whitetail deer grazing in the suburban yards raised their heads as the cruiser sped past.

When they were parked at the curb in front of Amanda's, Lacey let out her held breath. Exasperated, she asked, "Do you always drive that fast?"

"No, sometimes faster."

"Not many opportunities for high-speed chases in Dundee, huh?"

"Gotta get it out of my system somehow."

The ringing of Kathy's cellphone through the car's Bluetooth put their repartee on hold.

Looking at the Caller ID, she answered in her best detective voice. "Jensen here."

"Hello, Detective. This is Sally Stupine. If you remember, I'm the Social Worker at Wayne State Hospital."

"Yes, Ms. Stupine. How can I help you?"

"You asked to be kept informed if there was any change in Sandy Adams's status."

Kathy and Lacey exchanged surprised looks.

"Yes, I did. I assume something has changed."

"Why, yes. It's quite remarkable, actually."

After a few seconds of silence, Kathy rolled her eyes. "And what would be so remarkable?"

"Oh, well, Ms. Adams has begun speaking."

The social worker's nonchalance was in sharp contrast to Kathy's shocked reaction.

"Excuse me? Did you say she's awake?"

The other woman's tone turned pedantic. "Well, she's always been awake, of course. Technically, catatonia is not an unconscious mental—"

"Ms. Stupine, what did she say?" Kathy interrupted.

"Oh, right. Nothing too coherent, actually. She just mumbled something that sounded like random words. Ah, you may have misunderstood. She is not what you would consider *conscious*, per se. But this is the first time she has uttered anything since she was admitted."

Kathy's face was flushed, and her voice turned dark. "Is she exhibiting any signs of aggressive or violent behavior?"

"Oh, no, not at all. She still doesn't move on her own. Just sits there staring into nothing like she always has. The change is simply that on two occasions, she has uttered disconnected words."

Kathy asked, "So, she has spoken on multiple occasions?"

"Yes. Simple, one-word utterances at first, but the most recent was more like a full sentence."

Kathy took a deep breath, as if afraid to ask the next question. "What are the words she is uttering, Ms. Morrison?"

"Um, let me check my notes." Kathy and Lacey exchanged another exasperated glance while listening to the rustle of papers. "Again, they don't seem to be connected to each other in any way. Let's see. I wrote them down. Yes, 'dark' was one. And 'redemption.' That's an interesting one, actually. And one other. Apparently, it was hard to make out but sounded like 'Jack.'"

"Jack? Did you say '*Jack*?'" the voice of the deputy asked.

"Why…," the social worker looked at Samson, who nodded. "Why, yes. According to our orderly, who is here on the call with us, she said, 'Be gone,' to someone named 'Jack.' Of course, there was no one—"

Lacey gasped, and Kathy blurted, "Shit," before catching herself.

"Really, Detective. Such language." Ms. Stupine sniffed her disapproval. "At first, Samson—that's the orderly—thought she was referring to that boy who was with us for a while. You know, the one who ran away?"

Lacey's mouth hung open in shock, and Kathy said very slowly with her best professional tone, "Probably not. We've identified the boy. His name is Billy Saint-Germain."

"Oh. 'Billy' and 'Jack' aren't really that similar, are they?"

"No, Ms. Stupine. I suppose not."

Kathy looked in the rearview mirror as Jan pulled into Amanda's driveway.

"Listen, Ms. Stupine. I'll come by tomorrow to interview her, but in the meantime, Sandy Adams needs to be moved to your secure wing. If she is waking up…" Her voice dropped to a mutter. "…and talking to Jack." Then she caught herself and her official tone of voice returned. "Nevermind. She needs to be locked up."

Stupine's response was unexpected. "May I remind you, Deputy, that Ms. Adams has not be convicted of any crime, and we must assume she is—"

This was too much for Kathy. "Don't give me that bullshit. I saw what she did with my own two eyes, and my friend lives with the scars of her violent crimes every day."

But Stupine was adamant. "Patient Adams has never exhibited any violent tendencies."

"Maybe not as your *patient*, but when she was awake, she killed her husband and nearly killed my friend."

"Unproven allegations—"

Stupine's haughty tone was infuriating. "Enough! I'm ordering you, as the jurisdictional law officer of her case, to move her to the high-security wing of Wayne State Behavioral Hospital. Now!"

After a few seconds of silence, Stupine's officious tone returned. "As you *request*, Deputy. I will comply…once you have filed the appropriate paperwork, and I have reviewed it."

Unable to hold her tongue anymore, Lacey muttered, "Bitch," as the call ended.

"Holy shit," Lacey whispered. "Do you think she was actually saying 'Jack?'"

"If she was, that's a whole new wrinkle." She looked up to see Jan standing on Amanda's sidewalk impatiently looking their way. "Listen, Lace, let's not say anything to Jan about this, okay? He's got enough on his plate right now. The last thing he needs is to worry about Sandy waking up."

Lacey made her lips-sealed gesture.

82

Hestia
Friday, April 17th

Never once in her many months of catatonia was Hestia bored. Without the mental facility to perceive the passage of time, boredom is not possible. But as she extended her awareness to more and more of her senses, her body, and the outside world, the interminable hours of sitting staring out the window were becoming increasingly intolerable.

To relieve the boredom, Hestia paid close attention to the comings and goings of the staff, the big fellow called Samson, in particular. Thankfully, he had stopped waving that gun-shaped thing at her head every hour or so. He still hovered close by, though, apparently waiting for her to utter some profundity.

She had learned, for example, where the aides and orderlies took their breaks and had overheard some of the gossip when Samson stopped there to chat while wheeling her to and from her room.

And once inside her room for the night, Hestia fully explored her body's abilities. Although the visiting physical therapist had done her best to keep her muscles from atrophying, she still felt weak and barely able to stand the first time she slid out from under the covers of her hospital bed. The cold of the tile floor was disturbing at first, but she quickly learned to counter it with an infusion of Flame's warmth.

Over the nights since her awakening had begun, Hestia's first tentative steps became an impatient pacing around her room, and ultimately surreptitious prowling of the hospital's deserted hallways.

So, when Samson wheeled her into the social worker's office and she overheard part of Ms. Stupine's phone conversation with someone named Deputy Jensen, two thoughts filled her mind.

First, the voice coming through the phone's tinny speaker struck a familiar chord within Hestia. A flicker of memory—fleeting images and sensations—flashed across her mind. They were both pleasant and disturbing, raising even higher her need for redemption and…forgiveness?

The words that familiar voice said were much more alarming, though.

"Jack? Did you say '*Jack*?'" the voice of the deputy asked.

"Why…," the social worker looked at Samson, who nodded. "Why, yes. According to our orderly, who is here on the call with us, she said, 'Be gone,' to someone named 'Jack.' Of course, there was no one—"

"Shit," the deputy blurted.

The social worker's tone reflected her distaste. "Really, Detective, such language. At first, Samson—that's the orderly—thought she was referring to that boy who was with us for a while. You know, the one who ran away?"

The deputy's own tone turned professional. "Probably not. We've identified the boy. His name is Billy Saint-Germain."

"Oh. 'Billy' and 'Jack' aren't really that similar, are they?"

Apparently ignoring the social worker's comment, what the deputy said next chilled Hestia's heart.

"Listen, Ms. Stupine. I'll come by tomorrow to interview her, but in the meantime, Sandy Adams needs to be moved to your secure wing. If she is waking up…" Her voice dropped to a mutter. "…and talking to Jack." The tone of command returned. "Nevermind. She needs to be locked up."

Samson was taken aback by Kathy's vehemence, and Stupine sniffed her disapproval.

"May I remind you, Deputy, that Ms. Adams has not been convicted of any crime, and we must assume she is—"

"Don't give me that bullshit. I saw what she did with my own two eyes, and my friend lives with the scars of her crime every day."

The deputy's words stirred the Flame within Hestia, and a new feeling—guilt—washed over her.

But Stupine was adamant. "Patient Adams has never exhibited any violent tendencies."

"Maybe not as your *patient*, but when she was awake, she killed her husband and nearly killed my friend."

Friend? Husband? Killed? Though she had the sense that those memories were forever lost, the deputy's allegations rang true within Hestia.

Stupine was having none of it, however. "Unproven allegations—"

The deputy was done arguing. "Enough! I'm ordering you, as the jurisdictional law officer of her case, to move her to the high-security wing of Wayne State Behavioral Hospital. Now!"

Sally Stupine's reply was cold. "As you *request*, Deputy. I will comply…once you have filed the appropriate paperwork, and I have reviewed it. Good day."

"Bi—" a second voice came through just before she hung up.

Samson stared at Stupine, who returned a sly smile.

"I'm sure the deputy is furiously looking for the proper paperwork to file," she said, then snickered and checked her watch. "And I'm late for an appointment...out of the office."

She reached for her coat hanging on the back of her door.

Samson asked, "And what should I do with Sandy?"

"Same thing you've been doing since she got here. We'll deal with the deputy's *request* when I return to the office...tomorrow."

"Okay," he said with a smile, then wheeled Sandy out of the office. As they headed down the hallway, he leaned over her and whispered, "Enjoy your last night of freedom. I hear the secure wing isn't nearly as...comfortable."

As she rolled past the other patients' rooms, a plan was already forming in Hestia's mind.

83

Jan

Friday, April 17th

Jan, Kathy, Lacey, and Amanda sat around her small dining room table. She had made a full pot of coffee after Jan told her they were all coming. In his bedroom, Billy played with some twenty-year-old toys Amanda had found in her attic.

"Sorry, I don't have anything to feed you," she said after introductions were done and they were all settled. "Jan didn't give me much of a heads-up."

"No problem," Kathy said with a smile. "We've already had breakfast." She turned her smile on Lacey and took her hand, then turned to Jan, and the smile disappeared. "Okay, Jan, what's this super-secret plan of yours?"

Jan sipped his coffee before starting. "Amanda, I've decided to take the Board's offer."

She breathed a sigh of relief. "Oh, thank God. I'm glad you'll be done with those stuck-up ass—"

She stopped herself, looking embarrassed.

"—holes," both Kathy and Lacey said in unison.

When the laughter died down, Jan continued. "I'll send in the signed papers later today, which means I'll probably lose access to the mine as soon as they get the email." The others stirred uncomfortably, so he added, "Don't worry, though. We won't need to go down there for what I'm thinking."

Kathy huffed impatiently. "Doesn't matter. It's still a crime scene until they pressure Peterson to take the tape down." She made an impatient gesture to Jan. "Come on, Jan. Out with it."

Smiling slyly, he looked at each of the others in turn, then said, "A séance—of sorts."

Pausing, he gauged their reaction, but there wasn't any, so he turned to Amanda.

"Can you, ah, channel Mollie again?"

Reluctantly, she nodded.

"We need Tim to come through Billy," he added, and Amanda started to protest. But Jan held up a hand to stop her. "If we don't bring Tim forward, Jack will, right?" After a second, Amanda nodded, and he continued, "And we don't want that, do we?"

This time, Amanda shook her head, but even more reluctantly this time.

"That leaves Jack," Kathy said, trying to hurry Jan along.

"Right." He turned to Lacey.

"Oh, no," Kathy spat. "You're not involving her in this mess."

Lacey nudged her with her shoulder. "I'm already involved, Kath." Then she turned to Jan. "What do you need me to do?"

He pulled a whiskey flask from his satchel.

"Just a little day drinking."

He told them how Jack had gotten drunk-sick in Billy, but Tim didn't.

"Lacey, you said that you can hold off Jack, right?"

"So far. At least outside the mine."

"Can you let him in enough to get him drunk?"

"That's your plan?" Kathy was exasperated. "Get him drunk? And then what?"

Amanda spoke up. "Maybe if he's drunk, Mollie can convince him to move on."

"Can you convince Mollie?" Kathy countered.

Amanda nodded slowly. "Yeah, I'm pretty sure I can. She wants both of her sons to go with her. Tim, especially, but Jack too."

"I don't like the whole idea," Kathy muttered.

Jan was tired of her negativity. "I'm open to suggestions if you have an alternative."

"Yeah, I have one," she said. Her voice was defiant. "Dynamite both the shaft and tunnel. Shut the whole damned thing down and lock Jack inside."

"And Tim, too?" Amanda asked.

Before Kathy could answer, Jan said, "And what if Jack isn't inside when you set it off? We don't know how he moves around, but he's clearly been here." He looked at Lacey. "And at Mackey House, apparently. Maybe other places, too." He returned his stare at Kathy. "Can you guarantee he'll be inside when the charges go off?"

Her silence confirmed his suspicion. Sulking, she got up from the table, distancing herself from the plan.

Smugly, Jan said, "I didn't think so." Turning to the others, he added, "Okay, shall we get started?"

Amanda nodded, and Lacey asked, "Should I start drinking?"

"No!" Kathy said. She looked around, a little embarrassed by her outburst. "You need to be in control when Jack…comes to you. And you need to have him be the one drinking— Oh, my God, I can't believe I'm buying into this stupid scheme."

She flopped down in the far corner of the couch. The others followed her into the living room.

"Good." Jan turned to Amanda and had her sit in one of the chairs. "Now, Amanda, listen to the sound of my voice," he said in a soothing voice.

But Amanda held up a hand to stop him. Instead, she closed her eyes and took three deep breaths. Her body hunched over a bit. When she opened them, Mollie looked out through her eyes. Her affect was that of a much older woman.

"Amanda told me your plan," she said.

"That fast?" Kathy asked, amazed in spite of herself.

Mollie simply nodded in reply. "Your plan might work, although if I can take just Tim with me this time, I will."

"And leave Jack?" Jan didn't like the sound of that as a partial solution.

Neither did Amanda, who reasserted herself. "What if Jack doesn't need Tim to possess Billy anymore?" She paused, listening to Mollie inside. Then she said forcefully, "No. I will not let you exchange one boy for the other."

Mollie returned to the surface as Billy walked into the room. Except his purposeful stride told everyone it wasn't Billy in control.

"Mom," Tim's voice was clear. "I won't go with you. Not without Jack."

Mollie leaped from the chair and knelt in front of the boy.

"Oh, Tim, my beloved little boy. You can't mean that."

"I won't leave my brother!" Tim shouted.

"You tell her, Bro," Jack's voice growled out of Lacey's mouth.

Kathy gasped as all heads turned to stare.

"We're a team, right, Little Man? And we have our own plan, don't we?" Then he looked down at the body he was inhabiting. "Oh, my. How about these?" He laughed as he fondled Lacey's breasts. Then he jerked back as if he'd been slapped.

"Get out, you fucking pervert," Lacey said, retaking control of her body.

"Lacey," Jan called out to get her attention.

Then he pointed at the flask in her hand and made a drinking gesture. But instead of taking a swig, Lacey shook her head fearfully. Instead, she squeezed her eyes shut, and her whole body shook violently.

Her struggle to evict the evil spirit lasted nearly a whole minute. Curses, first in one voice, then in the other, spilled out of her mouth. Finally, her shaking stopped, but her eyes remained closed. From his vantage point, Jan couldn't tell which persona had won.

In the meantime, Amanda also struggled to evict Mollie, shaking her head from side to side. Their mumbled argument, in both Amanda and Mollie's voices, was joined by Tim, and lasted longer than Lacey's struggle against Jack. Jan picked up only the gist of the occasional phrase coming from Amanda and Billy.

Amanda: "…listen to your mother…"

Tim: "…I *want* to be good, but Jack…"

Mollie: "…no, you *are* a good boy, Tim."

All the while, Amanda's voice contorted with fighting Mollie's urge to keep control of her body.

Finally, Tim cried out, "Yes, Mommy! I'll go with you, just please stop crying."

With tears streaming down her cheeks, Amanda at last relaxed and caught Billy as he collapsed and fell into a deep sleep.

When Lacey opened her eyes, she let out the breath she'd been holding. "Jack's gone," she whispered, then dropped wearily onto the couch next to Kathy.

Holding her, Kathy looked Jan in the eye. "Never again," she swore.

Amanda looked at the others with the sleeping boy in her arms. "Mollie and Tim are gone, too. For good this time."

Looking at the exhausted, frightened, and angry fragments of his plan, Jan just shrugged half-heartedly.

"Well, that didn't work," he admitted.

84

Kathy
Friday, April 17th

Kathy stomped around the living room while Amanda put Billy to bed.

"My God, Jan. That was so fucking irresponsible. I can't believe I let you talk me into allowing that."

Her comment pricked a long-standing annoyance. "Allowing that? You're not in control here? I don't need your permission—"

"What you *need* is a voice of reason, dammit. And besides, you're not in control, either. Of anything."

"What does that mean?" His anger was carried in the spittle flying out of his mouth.

But he knew what she meant, and she knew he did. Since his near death, he had become adrift. For months, he wasn't even able to get out of bed without Kathy's help. Even his novel, which had given him his only positive recognition, was nothing more than a retelling of how he had lost all control over his life. And it had branded him as a victim as deeply as the scars covering his body.

"You know what I mean." Kathy's voice dripped venom. "I've been your maid and your babysitter, and then you wrote that *story* that made you a whole shitpot full of money. And what did I get out of it?"

Jan was aghast. "You were the fucking hero of the story! Yeah, you helped me more than I deserved. That's for sure. But what do you want from me? Half the royalties? I've got news for you. They don't amount to much."

"Oh, for Christ's sake," Kathy began, but Lacey interrupted.

"That's enough! Both of you. Kath, Amanda and I went along with the plan willingly. It didn't work out, that's all. We'll figure something else out."

"Some of it worked," Amanda said as she came in from the bedroom hallway, though her tone was anything but conciliatory. "Mollie and Tim are gone."

"Gone? You mean like, gone, gone?" Jan asked.

She nodded, then frowned. "No trace left. I hadn't realized how she had left some…residue…behind before. Like there was always her scent or a faint touch of her always around." She shook her head. "But now she's gone."

"Whispery Voice is gone, too," Billy said from the doorway.

The others stared at him until Amanda rushed over and gathered him into her arms.

"He can speak," Jan said in amazement. He turned to Kathy. "See? Not a total failure."

"Not a *total* failure?" Amanda shouted. "Your stupid séance put all of us in danger." She hugged Billy even more tightly. "Especially Billy."

"We all agreed—"

"Bullshit! You bullied us into it. I should have put a stop to it." She looked at Lacey, then focused on Kathy. "We *all* should have."

Kathy's expression was dark, but she kept her mouth shut for a change.

"That leaves Jack," Lacey said to break the tension. "We need to get him into the mine." She reached out and took Kathy's hand. "So we can dynamite the place."

The other women nodded their agreement, then they all turned to Jan, who took a deep breath and nodded as well.

85

Kathy
Friday, April 17th

Lacey stood on Amanda's back deck and stiffened when Kathy walked up from behind and put her arms around her. After a moment she softened and leaned back into Kathy's embrace.

"It's chilly out here," Kathy whispered in her ear.

Her hinting invitation was obvious, but Lacey didn't take the bait. Instead, she raised a vape to her mouth and drew in a hit, then offered it to Kathy.

Kathy pulled back a little. "Ah, can't. You know. Random drug tests."

Lacey blew out a cloud of smoke into the cold air.

"Right. Today, Deputy-Detective, tomorrow, Sheriff. That's what you're aiming for, right?"

Kathy's response was a little defensive. "If I play my cards right."

Lacey nodded and stepped out of Kathy's arms.

"But shutting down the mine will basically be folding your hand. You'll be making some powerful enemies around here. They'll blame you for losing their investment. And without their support, you'll never win an election."

Kathy's voice was cold. "You're not telling me anything I don't already know. What's your point?"

Lacey's voice was just as cold when she met Kathy's eye and said, "Somebody else has to take the fall."

"There's nobody else—"

She froze when Lacey nodded toward the house, where Jan and Amanda seemed to be arguing.

"Oh, no."

"Hear me out," Lacey insisted. "He's already tried to convince the Board to shut it down, so he's on record opposing it. Plus, he's got a reputation—"

"Stop! He took their buyout. He's done with them."

"I'm just saying that somebody's got to trap Jack deep underground so he can't ever get out again. Whoever blows the place up is gonna have to face the consequences. You have a future in this town. What's he got?"

Kathy shook her head in disbelief. "You want me to railroad my…my best friend. Hell, my only friend." She saw how her words stung Lacey, but didn't regret what she had said. "He could—no, *would*—go to prison." Her voice rose in pitch and volume. "And it would be my job to put him there!"

Lacey drew herself up to her full height. "As opposed to *you* going to prison? The mayor and his cronies will demand their pound of flesh, so someone's going to prison. Who's it gonna be?"

Kathy closed her eyes and shook her head violently. "No," she said, then in a whisper, "No."

Try as she might, she couldn't think of a way out of the dilemma, and Lacey's cold practicality solidified an idea that had been brewing in her subconscious and brought it to the surface. She attacked on this new front.

"You should leave. Leave Dundee. Leave Wayne County. Go back to New York, or wherever. Do your podcast thing."

"What are you saying?"

"Look, we both have our ambitions. I want to be Sheriff, and you want to expand your market. Maybe even get a real reporter job, right? Philly or New York, or even with a network."

"You're right. I don't want to be stuck in Podunk Dundee any longer than I have to be. But reporting on the mine and whatever happens next—"

She froze, having said too much, but Kathy nodded knowingly. She tried to hide her disappointment and hurt at the implied betrayal with surliness.

"I get it. Jan and me, and Amanda and Billy. We're collateral damage to your ticket out, right? We're your reputation maker to get a bigger gig."

Lacey stepped forward, trying to hold Kathy's hands, but her lover—former lover now it seemed—backed away.

"Get out." Kathy made a cutting gesture when Lacey started to protest. "This—" She waved her hand between the two of them. "—is done. *We're* done. You need to get as far away from the mine and Jack's reach as possible. You're the sensitive one, his conduit to get out here into our world. If we're going to trap him in there, you can't be around to give him a chance to escape."

Lacey shuddered, then nodded. "Just thinking about him inside my head and my body… It's disgusting."

"See? You've got to go."

The pain in Kathy's voice made Lacey sigh.

"I'm going to miss you. Maybe when it's all over—"

Kathy held up a hand to stop her. "Listen. When this is over, if I'm still standing and not in jail, you can have an interview. That's all. I can't be with someone who would sell out their friends for a better job. And if I'm not still standing, stay the fuck away, because that'll mean Jack is still out there. And he won't let go of you next time."

Lacey stood silently, a tear glistening on her cheek.

Feeling her resolve beginning to slip, Kathy snatched the vape from Lacey's hand, took a hit, and tossed it back to her.

"Now, go the hell home."

86

Hestia
Friday, April 17th

Two thoughts chased each other in Hestia's mind as she paced back and forth in her room.

A single word, "Redemption," echoed inside her like the tolling of a church bell. All memories of her past life were gone, ripped from her along with the monster that Flame once was. All that remained was this one thought, this determination, this burning need for redemption. Redemption for what, exactly, was beyond her ken, but that didn't lessen the desire to make amends. To set right whatever her previous incarnation as Sandy was guilty of. That need was all-consuming.

The other thought that drove her relentless pacing was the phone conversation she had overheard. That eerily familiar voice on the other end of the line had insisted, had commanded, that her Sandy body be locked up for everyone's safety. That deputy, for whom she felt both a kinship and deep regret, believed she was danger personified. And her voice fueled that sense of guilt that demanded redemption. Whatever it was that she must pay for, that deputy was a major part of it.

Hestia snickered at the stupidity of that Stupine woman. Ignoring the deputy's command, keeping her unrestrained—she tested the unlocked doorknob for the fourth time—and free to roam about the facility was the height of arrogance. But she knew her freedom was short-lived, and once taken from her, it would be impossible for her to achieve her goal. She needed to act to set her plan in motion.

She stopped her pacing and stared out the window at the fading light. Samson had stopped by to take her temperature a few minutes before, and she knew from watching his comings and goings that his shift would end soon. It was time.

Listening at her door, she heard no noises in the hallway, so she eased it open and peeked first one way, then the other. The hall was deserted. The overhead lights dimmed for the evening. It was medication time for the more unruly patients, and Samson and the other staff members had moved on to another part of the building.

Tiptoeing down the hall in her bare feet, Hestia peered around the corner of the intersecting hallway. It too was dim and deserted. Halfway down, the light from the employee break room fanned out across the darkened floor. With her first objective in sight, she hurried past the closed doors of the maintenance rooms and storage closets that lined the hallway until she reached the break room.

A quick peek inside told her it was deserted as well. Moving silently, she opened the room's coat closet, and began searching the pockets of the jackets hanging there. On her third try, she found what she needed—a set of keys. Grabbing them, she strode to the window—the only one on this floor without bars— and tried to open it.

The old wood had swollen over the decades, and the sloppily applied layers of paint made it fit tightly in its frame. Try as she might, she couldn't budge it. Frustrated but undeterred, she turned her attention inward to where Flame waited.

I believe you need to be redeemed as much as I do, she thought. *Maybe more. Time to do your part.*

Channeling Flame's heat into her hands, she ran her fingers along the edges of the sash, softening the old, dry paint until it ran freely. Then after a mighty push, the window flew open and the chilly, early Spring air flooded in.

We need your warmth, she thought, and Flame complied, making Hestia comfortable, even though she was barefoot and wearing only her hospital pajamas and robe.

Dropping the six feet to the ground, she ran along the side of the building to the back parking lot. Understanding of her surroundings came to her as she needed it, though her personal memories were long gone. So, when she reached the array of vehicles, she ran along the line of them, hitting the key fob's unlock button until a set of lights flashed and a doorlock clicked.

Climbing into the spacious interior, she smelled the familiar scent of Samson's aftershave.

Well, let's try not to wreck this thing. He'll be in enough trouble for letting me escape.

After a moment of fiddling with the seat controls, she put the vehicle in gear. Resisting the urge to peel out of the lot, she drove as discreetly as a large SUV could around to the front and down the long driveway to the main road.

At the "T" intersection, she faced a dilemma. Her plan was an *escape* plan, which she had executed flawlessly. However, she hadn't considered what she would do, or where she would go once free. In other words, how was she to achieve her goal of redemption? She didn't know, but one thing she was sure of was that it involved the evil Ghost.

With trepidation, she reached her own mental tendrils into the netherworld, seeking its essence, though careful not to arouse its notice.

There.

She sensed Ghost's ethereal presence, and using it as a beacon, she turned left and sped down the road.

87

Lacey, Kathy, Jan, & Hestia
Friday, April 17ᵗʰ

Lacey

Lacey couldn't stop the tears. It didn't make sense. She was a strong woman who had never been head-over-heels in love before. She'd never really been in love at all. And she wasn't even sure she was in love with Kathy. Oh, the attraction was there—had been there—for sure. Physical attraction for sure, but there was something more. A strength that went all the way to her core. But a softness, too, that showed itself only after you melted her hard exterior. But there was still that iron core that wouldn't break, or even bend. That combination had pulled her in like a magnet—or like a moth to a flame.

Tonight, that steel core showed itself through her loyalty to Jan, her not-boyfriend. They clearly shared a bond that went all the way to that core. That shared past, which Lacey knew only the barest hints of, was stronger to Kathy than a promising future with Lacey. It just didn't seem fair.

As she eased her car to a stop at a stop sign, she took a deep breath and held it. To her left lay the path back to New York, her apartment, and her small-market podcast. To her right, the road climbed the ridge, then dipped along Wolf's Creek and past the key to her future.

Down that road lay the answers to the strangeness of the past few days. She may have left a potential love affair behind, but she still had a job to do in Dundee. She had a story to report, and it was a juicy one. One possible future, sweet though it was, had become mist in her memory. But another, one that Kathy had skewered with that damned detective mind of hers, still lay before her. Down that way to her right lay the mine tunnel and the source of the story that would vault her all the way to the networks. Letting out her breath, she turned right.

Kathy

Once Lacey was gone, Kathy went back inside, where Amanda and Jan, arms crossed, were now standing in opposite corners of the room, while Billy calmly played with toy trucks. The scene looked so discordant, so out of balance, that Kathy's breath caught in her throat.

Earlier, she had envisioned a future where her best friend had found his forever family, and she was still…alone. Instead, though, the tension in the room was palpable. She let out a sigh.

Jan looked at her and said, "So, what do we do now?"

She shrugged. "Don't know. Lacey's…"

"Gone," he said. "We know. Look, we've done this before. Hell, *you've* done this before. We can do it again."

"You're not even considering going with her, are you?" Amanda protested.

Kathy could tell this was the latest foray in an ongoing argument.

Offended, Jan said, "Of course. I can't let her do this alone."

"Why the hell not?" Kathy spit out. She knew that if that vision of domestic bliss was ever to come true, she had to push him away. "I saved your ass last time, remember? I don't want to have to do it again."

Jan folded his arms across his chest. "And how do you propose to take Jack out by yourself?"

Kathy raised her chin indignantly. "I have a plan."

Jan raised an eyebrow. "You're going to seal him inside, aren't you?"

"Maybe."

Jan snorted and shook his head, then met her eyes.

"Well, there are two entrances, remember? Whatever your plan is, it'll take two people."

"Idiots," Amanda muttered.

"What?" Jan's voice raised in anger.

Before things could get out of hand, Kathy stepped in.

"Listen, I get it. You've got to protect Billy. That means staying as far away from that damned hole in the ground as possible. But it's my job to protect and serve the rest of this godforsaken town. Even if they don't want me to."

"And I need to protect Kathy," Jan said, barely above a whisper.

"Her?" Amanda asked, tears gathering in her eyes. "What about me? And Billy?"

"Don't make me choose between—" he pleaded.

Amanda's response was ice cold. "You already have. You did a long time ago."

They stood, staring at each other for several heartbeats.

Finally, Jan's voice was deadly serious when he said, "You'd better pack."

The others both looked at him questioningly, and he shrugged.

"If we fuck this up, Jack will be even stronger."

Kathy was nodding. "And even more pissed," she added. "He's right. You should pack up what you can and get the hell out of here."

"And go where?" Amanda protested. "If you don't get rid of Jack, …" She looked around the room at the pictures on the walls and the fire in the fireplace. "This is my home," she whispered.

Jan's voice had a hitch in it when he said, "You can make a home anywhere. Find a safe place for Billy."

Amanda opened her mouth to protest, then paused. After a moment, she shook her head and grabbed Jan's hands.

"I'm staying. I believe in you—in both of you. You call me the minute, the moment, you send the bastard to Hell."

Jan and Kathy exchanged a look, then he turned to Amanda. "Look, I'm leaving here. Leaving Dundee, and Pennsylvania, probably." He squeezed her hands. "Come with me. I have money now. Let's explore the country. Find a place to settle down—without fucking ghosts."

Amanda shook her hands free. The look on her face reflected both her devastation and determination. "How long have you been planning to leave us?" Her voice was cold.

"I'm not trying to *leave* you. I'm trying to take you—both of you—with me."

She turned away and wiped an angry tear. "Go. Go fight your demons. Both real and imagined." When Jan opened his mouth to continue the argument, she shouted, "Get out!"

Stunned, he stood frozen until Kathy gently grabbed his arm and nodded toward the door.

Once outside, she mumbled, "That went well."

"Fuck."

Lacey

The hike through the woods and across the rickety old bridge left Lacey wet and cold. But her ambition drove her to at least get some B-roll footage on the 4K camera she carried. And if she could find a suitable spot to prop the cam, she might even be able to shoot a remote report.

Slowly panning the small, hand-held steady cam, she smiled to herself as she visualized how to apply filters in the editing room to maximize the spookiness of the scene.

It won't take much. This is pretty damned spooky by itself, she thought.

With a good two minutes of her approach to the tunnel in the can, she propped the camera on a boulder to get an establishing shot of the tunnel door still wrapped in crime scene tape, then stepped into the shot.

"This is Lacey Devine reporting from the entrance to a previously unknown tunnel that leads into—"

She jerked and swayed as a wave of dizziness swept over her.

"Welcome, my dear. This is an unexpected pleasure."

Jack's words appeared in her mind like a whisper, but with each word, that whisper became stronger.

"Come closer—"

Get out of my head! Lacey fought back. She had managed to expel the lascivious ghost before, so she thought she could handle it again. She was wrong.

"Not so fast, Lover. You're in my domain now."

Jack's grip on her mind was cold, so cold. She opened her mouth to scream, but a terrified gasp was all she could muster. It was the last action of her body that he didn't control.

No! No…no.

Her voice, her thoughts, her very will faded to a background shimmer in her mind.

"Now, this is what I'm talkin' about," Jack's gleeful voice came from her mouth.

Her hands—his hands now—roamed over her breasts through her jacket. Unsatisfied, he unzipped the coat. Feeling the chill raise his nipples to hard points, he chuckled and walked Lacey into the tunnel.

"Let's see what I can do with this body."

Jan

Kathy's SUV sped away from the curb in front of Amanda's house. The parting from Amanda and Billy still had Jan's heart hurting. It had taken some harsh words to get Amanda to agree to take Billy and head for the hills. Words that couldn't be taken back. But that was a worry for tomorrow—if there was a tomorrow for him, or Kathy.

"Okay, I think I know what you're planning," he said, then had to grip the handle above his door as Kathy slid the car around a turn. "Jesus. Don't kill us on the way to our probable demise."

She chuckled. "Always looking for the artistic turn of phrase, aren't you?"

He shrugged and offered his own chuckle. "It's kinda what I do."

"Well, you'd better start writing this *story*." Her voice turned deadly serious. "It ain't likely either of us will be around this time tomorrow."

"Thanks for reminding me." He held on as she took another turn of the mountain road too fast. "So, how're we going to do this?"

Kathy glanced over at him, then nodded toward the SUV's cargo area. The back seat was folded down, and the entire space was filled with wooden boxes. He didn't really need to read the labels, but he lit his phone, anyway.

"'Hercules Powder Works,'" he read. "Wait, how old is this stuff?"

Kathy just shrugged.

"Where did you get it?"

"Evidence locker in the station basement. Pretty sure nobody knew it was in there."

"For how long?"

She shrugged again. "Paperwork on it's long gone."

"Holy shit! Dynamite destabilizes over time, doesn't it?"

Before she could answer, the SUV's right front tire hit a pothole that nearly bounced Jan out of his seat.

"Fuck," Kathy muttered and let up on the gas pedal a bit.

"Let's try to avoid blowing ourselves up *before* we get to the mine, shall we?"

"Yeah, yeah. Fuck off."

After a second, they both burst out laughing.

Lacey

Clawing at the edges of Jack's essence, Lacey tried in vain to regain control of her body. She watched, helpless, as he walked her like a puppet through the tunnel and into a dark room carved from the native stone. Using her muscle memory, he set up the camera facing a half-deflated air mattress lying on the floor and switched on its light.

Disgusted, she fought back as best she could as his fumbling hands fondled her body, all in full view of the video camera. The sour smell of stale blood filled her nostrils and, if she had had control of her stomach, she would have vomited.

Adrift, her mind tried to partition off what was happening to her body, but that only drew her farther back from the real world. Afraid that she was losing any connection to herself, Lacey felt like she was drowning in a sea of hopelessness.

But, as her last vestige of selfdom was shredding apart, she felt another presence reaching up from that netherworld that threatened to consume her. The presence had no voice, only a warmth that she somehow found reassuring, almost comforting. The warmth buoyed her up. She again had contact with the outside world, though only its sights and sounds. What she heard and saw both terrified her and filled her with hope. The terror came from watching her own hands clawing at her body. The hope came from the influence of that new presence, who at last, offered a name—Flame.

Hestia

Following Ghost's trail was easier than she expected. At each intersection of back roads, she knew instinctively when to turn and in which direction, as if she had lived in these mountains her whole life, which, upon reflection, she realized she probably had.

When her ethereal compass pointed off the road toward Wolf's Creek and the mountain beyond, she pulled over and parked behind another SUV. Unsure if the presence of another person was a good or bad sign, she set off down the overgrown path toward her destiny. And her redemption.

While Flame kept her body and bare feet warm enough, it could do nothing about the sticks and stones underfoot. Months of disuse had rendered the soles of her feet tender and soft, offering little protection. Undeterred, she plunged on, despite the self-inflicted assault. By the time she reached the ragged police tape littering the ground in front of the open door into darkness, her feet were leaving a bloody trail.

Stepping into the tunnel, Hestia let her eyes adjust to the darkness. In a moment, she could see a faint glow ahead. Ghost's presence was like a cold shadow permeating the very air, and Hestia shivered, despite Flame's warming touch.

The tunnel's rough floor did more damage to her feet as she sneaked forward, but she was past the point of even acknowledging the pain. She was solely focused on her goal, her redemption, which she now understood was ridding the world of Ghost's evil presence. And that goal lay just ahead.

The glow of artificial light came from a room ahead and to her right. When she stepped into the open doorway, she was disgusted by what she saw.

In the harsh glow of the camcorder's light, a woman lay on the floor upon a mattress stained, as were the walls and floor, with the blood of dead youths. The woman, Ghost's unwilling vehicle, was on her back, naked to the waist. One hand squeezed her breasts, while the other was buried between her legs.

"Pig!" Hestia shouted, startling Ghost, but only momentarily.

"Ah, you've awakened, my pretty! Come and join our party," he said through the woman's mouth.

Sneering, Ghost reached the tendrils of his possession toward Hestia, but she easily swatted them away. Instead, she called forth Flame, who lit flames from her fingertips.

"Get thee gone, Demon," she growled.

At the sight of the flames, Ghost drew back into the hapless woman, who pushed back off the mattress and across the stone floor until she was flat against the wall.

As Hestia stepped further into the room, she let Flame raise the fire even higher. The red glow of her flames mixed with the harsh light of the camera, making an orange radiance that suffused the space.

Another step forward. But then Hestia stopped her advance. The woman cowering in the corner stared at her in terror. Ghost had retreated far enough to let her fear show through.

A barely audible, "Help me," escaped her lips.

Lacey

When Flame reared up into the demon Jack's awareness, a wave of fear rushed from him down through her, and she recognized the room where she lay. She was gazing out into the room where the murders of those kids had taken place. The residue of those killings still lingered in the stains, the smells, and in the very air of the place.

But the fear that swept over her was not born of these things. Rather, its source was the terrifying figure standing in the open doorway.

A young woman stood with her arms extended. From the tips of her fingers, orange and red flames extended, reaching out for Lacey. Reflexively, she pushed herself backward until her back collided with the rough stone wall. The terror that filled her, though, was somehow cleansing. *She* had commanded her body to withdraw. It was *she* who raised her hands to ward off this new threat. Jack had relinquished control, hiding deep within her.

To the flaming woman, she whimpered, "Help me."

A response touched her mind, but it was not directed at her.

"Killing this innocent will not lead to our redemption."

The advancing fire woman stopped, acknowledging the thought. Then she answered Lacey's plea.

"We will help you. But you must hold onto Jack. Don't let him escape."

Although feeling Jack trying to slip away was a relief, Lacey understood the message. She must become the captor, not the captive.

The young woman, her fire extinguished, cocked her head as if listening, then backed out of the room. The sound of the latch being thrown sent a chill through Lacey, but also strengthened her hold on Jack.

Jan

Kathy slammed on the brakes and skidded to a stop barely inches from the bumper of another SUV parked behind a third one.

"Who—?" Jan started to ask, but Kathy was already out of the car.

Standing in the road, she scanned the other two SUVs.

"Fuck, fuck, fuck."

Jan came around to stand beside her. "What—? Oh, shit," he muttered when he recognized the first SUV in line. "What's Lacey doing here?"

All Kathy said in reply was, "Damn fool."

Then she headed down the path toward the tunnel.

Hurrying along behind her, Jan asked, "Whose is the other car?"

"Don't know."

"Shouldn't we bring the dynamite?"

Kathy stopped in her tracks and spun on him.

"Will you shut up and stop asking questions I can't answer? We need to figure out what's going on here before we start blowing shit up."

She turned and continued down the path while Jan nodded and shrugged. "Makes sense."

Under the cover of the trees, there was barely enough light from the full moon to see the ground, so Kathy fished a flashlight out of her pocket.

"You got another one of those?" Jan asked, but only got a derisive snort in response.

By the time they reached the tunnel entrance, scudding clouds obscured the moon, leaving it fully dark outside. But the darkness inside the tunnel was muted by a faint glow.

"Stay behind me," Kathy said as she turned off the flashlight, drew her service weapon, and clicked off the safety.

Got another one of those, Jan wanted to ask, but was afraid she might actually have one.

Pressed against the rough-cut wall of the tunnel, they slowly crept into the darkness. After half a dozen careful steps, Kathy froze as they rounded a bend to find the source of the light. A silhouetted figure stood in the lighted doorway of the murder room.

As the figure stepped into the room and its shadow was cast across the floor, Kathy and Jan heard a disturbingly familiar voice say, "Pig!"

A moment later, their eyes were dazzled by a fiery orange glow, which cut off just before the figure stepped out of the murder room and slammed the door shut. In the total darkness, Jan heard the heavy breathing of the unknown woman standing just feet in front of them.

Kathy raised her weapon, and her flashlight flared to life, pinning the intruder in its beam. What it revealed astounded them both.

Standing barefoot in torn and dirty hospital clothing was a petite, blond-haired young woman. Her right arm was across her face, shielding her eyes from the flashlight's glare. Jan didn't need to see her face to recognize her, though.

"S—Sandy?"

Hestia lowered her arm and squinted into the light.

"Not Sandy…Hestia."

A stunned Kathy found her voice. "No, you're Sandy. Sandy Adams."

Hestia slowly shook her head. "Not Sandy. She is gone. Only Hestia and—only Hestia remains."

Jan's mind was racing, putting puzzle pieces in place.

"Hestia. Greek goddess of the hearth. Keeper of the flame." His voice caught on the last. "Is Flora with you, too?"

Again, Hestia shook her head, more annoyed this time. "Flora is gone too. Gone with Sandy. Only Hestia remains."

With that, she spread her hands, palms up, and small balls of flame rose from her palms.

"Oh, shit!" Jan barked, backing up into the wall of the tunnel. "Shoot her, Kathy. Shoot her, dammit!"

Her voice shaky but her aim steady, Kathy said, "I'm not shooting anyone. Not yet." Then to Hestia, "Put your fire away, San—ah, Hestia."

After a moment, the fireballs winked out.

"Your voices are…familiar to me. You knew Sandy, and…Flora. Well, I think."

"You got that right," Jan muttered.

"But you fear them. Why?"

"Why?" Indignant, Jan stepped forward, pulling up his sleeves. He thrust his arms into the flashlight's beam. "This is why. These scars and all the others covering my body. That's why."

Hestia

Hestia staggered back. The voices and the scars shattered the wall that shielded her from her previous life. That dam broken, memories flooded over her, threatening to drown her in guilt and regret.

The screams of Dan, her husband, echoed in her mind as the memory of what Sandy and Flora immolated him.

Their final evil act—burning Jan alive—replayed itself in her thoughts.

Deep within, Flame cried out in anguish, and Hestia dropped to her knees, broken.

"Oh," Hestia moaned. Then, barely above a whisper, "That is what is to be redeemed."

"Redeemed?" Jan sputtered. "You can't *redeem* what Sandy and Flora did unless you can heal *me*."

"But you can save yourself," Kathy interjected, patting Jan on the arm to calm him down. She lowered her weapon and turned her flashlight on the door. "Lacey is in there, isn't she? With Jack."

Hestia nodded, kneeling on the hard ground. "Your Lacey, yes. I tried to drive Ghost—Jack—from her with Flame, but I still feel his presence." She stared at the closed door. "He is still with her."

Kathy jumped to the door. "We've got to save her from him."

Before she could unlatch it, though, Jan grabbed her arm.

"How? How do we get him out of Lacey without letting him escape?"

Before Kathy could answer, they were bathed in fiery red light, which was at first warm, then became a terrible heat. Backing away and shielding their own eyes this time, they felt and saw a terrible sight. Hestia, naked, her hospital clothes burned away, was sheathed in Flame. She rose from her knees and drove them further back toward the tunnel's exit.

Raising a hand, the murder room door burst into flame, and Hestia walked through it.

The gut-wrenching sound that followed was a combination of both a high-pitched scream and a deep growl.

Lacey

After struggling so mightily to rid herself of Jack's control, holding onto him to prevent his escape seemed, to her emotional self, stupid. But her logical self knew he must be destroyed, and if he disappeared back into the netherworld where he had existed for more than a hundred and fifty years, he would always be a threat. It was these doubts, the conflict between her thoughts and her emotions, that loosened her grip.

It was only a momentary lapse. Only a fragment of a thought's conception. But Jack somehow sensed her indecision and squeezed almost fully out of her grasp.

Clenching her eyes shut, Lacey gripped tighter, pinching his tendrils between her mental fingers. But, like trying to snatch a greased rope, she felt Jack sliding from her control. Terrified that she was losing the battle and focused solely on the internal mental contest, she didn't notice when the door reopened.

So, when Jack froze in shock, she imagined that her mental fingers were tipped with talons and she dug them in deeply. Only then did her closed eyes register the heat and brilliance of the fiery figure that had entered the chamber.

The petite and terrible woman from before, now naked and sheathed in flames, strode toward her. Fearing immolation, Lacey pushed herself along the wall into the farthest corner. The scream that filled the room was both hers and Jack's.

But her fear abated when the essence of Flame clamped an iron grip onto Jack, then gently opened Lacey's grip.

"We have him now," came through clearly.

And to illustrate the point, Flame dug his burning heat deeply into Jack. This time, the scream that followed could only be heard in the space between this world and the netherworld.

Lacey was free.

Kathy

The screams broke Kathy free of her shock. Rushing to the door, she was momentarily blinded by Hestia's fire-clad form.

"Holy shit."

She heard the epithet, unsure whether it was Jan or herself who had uttered the words. But seeing Lacey cowering in the corner sent her running toward her former lover. After two steps, though, Hestia's outstretched flaming arm stopped her in her tracks.

"Not yet," the burning woman said, her voice somehow more than human.

Reaching out her arms, her fingers became claws grasping the air. They slowly closed into fists and, as if she were dragging a heavy load toward her, her arms flexed.

"Take her now," Hestia said, and her voice rang like a bell in the enclosed space.

Sliding along the wall past Hestia's outstretched, burning arms, Kathy felt Jan grasp her hand. Together, they rushed to where Lacey lay, dazed. Helping her to her feet, they each slung an arm over their shoulders and turned to face Hestia. She drew her tight fists all the way to her chest.

"Run," she calmly said, but her voice shook the very air and made the rock around them hum.

Carrying Lacey between them, they made it through the door and were stumbling up the tunnel when a blast of heat pushed them along even faster. Thankfully, the fresh outside air revived Lacey enough for her to find her own footing, and the three ran down the trail toward the bridge over Wolf's Creek. As they crossed it, Hestia's voice echoed up and down the valley.

"I am *redeemed*!"

A blast shook the mountain and the ground they stood on, throwing them to their knees. It was followed by a deep rumbling that grew until they heard the unmistakable sound of millions of tons of rock collapsing into the voids left by those lost miners and the thousands of others who had carved caverns into the mountain by hand.

Dust and chunks of rock flew from the tunnel mouth like cannon shot. Hurrying across the bridge and safely away from the flying debris, Kathy, Lacey, and Jan collapsed onto the trail.

Lying on his back and breathing heavily, Jan managed to say, "I guess we didn't need the dynamite."

Lacey let out a barking laugh, and Kathy punched him in the shoulder.

Hestia

Her flames extinguished and her body pulverized by the mountain, the presence that was Hestia gathered Flame and the weeping essence of Jack into herself. But unsure how to finally achieve her goal, she reached out into the void for help.

The answer to her plea came immediately. Mollie and Tim reached out to the three-turned-one and gently guided them on to the next world.

88

Kathy
Saturday, April 18ᵗʰ

Kathy slouched in the chair in front of Sheriff Peterson's desk. He leaned back in his desk chair and propped his feet up on the old desk. With a wry smile, he raised his whiskey glass in a silent salute. With a nod, she hoisted her own, then sipped the brown liquor.

Wincing, she said, "You couldn't spare the good stuff for this celebration?"

"Is this a celebration?" He eyed her suspiciously. "Seems to me this town has just encountered quite a setback for the local economy."

He looked out the window of his office to the town square, where the stage for the gala announcement of the opening of the Lost Miners Coal Mine Tour stood empty.

Kathy shrugged and sipped her whiskey again—without making a face, this time.

"You know how I felt about that whole thing."

"Yeah. 'Blast the damned thing shut,' I think you said."

She nodded. "Something like that."

"And conveniently, it decided to *spontaneously* blow itself up."

Kathy didn't like the implication in either his words or his tone.

"A geologist from The U took a look this morning. Probably a buildup of methane gas, he says." When Peterson didn't react, she continued. "All the activity stirred up down there by the mayor's son might have caused a fresh out-gassing."

"Is that what your expert says?"

Kathy raised an eyebrow. "What's your point?"

Peterson shook his head. "No point. Just pointing out the coincidence. That one and the other one."

"The other one?"

"Yeah. How was it that you were the first one on-scene?"

Kathy thought back to the aftermath. Transferring the boxes of old dynamite to the stolen SUV and convincing Jan to drive them home and unload them into her garage at Mackey House. Saying a final—maybe—goodbye to Lacey before sending her away to help Jan and ditch the extra SUV, then waiting the scant few minutes before the patrol officer and Staties arrived to investigate the blast. She had been up all Friday night and most of Saturday coordinating the search of the scene.

Yawning and ignoring the sheriff's question, she changed the subject. "The job's not done, you know. The back entrance through the tunnel is completely blocked, but the main shaft is still open."

Peterson shrugged. "It's been that way for longer than anyone around here has been alive. What's *your* point?"

"It's gotta be awful tempting to sightseers and other…weirdos. We should blast the shit out of that hole in the ground, too."

To her surprise, the sheriff nodded. "Yup. Agreed. And, come to think about it, I believe back when I was a pup officer,

I encountered a load of explosives down there in the basement of this very building. I bet they're still sitting there."

Kathy paled, and her mouth dropped open. To cover her reaction, she said, "You mean we're sitting on top of old, like *really old*, dynamite?"

The corner of his mouth curled up. "Yeah, you should really do something about that."

"Me?"

Without answering, he took a sheet of paper out of a drawer and slid it across the desk.

"What's this?" Kathy said as she leaned forward, then she gasped when she saw the subject. Her head snapped up, and she stared into his eyes. "You really are retiring?" She read further. "As of tomorrow? For real?"

"Yep. Filed it with the county this morning, Interim Sheriff Jensen."

It took her a second to process the last.

"'Interim Sheriff?'" she repeated.

"That's right. It's my prerogative to name my replacement until approved by the county commissioners. Do me proud, Kaveetha. And don't fuck this up."

After they shared a laugh and a congratulatory drink, he eyed her over the rim of his glass.

"I agree your first order aught to be sealing off the mine entrance. I wouldn't use the stuff in the basement, though. It's been down there a long time. It's probably not very stable. Better call the state's bomb squad to have it removed."

His stare was like an eagle eyeing a rabbit.

"Ah, yeah. I guess I'd better call Dad."

"Not a bad idea." He sipped his drink. "And, Kathy—" He waited until she met his eyes. "—be careful. I never said it was dynamite."

89

Jan
Sunday, April 17th

Jan whisked the eggs and milk in a bowl. The scent of frying bacon filled the kitchen. It was probably the smell that brought Kathy out of her apartment. She was wearing a ratty bathrobe and fuzzy slippers. Her hair poked out from her head in several directions.

"You're…cooking?"

Jan pretended indigence. "I'm not a Neanderthal, you know. Besides," he said as he dipped the bread in the eggs, milk, cinnamon, and nutmeg mixture, "it's just French Toast and bacon. How hard can it be?"

Before the last words were out of his mouth, the bacon grease flared up into flames two feet high. Jan froze in shock. Grabbing a towel, Kathy slid the pan off the hot burner onto an unlit one, then smothered the flames with the towel.

"Jesus, Jan!" she said, then she saw the terrified look on his face and her voice softened. "Burner was too hot. No harm, no foul."

Letting out a sigh, Jan felt embarrassed and chagrined. "Sorry. I probably would have just stood here and let the place burn down around me." He turned off the burner and stepped away from the stove. "Don't like fire."

"Understandable," Kathy whispered as she retrieved the scorched towel from the pan. Picking up a piece of bacon, she popped it into her mouth. "Mmm. Smoky."

Feeling a type of love for this woman he had never experienced with any other, he put his arm around her waist and leaned his head on her shoulder.

"I don't know what I'm going to do without you."

She turned to face him and put her hands on his shoulders. Feeling his hands on her hips in a completely nonsexual embrace filled his heart.

Kathy must have felt the same way, because her voice had a hitch in it when she said, "So you're really leaving?" He just nodded in response. "I can't believe I'm saying this, but I really will miss you." She turned back to the stove, which broke their physical connection, but her words cemented their emotional one.

"I'll miss you, too." IIis eyes fell on the door to the basement, where so many bad things had happened. "Can't say I'll miss this place, though."

"I don't know. It's kind of grown on me."

He rubbed the scars on his arms. "Like a fungus."

Ignoring the jab, she asked, "So, no ties remaining?"

He knew what she was hinting at and shook his head.

"Amanda won't return my calls. I burned that bridge pretty thoroughly." He thought for a moment, then said, "I expected the Board to file a lawsuit to try to get their buyout back, but…" He shrugged.

"Given the possibility of criminal charges because of their incredible negligence for not clearing the very volatile methane gas from the second mine entrance, I think they have other issues to think about."

Plucking the still-smoking bacon from the pan, he chuckled, hearing the implied threat as clearly as the Board must have, and smiled. "Thanks."

Deflecting, she asked, "Where will you head to?"

Jan shrugged and flipped the French toast. "No idea. I'm just going to drive until I get tired of driving. I'm sure I'll find a nice, quiet place where I can settle down to write."

"Who'll be the hero in this one?" She paused, then said, "Sandy?"

He snorted and then got serious. "'Not Sandy. Hestia.'"

Kathy just nodded. "Right. And Flame. Don't forget Flame."

EPILOGUE

One Month Later

Jan checked off the last item on his list and locked the RV's rear storage compartment. He turned when he heard Kathy approaching.

"Snacks for the road," she said as she handed him a baggie of homemade cookies tied with a red ribbon.

He took the gift, and then without thinking, wrapped her in a bear hug. After the briefest hesitation, she threw her arms around his neck, and they squeezed each other.

"Shit, Dude," she said through tears. "It's not like you're dying." Suddenly, her face froze in terror. "You're not, right?"

"No!" he said, laughing. "I do feel like I need to be reborn, though. Like this is another trip through the metaphorical birth canal."

Kathy snorted. "Always the poetical turn of phrase."

"It's what I do."

He walked to the RV's passenger door and placed the gift bag on the seat.

"You know," he said without turning, "there's an empty seat."

Kathy smiled. "It's not for Amanda?"

He shook his head and turned around. "No. That never would have worked out." He touched the scars on his neck. "Too much baggage."

He held out his hands, palms up. Kathy looked down at them, then put her hands in his.

"I was serious about the empty seat," he whispered.

She shook her head. "Too much to do here."

Looking almost relieved, he said with a smile, "That's right. I understand congratulations are in order, *Sheriff* Jensen."

"*Interim* Sheriff. How'd you—"

"Oh, the word's all over town," he said, chuckling. Then he got serious. "Any problems getting elected? The 'owners' spawn' must be pretty pissed."

She shrugged. "An exploding mine could have gotten a whole lot of people killed."

"Not to mention the mayor's son's *activities*."

"Right. I expect their full support."

After slamming the door, he opened his arms again. Accepting her hug, he whispered in her ear, "Well, if it doesn't work out, shotgun will always be yours."

Stepping back, she wiped a tear from his cheek. "The way you drive?" Then she wiped away her own.

Their shared laugh would be their last memory…for a while.

THE END

It was great spending a few months with Kathy, Jan, Barb, and Jim again. And getting to know Amanda and Lacey was a blast as well. If you haven't read the first book in this "series," *The Ghost of Mackey House*, you should check it out. I hope I didn't spoil it too much in this one.

The plot of *Mollies' Ghost* (and I hope by now you understand that the apostrophe is *not* in the wrong place) is inspired by an actual mine disaster that took place in the Plymouth Township in the anthracite coal region of Northeastern Pennsylvania.

In 1869, the Avondale Collery, was configured just as I described the Avon Hill Mine—a single shaft with the breaker building built right above it. At the end of a miners' strike, during which the Mollie Maguires and Pinkertons were violently active, the wooden cribbing and walls of the single hoist/ventilation shaft caught fire, trapping one hundred and twenty-two men and boys within the mine. All perished.

Two more men were lost when they were overcome by the poisonous gas while trying to recover the bodies. The loss of those one hundred twenty-four lost souls constituted the worst mining disaster in the history of anthracite coal mining.

The source of the fire—whether incorrectly stoking the ventilation furnace; the Pinkertons, operating on the owners' behalf, punishing the miners; or sabotage by rival miners or mine owners—is still a controversial subject in Plymouth. I witnessed this firsthand when I attended an annual remembrance ceremony and a mining engineering professor from Penn State made a pretty unconvincing presentation that argued it was the miners' fault.

The living and working conditions of the miners and their families are well-documented in a variety of books that I used for reference, for example, *Tragedy at Avondale: The Causes, Consequences, and Legacy of the Pennsylvania Anthracite Industry's Most Deadly Mining Disaster, September 6, 1869* by Robert P. Wolensky and Joseph M. Keating, and others. The level of brutality and disregard for life and limb that they faced is, to today's more enlightened eyes, frankly appalling.

At the end of *Mollies' Ghost*, Jan and Kathy go their separate ways alone. Whether they stay that way forever is open to debate and, since I control their fate, right now is simply taking place within the confines of my twisty mind. I'd love to hear your feedback, though, Faithful Reader, on what their future may hold.

Until next time…

R.A. (Rob) Johnson
April 2026

Acknowledgements

As always, there are several people to thank for their help in putting this novel together. First and foremost is my daughter, Carly. She is perhaps the most objective critique of my work, and without her feedback, this would be a much weaker story.

Similarly, I'd like to thank my other beta readers, Carol, Adele, Emily, Steve, and Ka'u'i, who all gave me their insights and feedback.

A special thanks to the folks at the Lackawanna County Coal Mine Tour for their inspiration and for patiently answering my innumerable questions when I visited. I'm very happy they let me use the entrance to the #190 Shaft on the cover, and for their enthusiastic support.

Finally, I'd like to give special thanks to Carol, my biggest fan, for her love and support.

So, what's next? Look for a serial science fiction novel, *Roanoke Colony*, coming sometime in 2026. After that, along with sort-of-weekly flash fiction pieces and hopefully-monthly short stories, who knows?

If you want to keep up-to-date with my writing journey, you can subscribe to my monthly newsletter at https://rajohnsonauthor.com.

You can reach me directly via email at rob@rajohnsonauthor.com. I'd love to hear from you.

As always, a review with lots of stars wherever you found *Mollies' Ghost* will be greatly appreciated and very helpful. Thanks in advance for your support.

R.A. (Rob) Johnson
April 2026

Titles by R.A. Johnson

Fiction

Ghostly Poconos Series
The Ghost of Mackey House
Mollies' Ghost

The Enclave Series (Historical Thrillers)
#1 The Templar Lance
#2 Lady 355: Mother of Freedom
#3 Shroud of Doubt

Fantasy
Tales from the Wood

Science Fiction
Roanoke Colony (coming Summer 2026)

Collections
Starside Interlude and Other Stories

Non-Fiction

*Mental Crudites: Appetizers for the Creative Mind Series,
Getting the Science Right and the Fiction Plausible*
#1 Get Your Stories Off the Ground (coming Spring/Summer
2026)

To connect with Rob, check out his website www.RAJohnsonAuthor.com. There you will find his blog, which contains dozens of flash fiction pieces, and you can join his email list to get monthly newsletters and special offers.

You can contact him directly at rob@RAJohnsonAuthor.com.

CROW Books

www.ingramcontent.com/pod-product-compliance
Lightning Source LLC
Chambersburg PA
CBHW032143050726
47591CB00001B/59